A VERY PRIVATE ENTERPRISE

Elizabeth Ironside

All the characters and events portrayed in this work are fictitious.

A VERY PRIVATE ENTERPRISE

A Felony & Mayhem mystery

PRINTING HISTORY
First UK edition (Hodder & Stoughton): 1984
Felony & Mayhem edition: 2008

ISBN-13 978-1-933397-94-8
ISBN-10 1-933397-94-2

Manufactured in the United States of America

FOR DAVID

The icon above says you're holding a copy of a book in the Felony & Mayhem "British" category. These books are set in or around the UK, and feature the highly literate, often witty prose that fans of British mystery demand. If you enjoy this book, you may well like other "British" titles from Felony & Mayhem Press, including:

Death on the High C's, by Robert Barnard
Out of the Blackout, by Robert Barnard
Death and the Chaste Apprentice, by Robert Barnard
The Skeleton in the Grass, by Robert Barnard
Dupe, by Liza Cody
King and Joker, by Peter Dickinson
The Old English Peep Show, by Peter Dickinson
The Killings at Badger's Drift, by Caroline Graham
Death of a Hollow Man, by Caroline Graham
Murder at Madingley Grange, by Caroline Graham
Death in Disguise, by Caroline Graham
Death of a Dormouse, by Reginald Hill
A Clubbable Woman, by Reginald Hill
Death in the Garden, by Elizabeth Ironside
The Accomplice, by Elizabeth Ironside
A Back Room in Somers Town, by John Malcolm
Death's Bright Angel, by Janet Neel
Death in the Morning, by Sheila Radley
The Chief Inspector's Daughter, by Sheila Radley

For more about these books, and other Felony & Mayhem titles, or to place an order, please visit our website at

www.FelonyAndMayhem.com

or contact us at

Felony and Mayhem Press
156 Waverly Place
New York, NY 10014

A Very Private Enterprise

Chapter 1

IT WAS A BEAUTIFUL EVENING for a party, the night Hugo Frencham was killed.

It was April and the soft tropical darkness lay over the city like a cashmere shawl on a bare arm, trapping the warmth rising from the earth, meshing with the trees and buildings as filaments of wool with the fine hairs of the skin. In the Turnells' garden, where the party was to be held, tiny lights glimmered under pierced terracotta lids. Visible as darker masses against the sky, the trees and shrubs enclosed the lawn with a heavy scent only bearable diluted by the warm, dark air.

Later, Janey was to assert that no one could know what happened that evening; that only Hugo and one other could have any real knowledge of what had occurred, and that even for them, perhaps, it had been hard to understand, confused, unreal.

Had Hugo any foreboding of his own death? He was

certainly uneasy, revolving many cares like a prayer wheel in his mind. He had, rather reluctantly, arrived at the party early. He had had to leave several interesting objects which he had just bought from a dealer that evening. If he had been free he would have spent a far pleasanter time examining them in detail, the spotlight shining over his shoulder on the liquid gleam of the silver, the intricate surface lifted into clear relief under the huge eye of the magnifying glass. But it was expected of him, as a friend and neighbour, to be among the first and he had accordingly set down the tranquil figure of the Buddha placing beside it the knife with its slim, pointed blade and elaborately patterned handle. As he left the house he had glanced at the statue and the knife lying on the side table in a pyramid of light from the lamp. The fascination that they exerted lay in the retreat they offered from the problems closing in on him. Both through the philosophy they stood for and the artistry with which they had been created they offered the spirit an escape. Perhaps that was a form of premonition.

The rest of the house was in darkness as he locked the door behind him and strolled along the road to the Turnells'. Tables were set out under the trees. The candles on them burned evenly in the still air, their flames like golden tear drops in the centre of a haze of light. The glow glossed the talking faces, the eating hands. The waterfall noise of voices was a background to the sharper chinking of glass and silver.

Hugo's head was bent to listen to his neighbour; his face was intent as if absorbed in her words, but his mind was on the objects left in the lamplight next door. Concentration on them could blot out the many other things which he did not wish to think of in a way that the conversation never could. His glass was refilled and he lifted it, nodding in agreement with he was not sure what. As he took a mouthful he looked through the trees at the dim roofline of his own house. No light came from it; inside, like gold in a box, were the figure and the ritual knife which in a few hours he could examine again.

The buffet was laid out in the dining-room and soon people began to move in to help themselves to pudding. Hugo stood on the verandah talking in a group of men as the women gathered round the table. This time as he glanced at the end of the garden he saw a light shining through the branches. He made no move until his hostess came to urge them to take some food. He waited while the others went into the dining-room before saying, "Maggie, I'm so sorry. I shall have to go. I'll just slip away. Apologise to Alan for me."

She looked a little startled and said, "Of course. Are you all right?"

"Yes, yes. I'm sorry about this. Goodbye." He edged away along the verandah leaving her looking momentarily bewildered.

At the door he was caught by Ranjit Singh. He had avoided him thus far; there was now no escape. So it was another twenty minutes before he was able to let himself out of the Turnells' front door and walk rapidly down the drive. He saw no one, only the feet of a sleeping driver projecting through the open door of a parked car. The noise of the party was a muffled blare behind him as he approached his own house.

The door was still locked. He let himself in and looked into the drawing-room in front of him. It was empty. The verandah doors were open, and the Buddha and the ritual knife lay still in the circle of lamplight.

"Where are you?" he called. He had projected his voice at the stairs and was looking in that direction as he hesitated by the little table. So he had to turn when the reply came from behind him.

"Here."

Beyond the verandah a figure moved in the darkness.

"I'm here."

She was standing on the lawn looking at the sky. Hugo paused a moment longer, then, picking up the two silver objects, he walked slowly outside.

"When did you get here?" His tone was reproachful, reasonable rather than angry. "What are you doing? You should be in bed, you know you should." She turned towards him; she was outside the fall of light from the drawing-room windows, merely a darker shape against the dim garden.

"Hugo, I had to see you."

Hugo sat down on the cane sofa facing the lawn. He put down the statue and the knife on the glass table and placed the Buddha full-face towards him. He touched the top of its head with his finger-tips. He wished she would go. She was speaking torrentially now. Why couldn't she leave it? Women always wanted to rake things over, discuss them, when they were finished and better left for dead. At this point his mind swerved; he lifted the Buddha and started to revolve it in his grasp.

His obsession with the statue and the knife was the only warning that he received of his imminent death. For Hugo the last few minutes of his life were a series of sensations so rapid that the mind could only register, not interpret, them: a silver arc flashing into the night, his surge of rage and desire as he leapt to find it, the searing pain and the fall into darkness.

So, as far as Hugo was concerned, Janey was probably right. Perhaps there was a split second of understanding that what had happened to him was death; or perhaps it was incomprehending blankness that engulfed him and he, like so many others who became involved in the affair, never knew what happened.

Chapter 2

THE HEAD OF CHANCERY, Hugo Frencham, was found dead on the morning of Tuesday 1 May. His body was discovered at about 6.30 a.m. by his bearer, Jogiram, in the garden of his bungalow within the High Commission compound.

The body had been disturbed by the time that the High Commission doctor, Dr Mason, arrived on the scene at approximately 7.15. Its original position was some ten feet from the edge of the covered verandah, lying on the lawn facing the house. The cause of death

As soon as the ticking of rapid two-fingered typing ceased the hushed roar of the air conditioning swelled up to replace it. The typist rolled the paper up a couple of turns in the machine and leaned back to look over what he had written. He was a tall man on the verge of middle age, the signs of which were visible in the fading blond hair receding from his forehead, giving his bony face a highbrowed appearance it had probably lacked in his youth.

His eyes moved from his paper to the garden. Framing the view of the lawn was the harsh pink of bougainvillea which climbed the posts and sprawled along the roof of the verandah. It was just under the lower sprays that Jogiram had found his master's body.

Sinclair had taken him over his actions and reactions time and again until the scene became so clear to him that it seemed a carefully choreographed ballet shown in slow motion.

Jogiram in his white uniform and silent bare feet comes on to the verandah carrying a tray of tea, places it on the cane table and says to no one in particular, "Chhota-hazri, please Sahib." He pads back to the kitchen where he sits on a stool for some minutes. Then, disturbed by the silence, he looks out into the hall. He sees the tea tray untouched so he climbs the stairs to the bedroom. Listening at the door he can hear nothing, none of the splashes, grunts, mucus-clearings of awakening, so tapping softly he goes in. The bed, which he had neatly turned down the previous evening, is unslept in.

Jogiram slowly descends the stairs, unworried, hardly puzzled. He goes to collect the unwanted tray from the verandah. Then, not knowing why, he walks into the garden a few steps, sufficient for his view to clear the mass of the bougainvillea and to see the body beneath it.

Sinclair sighed, and looked again at what he had typed. He would not have said he was an imaginative man and certainly his appearance and manner did not suggest to others that he was. Yet into the elaborate physical reconstructions that were part of his technique of investigation, there always seemed to enter the ghosts of the emotions felt by the participants of the original scene. As his mind followed Jogiram's actions of that early May morning he could sense the instant of discovery and panic when Jogiram, from a routine-dulled blankness, suddenly lurched to recognition of what he had seen lying under the bougainvillea.

Sinclair continued to stare at the bald sentences of his memorandum. They conveyed nothing of the suddenness and strangeness of that day which he had understood so clearly from Jogiram's broken, vivid English. That was his assignment: to smooth over what had happened, to make those horrible and hurried events anodyne and comprehensible for Whitehall.

❀ ❀ ❀

Anderson, who had briefed him for the journey, had already made up his mind not to allow events so far away to affect him on either a human or a professional level.

"The Head of Chancery at the High Commission in Delhi has been bumped off," he had said. "Ever come across him? No? Well, no reason why you should, I suppose. Hugo Frencham was his name. I knew him years ago in India in the old days. He went back there as H. of C. a few years ago and now he's got himself killed, knifed apparently. It's probably nothing much."

Anderson was a Scot with a rough red-brown head like bracken and a huge nose, ferns of hair curling from the nostrils. Thus dismissing the violent death of an old acquaintance, he ruminated for a time, then said, "Sex, possibly."

Sinclair looked vaguely enquiring.

"They get into a lot of mischief like that in the subcontinent. The heat you know. Can't think why they're calling us in. Davey Simpson-Smith of Southern Asia Department in the Foreign Office is pissing himself about it. Ever come across him? No? Well, he's a wee body with a great voice. 'We can't lose a Head of Chancery in such a fashion.'"

He parodied the deep tones of Davey Simpson-Smith, exaggerating the pedantic exactness of the consonants. Like a lot of the senior men in the Security Department, Anderson was ex-Army and had the military man's contempt for the effeteness of all civil servants and the Foreign Office in particular. He laughed at his own mimicry, plucking his nose and leaning back in his chair in high good humour.

"I've called for Frencham's file. Last positive vetting seven years ago. Looks clean to me. But they're flapping about something over there and I'll have to send somebody. I'm giving this to you, Sinclair, because there's not much in it from what I sense and you could do with a break. You've had a bad year or two so a change will do you good. Get away from London." He was now carried away on the flood of his own generosity. "Sort Delhi out as quickly as may be. Write a good clean report to calm all the old women down and then take some leave, why don't you? Kashmir, you know, wonderful at this time of year. Ever been there? No? You should go. I'll tell you what. We'll not expect you back for a month. Come back to the office next month fit as a fiddle after your nice wee holiday."

Sinclair knew too much of his superior's capacity for self- deception to believe that the trip to Delhi was compensation for a bad couple of years in his personal life.

The time of year, May, was the source of his first suspicion, quickly confirmed by a glance at the list at the back of *The Times* giving the temperatures of the world capitals. The previous day Delhi had recorded forty degrees Celsius. The second suspicion was about the nature of the case. Anderson's judgment that there was not much in it except the sexual excitements of a lively international community was based, Sinclair guessed, on no hard evidence, merely on his superior's memories of the bored wives of Simla in the last days of the Raj. Probably his time as a young subaltern in the Indian Army attached to the Viceroy's staff had been Anderson's sexual heyday, accounting for his curious coupling of heat and sex.

Sinclair's own experience did not bear out this theory. The time he and Teresa had gone to Morocco leaving the four children with her mother had been terrible. She had been made languid, he irritable, by the heat. Admittedly Dominic, their youngest child had been conceived there, but he had not brought greater harmony to their household.

Superficially there was the sexual difficulty. Teresa was a devout Catholic for whom abstinence was the only acceptable way of limiting the size of their family. This deprivation was not, Sinclair found, the immense hardship which society with its obsession with sex would have people believe. Nevertheless, it exacerbated the differences between Teresa and himself. His rationalism and agnosticism became more pronounced and their views continually conflicted. Abstinence from conversation as well as sex followed and eventually Sinclair moved out of the house; living with a furiously silent woman had become unbearable. One of Teresa's complaints was that he took no notice of his family, immersing himself in his work, so she was surprised when the hostile atmosphere took effect. For Sinclair it was Teresa's forgivingness, her attitude that her absolute rightness would one day be revealed and he could be sure of her compassion and understanding until then and beyond, that finally drove him away.

He said nothing of divorce, nor even of legal separation; indeed, he did not particularly think about them as there was no one else he wanted to marry. Teresa continued to live in the shabby, roomy house in Tulse Hill while Sinclair rented a two-roomed flat in Kennington from where he could walk or cycle to work. Teresa, not unexpectedly, took it very badly, wept, became hysterical. Mothers and sisters from both sides of the family rallied round to support her and she eventually constructed in her mind a monster for a husband whom she was glad to be rid of.

This was the 'bad year or two' for which going to Delhi in May was to compensate. Sinclair would have kept such domestic friction and his lack of success in marriage hidden from his colleagues; Teresa at her most distracted and enraged had taken to telephoning the office to abuse him and to disabuse those around him of their belief in his integrity. The idea of Sinclair's 'hard time' and 'bad year' was general within the office, with an accompanying suspicion that he had, in fact, behaved rather badly to his wife.

❀❀❀

Delhi, as Sinclair had rightly surmised, was by no means the light holiday task in pleasant surroundings that Anderson had implied at the briefing. For a start, the heat was tremendous. The sky was an open furnace from which, although it was often overcast, a shrivellingly hot breath came at all times of the day. The very morning of his arrival there had been a dust storm and the hot wind had acquired a fierce rasping edge which grazed the skin like sandpaper and filled the nose and mouth with grit.

What made it worse was that he had no suitable clothes. In his loosest trousers and with rolled up sleeves he sat in the air conditioning and vowed that tomorrow he would ask Jogiram to show him where to have some cotton shirts and trousers made.

Jogiram seemed to Sinclair the only source of help and information he was likely to find. Those representatives of the High Commission that he had met so far had treated him with a wary reserve, palpable even in their automatic welcoming rituals.

He had arrived very early in the morning and had been met at the airport by a man called Markham from the Administration Section of the High Commission who knew how to cope with the elaborate bureaucratic processes of the Indian customs service. Markham moved with assurance from one documentation check to the next, thrusting aside the other bewildered passengers from Sinclair's jumbo jet, until he released Sinclair into the blinding glare of the early morning city.

Sitting in the back of the High Commission Cortina Sinclair listened to the arrangements that had been made for him.

"We've put you up in the Head of Chancery's bungalow in the compound," Markham told him. He saw a look of surprise on Sinclair's face and said, with a warning glance at the driver to prevent any comment, "We thought it would be useful for you to be on the spot, you know." Then, after another pause, "And, anyway, we've had instructions from London about not putting civil servants into hotels. They have to be accommodated by officers *en poste*. To save subsistence."

In the jerky explanation Sinclair could hear the curt sentences of the memo, probably headed: 'Accommodation of Visiting Members of the Civil Service Under Grade 4: Reduction of Subsistence' with ten numbered points to follow. He knew from his reading of the personnel file that the dead man was divorced and had no family living with him in Delhi, so such an arrangement would not intrude upon a widow. He would be alone.

"There's someone else staying there as well," Markham went on. "A woman called Jane Somers, an archaeologist I think she said. She was going to visit Hugo for a few days apparently. She arrived the morning he was…the day he… well, a few days ago. She has some work to do in India I believe. We've asked her to stay until you have seen her. She's been interviewed by the Indians of course."

"Can you tell me what the Indians have done so far?"

Markham again frowned at such lack of discretion in front of the driver.

"Bryan Lenton, the acting Head of Chancery, has asked to see you after the morning meeting. I'll take you over to see him. He'll be able to brief you on that side of things."

Sinclair could only put Markham's exceeding caution down to his horror of the Security Department and forbore to question him further. Markham volunteered no comment of his own until the car bumped over a railway bridge and was running along a straight, broad-verged avenue.

"Almost at the compound now," he informed the new arrival. "This is the diplomatic area round here. That's the

Russians' over there. Ours is not so big, but very convenient: office, houses, swimming pool, hospital, club, all on one site."

Sinclair thought it sounded like a diplomatic Butlin's camp.

"You like compound life?"

"Oh, yes. It's very nice for the wives and kids. You feel safe," was the reply as they halted at a lowered barrier. A Gurkha, after peering inside to view the occupants of the car, saluted and allowed them in. "Or, at least, we did until this last week."

Markham went off to his breakfast after leaving Sinclair at the Head of Chancery's house in the charge of the bearer, a thin man in white shirt and trousers who had been waiting for them to arrive.

"I am Jogiram, Sahib. I show you your room." He set off up the stairs with Sinclair's bag. "That Frencham Sahib's room. That Miss Sahib's room. She sleep late; very late home last night. This your room, Sahib, and bathroom, please." He efficiently placed the case on a small rack ready to be opened and regarded the jet-lagged and crumpled Sinclair.

"I make breakfast. Tea, coffee for Sahib?"

"Oh, coffee, please. Thanks."

Sinclair showered and changed and went downstairs to the dining-room where he was given Jogiram's idea of a good breakfast: sliced mango, bacon and scrambled eggs, toast and jam, coffee. The mango and coffee were superb, the toast flabby and inedible, the bacon and eggs reviving after the long flight. Jogiram cleared away the breakfast things and Sinclair, correcting his watch by the bracket clock on the bookcase in the drawing-room found that it was only half past eight.

Looking round the room he gave himself to estimating

something of the late occupant from the furnishings. The carpets, covers, curtains were all a heavy and slightly unpleasant shade of blue; Sinclair knew these were standard government-provided items of a type laid down as suitable for the rank of counsellor and of a colour favoured by the clerk in charge of the properties. The solid, self-satisfied air of the chief pieces of furniture contrasted curiously with the ornaments which were many and fine. Sinclair was no judge of antiques and could not assess the quality of the late Hugo Frencham's *objets d'art*. He was, however, able to recognise the care with which each object was spaced in relation to others. The fact that some of them were damaged also spoke for their value.

On one wall was a long painting on cloth, the subject of which Sinclair was unable to understand. It seemed to be of a monster supporting a wheel with its jaws, hands and feet. The wheel was segmented and in each sector were scenes full of activity and torment. The picture was bordered with dark red silk, much frayed and torn, and was clamped between two sheets of glass, obviously to prevent further damage to the fabric.

Hugo Frencham had been interested in antiquities of many kinds: paintings, sculptures, bronzes, silver; so much was evident. He had been acquisitive; the room was so full that the walls with their load of treasure appeared to lean in towards the visitor. There was a preciousness and self-consciousness in the arrangement of the objects which spoke of a man very aware of visual appearances and the power of impression on others. He must have had money. Private means? Making a mental note to look into Frencham's finances, Sinclair dozed until Markham arrived to escort him to the High Commission, a walk of a hundred yards or so.

Sinclair's meeting with the acting Head of Chancery clarified a number of things about the investigation that had been puzzling him. The death of a senior diplomat in violent and mysterious circumstances called for some kind of enquiry, but it might be assumed that, without further evidence of security breaches, a police investigation would be enough to clear the matter up. Indeed, the Foreign Office was usually extremely anxious to keep the Security Department from meddling in its affairs unless ministerial or public pressure for the Department's involvement was overwhelming. So why had Davey Simpson-Smith been so quick to call Security in? At least part of the answer, Sinclair soon established, lay with Bryan Lenton.

He was a youngish man, in his early thirties, with a forceful style of speech and a rancorous dislike of his late superior evident from his first sentences regretting his death. He was also charged with an excitement that Sinclair had often noticed in people peripherally caught up in security or police cases, a prurient interest in death and scandal where their own emotions of grief or fear were not aroused. Lenton shook hands with Sinclair across his desk and began to speak at once of his predecessor.

"He will be much missed here. A great tragedy. A real old India hand, you know, steeped in the old ways. He was here during the War in the Indian Army and then stayed on for a year or two after Independence in '47, teaching at a school in the Hills or Kashmir, somewhere like that."

Sinclair registered the repeated 'old' and reinterpreted it as it was meant to be understood. Old Hugo had bored Bryan with stories of the Raj and had refused to adapt to the needs of diplomacy with an independent state.

"He was always going off to stay with old Army friends,

mostly retired now and really not of much use as sources of political or military information. But he had a lot of contacts: Indians are amazingly hospitable, you know."

"He sounds the ideal diplomat for the country."

Lenton frowned judiciously, a pretence at being fair.

"Well, *de mortuis* etc but…" Sinclair waited for the dirt which he knew would follow. "It's all very well, you know, but this indiscriminate socialising needs to be coupled with some political flair for making sense of what you hear. Now that's what old Hugo lacked. He just wasn't interested in coming back from his trips with some ideas about how the Congress is doing in Uttar Pradesh for instance. More concerned with another piece of junk from a bazaar."

"What about in Delhi?" asked Sinclair. "Did he mix much here?"

"The usual thing—National Days and so on, not much more than that. Though, of course, he did see a lot of Dolgov, the Russian Counsellor."

"Oh yes?" Sinclair did not betray any special interest.

"Dolgov is our licensed Russian in Delhi, goes to all the Western cocktails. I don't know how or when he and Hugo became pally—I've only been here nine months—but they certainly are, were. Used to play chess together; every month."

Sinclair changed tack. "Can I ask now about the police work that's been done so far? How much has gone on?"

"Indian police work, you know." (Sinclair knew little about either Indian police methods or diplomatic life but Lenton's reiterated 'you know' implied he knew everything and was one of the family.) "It's rather crude normally. They take in the witnesses and beat them until they confess to something; that's the usual technique.

They've been very circumspect so far with this case. They've interviewed Hugo's servants and the Gurkhas on duty and Miss Somers. The weapon hasn't been discovered, as far as I know and, of course, no arrest has been made yet." A note of annoyance crept into Lenton's voice. "They didn't interview me. I wasn't anywhere around, of course; I live off the compound but… Well, perhaps it is better that you're here so that the more confidential background information can be given to you." He hesitated as if looking for encouragement; he received no more than a mildly questioning stare. "I feel I as acting Head of Chancery should be the person to put this to you. It may have a crucial bearing on your investigation. It's…boys."

The pause was a long one until Sinclair said, "Yes? What boys?"

"I'm not sure what boys or which boys as individuals. I'm just pretty sure that old Hugo was queer. And that may have something to do with what happened. Hugo had been divorced for a long time, you know," he went on without noticing the irrelevance, "and he was rather a pernickety old woman—all those damn bronzes arranged just so."

Sinclair gathered the divorce and the bronzes were adduced as evidence of effeminacy and so of homosexuality. He could only hope that Lenton's political assessments were based on better foundations than his personal judgments.

"That kind of information could be significant," he said cautiously, "and I think it is probably better for me to hold it rather than the Indians at this stage, unless you have any knowledge of a particular boy being at the bungalow on the Monday night."

Lenton seemed relieved to have dropped his two hints and went on in more relaxed style, "I expect you'd like to talk to the police. I've been in touch and told them you're here and arranged a meeting for this afternoon. I'll have a car ordered for 2.15 to take you round there. It is an Inspector Battacharia who'll see you."

"I'll need to have a look round Frencham's office," said Sinclair, "and make a digest of papers and topics he had been working on in recent months. This is all routine. And I should like to send a message to London today."

At this list of requests Lenton looked sheepish, and started his reply with the last item.

"Sue, my secretary can type up anything you want sent. Now, Hugo's work," laughing, "making a list of that won't be too demanding a task. Sue can do that for you. I'll get Registry to help her. And the office—well—this is Hugo's office. My old one is a bit smaller and, in fact not so close to the High Commissioner." This line of argument seemed to please him and he elaborated it. "So it was better, you know to be a bit further up the corridor."

"I'd like to have a look around all the same," Sinclair repeated. "I always find it very revealing. Perhaps when you're at a meeting so I shan't inconvenience you. I'll bring my telegram over this afternoon when I go to see the police."

❀❀❀

Sinclair sat at his typewriter and considered Bryan Lenton. He wondered whether anything the man had said could be believed. His display of dislike was so obvious that Sinclair was inclined to be sceptical of most of what he said. Lenton's intelligence had to be taken on trust as there was precious little evidence of it, except in efficient denigration of his late boss. So perhaps Anderson was going to be right. If the source of suspicion of Hugo Frencham was a subordinate's ambition and enmity there might be 'nothing in it' after all.

Chapter 3

THAT AFTERNOON Sinclair was taken by car to the Police Headquarters where he was led along a stuffy corridor lined knee-high with bundles of papers, through several anterooms filled with clerks, to the sanctum of the inspector in charge of Hugo's case.

Never before had Sinclair seen so much paper in a single room. Every written word, it seemed, was treasured and had multiplied. The papers could not be confined within the filing cabinets that lined the walls. They had long since overflowed all cabinets and drawers, spilled onto window ledges, shelves, desk tops, tables, chairs, and finally taken over the floor. The papers were all a yellow-cream colour which matched the dirty walls, the police uniforms and even the light that filtered through the lowered cane blinds. They stirred restlessly with the movement of the sluggishly turning fan, trying to escape from the bonds of tape and weight to occupy the air, the only space they had left unfilled.

The dusty piles of past, or even current, cases had no depressing effect on the inhabitant of the office. Battacharia was a lively, friendly, talkative Bengali who professed himself delighted to see Sinclair. He shouted for tea which soon came, creamy-beige like the uniforms and the papers. The first startlingly sweet sip brought beads of sweat onto Sinclair's forehead which the fan was too slow to cool before they evaporated.

"This is terrible business of Mr Frencham," said Battacharia releasing a small spurt of dust as he made space for his tea cup. "We shall be grateful for thoughts on the matter."

"I don't really have many ideas about the affair. I was simply hoping you might tell me what you have managed to find so far."

Battacharia, having established that all was within his power and that Sinclair had not come to dictate methods to him, launched into an account of the case.

"One of our men, Arjun Ram, who was on duty outside the British High Commission, was called to Mr Frencham's bungalow at about seven thirty on Tuesday 1 May. He found the body lying on the grass near the verandah. Mr Frencham was dead with stab wound in the chest. High Commission doctor was already on the scene and it seems from medical evidence that he died round midnight and had been lying there all night.

"We have statements from Jogiram, bearer; Barua, cook; Babu Lal, sweeper; Miss Somers, guest; Mr Turnell, Minister at the High Commission. We are knowing that Mr Frencham went to a big party at Mr Turnell's house on Monday evening so he had dismissed his servants early in the evening. They did not wait up for him. The servants live in quarters on the other side of compound, so they did not know or hear any thing. All were playing cards—gambling too I am thinking, until late at night."

"When was the last time Frencham was seen alive?"

"Mrs Turnell said he was leaving her party a little early, so we must be saying between eleven and eleven thirty."

"And what about the other guests at the party?"

Battacharia shuffled his chair closer to his desk and became confiding.

"We are having the guest list kindly given by Mr Turnell and we are making enquiries. I am telling you, Mr Sinclair, it is delicate. Delicate. On this list are important people, members of Parliament, a Minister, a very great business man, officials." He sighed. "Now for the servants, the guards, people like that we can get statements quickly, easily. To be getting an interview with these people is harder. You are waiting all day. At last they are giving you ten minutes. 'I left at twelve or twelve thirty.' Who can confirm? 'My wife, my driver. I went straight home.' You cannot press them. It is very delicate. Let me show you list."

Files and papers were rumpled as if they were dirty bed clothes until Battacharia had found what he wanted. He held it out for Sinclair to see, keeping one corner in his grasp. It was a copy of a guest list entitled: BUFFET DINNER TO BE GIVEN BY THE MINISTER AND MRS A. TURNELL ON MONDAY 30 APRIL.

It was typed in two columns headed 'Indians' and 'Home side' as if for some team game. 'Home side' read: Host and Hostess, Mr H. Frencham, Mr and Mrs B. Lenton, Squadron Leader and Mrs J. Fox. 'Indians' was much longer, about fifteen names, most of them of married couples.

"Look at this, Mr Sinclair," wailed Battacharia. "Mr

and Mrs R. Singh: he was in the Army very high up, now he is business man, very rich; he lives in the Prithviraj Road in huge house. And this: he is top man in Tata in Delhi; Mr and Mrs R. K. Sinha: he is MP, she is MLA, both powerful people. What to do?"

Sinclair felt he had got the gist of the problems involved so he turned to another aspect: intruders. An Indian police man on diplomatic protection duty and two Gurkhas in British employ had been on guard on the west side of the compound that night. All three were quite sure that anyone climbing in or out would have been noticed; no one had been seen. The Gurkhas' log book at the main gate had recorded the entrance of late party goers around 1 a.m., the departure of a car to fetch Miss Somers at 5.30 a.m. The second Gurkha had seen all thc gucsts out of the Turnells' private entrance before locking it securely at 12.45 a.m. Sinclair agreed that a casual intruder or an interrupted burglar seemed unlikely.

"Is there anything missing from the house?" he asked. "I noticed that Mr Frencham had a large collection of antiques of various kinds."

"Now this is very strange, Mr Sinclair. Yes, there is some thing missing or rather three things, according to Jogiram the bearer. Now what would you think in such a house a burglar might be taking?"

"Money," suggested Sinclair. "He would look in drawers and desks for money."

"No, no," cried Battacharia delightedly. "You are wrong. No searching. Nothing displaced. No vandalism. The criminal perhaps met Mr Frencham first, killed him and then was too frightened to stay to search. No."

"Well, small things then. Silver. There was a table covered with silver boxes and gewgaws."

"You would be a good thief, better than this man. No. Of the three items missing two are quite large, not a size that you could put in pocket or tuck into fold of your dhoti. They're all Tibetan things and two of them Mr Frencham had bought that very evening from a dealer in such objects who had visited him at the house. He was a collector, Mr Frencham, a rich man evidently. The dealer has been questioned and has described the objects to us. One was silver figure of Buddha, in earth-touching pose," Battacharia noted pedantically. "Not too big, but awkward to hide, I am thinking. The other was a knife with a silver handle and blade five-six inches long, sharply pointed. Medical evidence is suggesting this could have caused the wound Mr Frencham received. The third thing was a big conch trumpet with mounting of silver and gilt studded with turquoises. Nothing else was taken. What are you thinking of that?"

Sinclair considered. "It is possible, as you say, that a burglar was discovered by Frencham, stabbed him and simply seized anything in his fear and haste, to make something of his venture. Alternatively we could hypothesise that the objects were taken, in haste admittedly, in order to make it appear that theft was the motive for the crime. In that case, though he could not carry much, he would want to be sure that whatever he took was missed."

"That is good, that is very good." Battacharia was now bouncing in his seat, his little round face and snub nose glowing. "I am thinking this also. Which means intruder can go. It is friend, colleague we are looking for." He looked solemn again. "So now, Mr Sinclair, I have been telling you what we have been doing and there is remaining only one more area to be investigated: this is the people in the compound. Now if it is an Indian citizen who is doing this dastardly act it is my duty to pursue him and capture the badmash. But if it is an English person, colleague from High Commission, I cannot interfere. Some have diplomatic immunity, some have not. So I am feeling, and my superiors are feeling, that the investigation is best done by British officer. When the criminal is apprehended then the lawyers must be working out what courts British or Indian can take cognisance."

Sinclair came away from the Police offices considerably cheered. The lively little Bengali amid his sea of paper had been amusing and stimulating after the sterile carping of the morning's meeting. He would have to see Lenton again to break the unwelcome news that enquiries had to be made on the doings and whereabouts of all the people in the High Commission. He was going to have to do a good deal of straight police work for the murder investigation and without any of the help that Battacharia had from his subordinates.

At the High Commission the girl at the reception desk, a beautiful Indian with long hair coiled at the nape of her neck and a diamond in the curve of her nostril, gave him the telephone extensions for the secretaries of Alan Turnell and Bryan Lenton. Lenton's secretary, Sue, said he was rather busy and six o'clock would be his earliest free moment. Sinclair shrugged and accepted the offered appointment. Margaret for Turnell said her boss would be free in ten minutes' time. Sinclair made his way up to the Chancery where Margaret met him and he used the ten minutes to have a photocopy made of the guest list of the party of 30th April. Armed with this he went in to see the Minister.

Alan Turnell was the second in command of the High Commission and fulfilled all that imagination could conceive of a diplomat. He was tall, slim, silver haired, patrician featured and was in fact a grammar school boy who had started work as a clerk. He was elegantly dressed in a cream bush suit and his manner was engaging and welcoming. Everyone who met him felt that he had made a distinct and favourable impression in those interested blue eyes.

Alan advanced to meet Sinclair, saying, "Hard at it already? You only arrived this morning, didn't you? Sit down and let me ask for some tea. Or do you prefer coffee?"

They settled into some black imitation leather chairs, while tea was produced.

"What do you make of all this? And how are we going to cope with it?"

Sinclair sketched his visit to Battacharia.

"There are a number of lines of enquiry at present. The casual intruder; the guests at your party; other visitors to the compound during the evening; the servants who have quarters in the compound; and finally the High Commission staff. The first four groups the police are dealing with. The last I have agreed to question. This line, if it proves the true one, which I hope it won't may lead us into legal quagmires. There is the question of diplomatic immunity, for the killing took place on diplomatic soil. Leaving aside the security aspect, I am sure it is best if I do undertake to deal with the home-based staff. In any case, I should like some work to be done on the legal side of all this."

"Ye-es. I can see all this is going to be extremely tricky. We'd better get something off to the Legal Department in London, so they can advise us. And yes, you're right that you should make the enquiries, at least initially. I had hoped it would not come to this. I had been putting my faith in the early arrest of a casual intruder."

"It could be an interrupted burglar, though there are one or two small pointers away from that at this stage. Now, if I could trouble you, I should like your help on two things. First, I have here a copy of the guest list of your party which Frencham attended the evening he died. Could I ask you to cast your eyes over it and mark the names of the people whom you know he was friendly with."

"My dear chap," taking the sheet from him, "that's no use. Hugo knew everybody. I don't expect there was anybody here that Hugo didn't know. Except perhaps, here yes, Mr and Mrs D. K. Narayan. He wouldn't have known them. Padma is a Bharatnatyam dancer, not Hugo's style, rather young for him." The slightly self-satisfied expression on Alan's face led Sinclair to guess that he was more susceptible to the beauties of young Indian girls than the late Hugo, and prided himself on his charm.

"Let me put it another way then. Could you mark any of your guests who were particularly intimate with Frencham, any close or old friends."

Turnell took the list and made small ticks against about half a dozen names, then handed it back. Sinclair glanced down at the marks: Singh, Beg, Mohan, Kant, Sharma.

"And what was the second thing?"

"Just your personal impressions of Mr Frencham."

There was some reluctance in Turnell's voice as he said, "What kind of impressions were you thinking of?"

Sinclair recognised the signs of discomfort in the presence of bad form and made it easier.

"What was he like as a colleague, for instance?"

"Oh, very sound, very knowledgeable about India. Plenty of contacts, always out and about, you know. And in the office, reliable, hard working, a real eye for detail. A pity about his career. Hugo was not originally mainstream

Foreign Office. He joined the Colonial Office quite late and sideways moves brought him to us. He was rather bitter, felt he should have risen higher than a grade 4. They weren't going to promote him, though. He'd only one more posting before retirement. A pity. He was certainly clever enough, or at least shrewd, I'd say. Not an intellectual, Hugo, but sharp, especially where money was concerned. His collection must be worth something."

Sinclair's last interview was with Lenton who kept him waiting ten minutes after the six o'clock appointment. Lenton was annoyed at the idea of all home-based staff having to be interviewed, in spite of Sinclair's soothing murmurs of 'routine'.

"They won't like it," he said irritably. "They'll complain and as Head of Chancery I'll be on the receiving end."

Sinclair offered no comment of consolation or apology, saying merely, "If I could have an office I'll start tomorrow."

He extracted a promise that Sue would help by setting up a system of appointments and then dragged himself back to the house.

He had no key and, as he waited for Jogiram to let him in he thought he would perhaps now meet his fellow guest in the dead man's house, Miss Somers, asleep at breakfast, out at lunch-time. In the hall the cool rush of air revived him.

"Miss Somers on verandah, Sahib," Jogiram informed him. "Miss Sahib say dinner at eight. Is that right for Sahib?"

"Yes, yes, that's fine. Thank you, Jogiram. I'll go and—er—introduce myself."

At first, as he pulled back the doors and stepped into the soupy outside air again, he thought there was a mistake. For no good reason, he had expected the archaeologist, Miss

Somers, to be Hugo's contemporary as well as his friend. He had visualised a stout-calved academic, complete with spectacles.

She was wearing spectacles, enormous dark ones with white rims, under her untidy, luminously red hair. She stood up as he came out, taking off her glasses as she rose and holding out her hand. She was tall, almost as tall as Sinclair, thin and young, dressed Indian-style in tight cotton trousers and a loose knee-length tunic.

"Hello," she said. "I'm Janey Somers. We've been playing Cox and Box all day."

If they'd called her Janey Somers, thought Sinclair, I'd have been prepared. No one over forty is called Janey.

"You look whacked." She pulled out a long planter's chair. "Let's order a nimbu for you."

When Jogiram had brought the lime and water Janey went on, "You're the sleuth sent out from London to clear up the mystery of poor Hugo, aren't you?" Sinclair agreed to this definition of himself. It was better to be seen as involved in a murder enquiry rather than a security investigation.

"How is it going?"

"Just sorting out the bare facts at the moment. I need to talk to you about what you saw. You arrived at the moment Jogiram found him, didn't you?"

"Yes, I think I arrived here at about a quarter to seven. Jogiram was in a terrible state. He and Barua and Babu Lal, the sweeper, were about to rush round to the next bungalow when the car drew up. They were very upset. It took me some time to calm them down enough to tell me what was going on. Jogiram hadn't touched Hugo. I should think he just assumed he was dead because he knew he hadn't been to bed and so must have been there all night. At first all they would say was, 'Sahib very bad. Sahib very ill.' When I asked if the doctor had been called they looked sheepish and quite clearly 'very ill' was a euphemism for dead."

"Where was all this happening? Did you go to see the body?"

"It was all taking place in the drive outside the front door. I was rather confused by everything, so I sent Babu Lal next door for help and Jogiram took me to Hugo."

"Where was he? Would you mind showing me?"

Janey stood up and walked round the mass of the bougainvillea.

"He was lying here facing in towards the house. You couldn't see very much except his back, so I took his shoulder and rolled him over and that's when we saw what had been done to him. His bush suit was all bloody; there was a small tear in it; and his hands were bloody, too, as if he had been holding the wound. It was dry and dark, of course, not wet and flowing and, considering that the wound killed him, there wasn't all that much of it. His face was awful, all screwed up. I'd never seen anybody dead before. I didn't realise they would look like that."

They turned back to the verandah.

"Do you mind if we go in," said Sinclair. "This heat is too much for me." He was flushed, his fair hair slicked down with sweat.

"I'm sorry," she said. "I love the heat. We'll go into the air conditioning."

Sinclair's head cleared as they went in. Janey Somers was a cool lady, in spite of her youth. She looked unflustered by the temperature and her description of finding the murdered body of a friend had a grim matter of factness to it.

"How did you know Hugo Frencham?" Sinclair asked.

"I met him about three years ago. I had an introduction to him through the mafia of Tibetan scholars. He was marvellously kind to me. I've come to India every summer while he's been here. He always let me stay with him while I was in Delhi and was very helpful in fixing me up to see people to obtain permissions for things."

"What permissions do you need? What are you doing in India?"

"I'm a student of Tibetan, that's the simplest way of expressing it. I'm studying some paintings and documents in a couple of monasteries in Ladakh."

"And where's that?"

"It's a bit of Western Tibet, sometimes it's called Little Tibet, which for accidental historical reasons has ended up inside India. It's due north of Delhi beyond Kashmir. It's a rather sensitive area as parts of it are disputed with China and parts with Pakistan, so much of Ladakh is now a huge Indian Army camp. It's important to do as much work as possible before the way of life of the Ladakhis is quite destroyed, and the monasteries are despoiled."

"I was told you were an archaeologist," Sinclair said, "I imagined a stout elderly academic lady."

"Not an archaeologist," Janey agreed. "But I am an academic lady."

Sinclair forced himself to concentrate on Hugo Frencham. "Hugo. What kind of man was he? How did you get on with him?"

"We got on fine," Janey said in the confident tones of someone who gets on well everywhere she goes. "He was a funny guy, Hugo. He seemed to love India and Indians. There were always people in and out of the place without invitation, free house to friends. But he wasn't an easy-going person at all. He had a raging fastidiousness in spite of the bonhomie, especially over his collection. He was once furious with me for moving a whole lot of his knick-knacks in order to put a pile of books on a side table."

"What about his collection, is it good?"

"I don't know much about saleroom values. His Tibetan stuff is superb. I was always trying to persuade him to leave it to a museum. I don't know what'll happen to it now. There's so much of it. Hugo had an acute case of acquisitiveness. And talking of acquisitiveness, Andrea Lenton rang to ask you to dinner tomorrow night. I'm going so if you've nothing better to do you could come to lend me moral support."

Chapter 4

THE NEXT MORNING Sinclair found that his requests had been attended to and that a small office on the second floor of the High Commission had been given over to his use. Lenton's secretary, who indiscreetly admitted she had very little to do, came to help arrange a timetable. She had already prepared a list of British staff which Sinclair regarded with horror.

"My God, how many of you are there here?" he demanded, flicking through the sheets of neatly typed paper.

"Seventy-two home-based officers, fifty-five of whom are married and accompanied. There's a total of sixty-one offspring, but only eighteen of those are in Delhi now. There's also the British Council with ten British staff members and there were a number of visitors staying in the compound when Hugo died. So I'd put the total somewhere around a hundred and sixty. One hundred and sixty-five," she said after a moment's mental arithmetic. She did the enumeration with glee; the prospect of Sinclair's interviewing all those people was obviously highly entertaining for her. Sinclair started to slash at the list.

"These eighteen kids. I don't want to see them. Or at least," with memories of Lenton's 'boys', "how many are teenagers out of that lot?"

Sue reluctantly admitted that there was only one teenager, the High Commissioner's step-daughter who was between school and university and she did not live in the compound. The rest were of primary school age.

"So we're rid of eighteen of them. How many of the rest of the list live off the compound?"

All the members of the British Council and a further ten officers and nine wives were dismissed in this way.

"Put them on one side. We can come to them later if necessary. Now what have we left?" The list remained at over the hundred mark.

"You'd better bring the wives in at the same time as the husbands," Sue advised. "It's the wives that you'll find the difficult ones. I'd better go and start phoning. How would you like them?"

"Alphabetically is as good a way as any. I see you've put on the list what each one does and where they live: that's a great help."

"Right. I'll start like that, but there'll be so many problems with shopping and lunches and sewing bees and ayahs' afternoons off that you'll probably have to do all the singles—" Sue's contempt for the married woman was interrupted by the telephone which she seized in mid-sentence.

"Mr Sinclair's office… Yes, Mrs Turnell… No, that would be fine… Right, I'll tell him to expect you in five minutes." She put the receiver down. "That's Maggie Turnell. She has to go out today so she's volunteering herself early. I said to come at once. You might as well start with her while I telephone."

Sinclair meekly agreed. "No problems with ayahs or hair appointments there," he remarked.

"No, Maggie Turnell's all right. She's a sensible woman."

This commendation was borne out by Maggie's appearance. She had curly greying hair surrounding a plump, pleasant face; a loose cotton dress flapped about a stout body. She was a surprising partner for Alan Turnell, Sinclair thought, remembering the studied diplomatic elegance of her husband.

"I heard you were to interview us all and I thought I would try to dash in before you started as I'm out all day." Sinclair later learned from Sue that Maggie was a nurse and spent two days a week working at a mothers' and babies' clinic in Old Delhi.

"I'm pleased to see you first," said Sinclair. "As you were one of the last to see Hugo I expect you will have more of interest to tell me than the rest of the High Commission put together."

This expectation was not fulfilled. Maggie Turnell could tell him little more than he had already learned from Battacharia. Sinclair went carefully over Hugo's departure from her party.

"You told Inspector Battacharia that Hugo left your party early."

"Yes, that was odd. I mean, it is normal practice for Brits to stay to the end, not to leave until all the Indians have gone, and it was only about eleven when Hugo came to me and said he had to go, giving no reasons either."

"What time did the party end?"

"About half past twelve I should think. But Hugo didn't actually leave at eleven. He was caught by one of our guests; I saw him chatting, with Ranjit Singh I think it was, about twenty past eleven."

"Did he seem himself at the party? Not depressed or nervous or excited?"

"Yes, quite normal. That's why I was surprised about his leaving early. Anyway, Hugo would usually soldier through whatever he felt like."

"There were no disagreements with any of your guests?"

Maggie Turnell laughed. "Who then jumped over the hedge and stabbed him? No, no, Mr Sinclair, it was a quiet and decorous diplomatic party."

"Mrs Turnell, how do you account for Frencham's death? Why would anyone kill him?"

"Surely Hugo wasn't killed for being Hugo. He just was in the way of a burglar. If he'd stayed at the party longer he would have gone home to find he'd been robbed, but at least he would not have been killed."

His last question Sinclair put to all the people he interviewed during that long day and from almost all he received answers similar to Maggie Turnell's. The entire High Commission was united in attributing the tragedy to a casual intruder. If Sinclair ventured to point out that they were exceptionally well protected with a six foot perimeter wall, a ditch, an Indian policeman and a detachment of Gurkhas to guard them, he was met with tales of the violence of Delhi, of old ladies murdered in respectable suburbs, of dacoits who robbed women of their jewels on the city streets. The murder had frightened them and Sinclair saw that in a community living behind walls, fear could quickly grow. The British staff were indulging their fear, giving way to it as a novel and refreshing disturbance of their routine. None of them entertained the idea that Hugo's death might have had any connection with the way he had lived. It was a random blow which could equally have fallen on them.

To most of those he interviewed Sinclair's questions were simple and simply answered. Where had they been on the night of Monday 30th April? What witnesses did they have? Had they passed the bungalows at any stage of the night? Had they noticed anything out of the ordinary there? Had they any comment to make on what had happened?

For the Chief Security Officer, the Head of Registry and one or two others, Sinclair had special questions.

Hipkin, the Chief Security Officer, was a burly ex-NCO from the Royal Green Jackets. He was a sharp-minded, toughly built fellow now running to fat in the soft life of the foreign service. He was angrily defensive towards Sinclair, bitterly blaming the Gurkhas for letting in an intruder at the same time as complaining of the impossibility of patrolling the boundary wall adequately.

"Not built proper," he grumbled. "Now, they should have had the bungalows built inside the perimeter road, not with their gardens up against the wall. It's obvious to anyone that's unsafe. If they'd built it like I say we'd have no trouble with the buggers."

Hipkin seemed to be imagining himself in a new siege of Lucknow. No doubt he was visualising a squad of Green Jackets patrolling the wall with check posts every thirty yards. He was calmed by Sinclair's civilian quietness, his deceptive vagueness. A trace of contempt crept into his attitude as he assessed his interviewer; his bluster grew more cheerful and less persecuted. After twenty minutes he rose full of condescending goodwill. Apart from achieving that, Sinclair had learned nothing from the interview.

❀❀❀

Amid the indulgence in fear, the nervous hostility and the excitement that even a minor break in routine can produce in procedure-bound organisations, Sinclair noticed one young woman in particular because of her tearfulness. She was the wife of a commercial official and her husband was suffering from suppressed irritation with her. Ruth Quinton was in her early thirties and, to Sinclair's eyes, positively ugly. She was plump in a way that made her skin look as though it had been pumped full of air or water very close to bursting point. Her face was shiny, her hair scraped back from her brow, and she wept uncontrollably from the moment Sinclair asked his first question. He disliked feminine tears, though as he was more used to them than many men, he ploughed on with his interview undaunted.

"Your wife has been very affected by the murder?" He directed his question at the husband as Mrs Quinton was clearly in no condition to answer. "Or is she…?"

"No, she's not usually like this. Ruth, please. Will you pull yourself together. Yes, she was very upset to hear of Hugo's er—um. She couldn't bear the idea of someone getting into the compound. She took it all very hard."

Apart from these unilluminating remarks Frank Quinton could offer no additional information about why his wife should react in such a way. Sinclair rapidly established that Frank Quinton had been on a commercial tour of the Punjab and had only arrived back in Delhi two days after Hugo's death. Mrs Quinton had been ill for several days before the murder and had not risen from her sick bed until after her husband's return. Sinclair wrote 'neurotic' in his secretive hand next to Quinton on the list and at lunchtime said to Sue, "Mrs Quinton, what can you tell me about her?"

"Ruth Quinton? Not a lot. What do you want to know? She's about thirty-two, I'd say. Been here about two years. Good sort, not a leader of men—or women. Doesn't work but helps with costumes for plays and with the library. No children."

"Any reason why she should be particularly upset about Hugo? Or is she a bit neurotic, do you think?"

Sue rose to that one. "I shouldn't be surprised," she said scornfully. "All the wives are bored to death, stuffing tranquillisers." Then her sense of justice reasserted itself. "But I wouldn't have thought it of Ruth Quinton. Hang about though, doesn't she do photography? I've a feeling someone told me she was photoing Hugo's collection for insurance, perhaps that's how she came to know him well."

Sinclair could not feel his query was answered definitively and made a note to see Ruth Quinton on her own at some stage.

No one that he talked to had any useful observations about murderer or victim. For the crucial hours after eleven thirty everyone had been at home, in bed or at other parties. The whole exercise was going to be fruitless, Sinclair thought at six o'clock that evening. He had managed to see a large number of the people on his list and had remarkably little to show for it.

Battacharia rang at six fifteen and his tale was similar to Sinclair's. He seemed quite cheerful nevertheless. Speed did not appear to be an important concern in an Indian enquiry.

"I am leaving the big shots for the moment," Battacharia shouted over the crackling on the line. "I am concentrating on the servants and the drivers at the party. I am looking out for gossip, you know, any scandals Mr Frencham was involved in, to give us leads." Sinclair fervently hoped none would be uncovered or, at least, not before he had found them first.

"How are you progressing, Mr Sinclair?"

"Not very fast, Inspector Battacharia."

"Now you should be calling me Pratap."

"Thank you, er, Pratap, and please call me Sinclair." There was a moment's silence while Battacharia tried to work this out. Sinclair explained, "All my friends call me Sinclair. Nobody calls me George—not even my wife." Battacharia absorbed this puzzle while Sinclair went on, "Pratap, if you should come across any—er—scandals as you call them I should be most grateful if you could—er—tip me off. Not that I want to interfere in the course of Indian justice, you understand, just that the British government would not like to be caught unawares, so a timely warning…"

"I am understanding you, Sinclair," yelled Battacharia. The line suddenly looped into gobbledy-gook, the crackles dying away a few seconds later for Sinclair to hear, "…plenty of time in advance." Reiterating gratitude and hopes of continuing co-operation Sinclair thankfully put the phone down. Sue's head appeared round the door.

"I'm off for a swim now. First interview nine o'clock sharp. We'll have polished the lot off by this time tomorrow. Not much in them, is there?"

"One thing, Sue, before you go. I'm going to start on the house this evening. Do you know if there is a safe and where it is?"

"Yes," replied Sue promptly. "Behind a picture on the right-hand wall of Hugo's bedroom, as you face the bed. I'll go and find the combination for you. Just a tick."

Walking back to the house Sinclair was filled with depression. He had been in Delhi for two working days now and had discovered nothing that Battacharia had not found out in his initial questioning. He was bogged down in useless interviews with resentful British staff. But if he were not doing that what should he do? He had no other real lines to follow up—the boys and the Russian had not figured in anyone's comments on Hugo apart from the venomous Lenton's.

Janey was on the verandah reading and making notes when Sinclair came in.

"What time is this dinner tonight?" he asked from the safety of the air conditioned drawing-room.

"We're asked for eight fifteen but no one'll be there before nine; everything's quite late in Delhi. Indian time runs an hour later than the time fixed. Let's leave about a quarter to nine. We can call a taxi from the Ashoka Hotel across the road."

Sinclair looked at his watch. He had an hour and a half to begin his search of the house, and he was strangely reluctant to start. He still hadn't done anything about cotton clothes.

"Do come in, Janey. I'm not sitting out there in this heat." She picked up her books and moved inside. "Where do I find some cotton shirts and trousers?"

"If you give me a shirt and a pair of trousers I'll have them copied in cotton in Khan Market. What colours would you like?" Seeing Sinclair look vague as though he had never realised his clothes were coloured, she said, "Forget it. I'll choose something suitable."

"Not too gaudy," said Sinclair, gazing doubtfully at her brilliant pink tee-shirt. "Another thing, Janey. Was Hugo queer?"

Janey gave a yelp of laughter. "What an extraordinary range of topics you've covered already this evening. About Hugo, I should say not actively, more like gay, retired. He was certainly not much interested in women, but neither did he have orgies with beautiful Indian youths, at least not while I was here."

"Then if you've no evidence why do you think he was that way inclined?"

"Just the way we got on with one another, I think. First, he didn't see me as of any sexual interest, though you might not think that's anything to judge by. And we used to have such good gossips together. I've an old friend from Cambridge who's gay and we get along together in the same way. So companionable and so restful. None of this awful eyeing up the talent or the competition." Sinclair guiltily moved his gaze to the pattern on the curtains.

"Anyway, does it matter if he was queer? So what, nowadays? It's not illegal."

"Don't be naive, Janey. You know quite well it's not a question of illegality. It's just blackmailability."

"If no one minded and no one made an absurd fuss he couldn't be blackmailed. The more people like you go prowling about saying if you're queer in government service you'll be blackmailed the more likely it is to happen. It's a self-fulfilling prophecy. Have you never noticed that there are plenty of people who are gay and don't give a damn who knows it?"

"You can say that and mean it and so can all the brave young things of Gay Liberation, but you've got to think about it from the point of view of someone of Hugo's age and background. He's the one who would want to conceal it."

"Yes, he would, poor lamb. And not just being gay; affairs with other people's wives as well, and money troubles. A more secretive generation, I suppose."

"Don't get this out of proportion. It was a purely theoretical question. It's just that you're a friend of Hugo's, the rest are his colleagues, so you seemed the best person to ask." Sinclair started his search in the study, a small gloomy room at the end of the house. The desk was a model of civil service order and tidiness. On the left was official stationery, private letter paper and envelopes, boxes of copperplate invitations: Mr Hugo Frencham requests the pleasure of the company of… The right-hand side was more personal, but not much: bundles of bills; the servants' pay book; cheque stubs. Sinclair went through each pile meticulously and from the pad of rough paper ready for use on the desk he took a sheet and wrote:

letters—check Bag Room
bank statements?—chase London
diary—check office

The filing cabinet added something to his knowledge of his dead host's life and background. He had had a flat in Westminster; his ex-wife lived in Wiltshire. He had had an account at Hatchards and used it regularly. Sinclair sighed with boredom, slammed the bottom drawer shut and looked at his watch. He had time for a whisky before he showered.

When Jogiram brought his glass Sinclair said, "Did Mr Frencham do a lot of work at home, Jogiram?"

Jogiram considered this for a time. "Some work,

Sahib," he said at last. "Some work, some times. Not lot, not all times. Then he always do burning."

"Burning?"

"Yes, Sahib. Frencham Sahib some evening do plenty work, write plenty letters, use machine." He indicated the calculator. "Then when finished, very tidy, Sahib burn in mali's bin."

'Mali's bin' turned out to be a neat dustbin-like incinerator used for garden refuse in the vegetable patch at the side of the house. Sinclair poked inside it in a desultory way with a bit of stick. Wood waiting to be burned was all that was visible. He had not expected anything else. No one who went to the trouble of burning papers would omit to see that the job was done properly.

He turned away from the hot smell of decaying compost which rose from the nearby heap. Papers could not be burned in the bungalow itself, he thought, as there was no fireplace. Somewhere in the compound, however, there must be facilities for shredding classified waste. Why did Hugo not add his private waste paper to his office stuff? Then Sinclair remembered the immaculate neatness of the study. Hugo's nature would not tolerate the untidiness: anything to be disposed of would go at once. That still left the question of what was so secret and so private that it had to be burned at all.

Sinclair came back into the house through the kitchen door where Jogiram and Babu Lal had been standing and watching him. He stopped inside the door and said, "Did Mr Frencham burn all his papers, Jogiram, always? Did he never leave things in his waste paper baskets? Or did he only burn them occasionally?"

Jogiram said with dignity, "Waste baskets is Babu Lal; Babu Lal sweeper."

He turned away to arrange cups in a cupboard and Sinclair, rebuked, addressed Babu Lal. But Babu Lal was deaf that evening and had to have the questions repeated.

"Did Mr Frencham leave a lot of paper in his waste paper baskets in the study? Or did he always burn the paper himself?"

Babu Lal giggled nervously and kept casting his eyes towards Jogiram. An older man than the bearer and lower in the social hierarchy, Babu Lal seemed to need his superior's help. Jogiram offered him no assistance and at length Babu Lal said, "Before Frencham Sahib not burning. Plenty paper in basket. Then burning own paper, no more in basket."

"How long has he been burning his own waste paper, Babu Lal?" The sweeper had overcome his nervousness, or whatever else it was and replied with a promptness which Sinclair was only to remark sometime later.

"One year, Sahib. One year June no more waste paper."

Sinclair went upstairs, looking at the slip of paper which Sue had given him. He had just time to have a quick glance in the safe, though with the model of the study in front of him he could hardly expect anything of interest in it.

He hesitated a moment before opening the door into Hugo's bedroom, then, rejecting the feeling of intrusion, he pushed it wide and went in. It was orderly and dusted, as though Jogiram were keeping it tidy in the expectation that his master would soon return from leave. A book lay on the bedside table; *Can You Forgive Her?* by Trollope. Sinclair put it down and lifted the picture from the right-hand wall. It was a hideous seascape, government issue not Hugo's own, he was sure. Behind the picture was a neat rectangle with a central boss. Sinclair set the knob, moving it back and forth carefully until it yielded. The safe went back further than he expected and he realised it must form part of the cupboard which opened onto the landing. It was also surprisingly full; there were several bundles of papers secured with rubber bands and at the back two black boxes with handles.

A door in the passage clapped to and Janey's footsteps flip-flopped from the bathroom. She peered round the door.

"What's going to happen about Hugo's stuff, all his clothes and things? No one's making any effort to pack them up."

The first of the boxes which Sinclair was trying to pull out of the safe was astonishingly heavy and awkward. He was having to drag rather than lift it out.

"I suppose they're waiting for instructions from executors. I assume that next of kin have been notified and the will has been read by solicitors and that the usual machinery of death is grinding into motion."

He had by now manoeuvred the box to the edge of the safe and, wedging his fingers underneath it, he brought it out and carried it to the bed.

"What's in there?" asked Janey with the tone of one not much interested and aware that Sinclair did not yet know and could not answer her question.

The box, though it had a keyhole, was unlocked, and the lid fell back under Sinclair's fingers. It was not full in spite of its weight and a crumpled piece of fine leather rather like chamois filled the space at the top. Sinclair removed it, feeling the slimy softness clinging to his fingers, at the same time as the jolt of realisation and disbelief went through him as he looked at the contents of the box. For, unfamiliar in shape, it was instantly recognisable in substance.

Janey had sat down on the bed and was peering into the box. To her recognition had come at the same time as to Sinclair, but she was the first to put their common thoughts into words.

"Gold," she breathed. "What the hell is Hugo doing with a safe full of gold?"

Chapter 5

THEY WERE LATE for the Lentons' party, late even by Indian standards. No one arrived after them and, though they were served with drinks, they were not allowed time to finish them before dinner was announced by the bearer. They had clearly broken several diplomatic conventions and were out of favour with their hostess. Sinclair guessed that he and Janey had gone down on the 'Home side' on the guest list and had been expected to arrive promptly and to perform amusingly for the rest of the party. There were probably several other things amiss with them but he did not know the rules well enough to work out what they could be.

Bryan Lenton's wife was tall and, though her face and figure showed her to be young, her hairstyle and clothes were prematurely middle-aged. She seemed to be rehearsing for the time, in twenty years, when she would be an ambassador's wife. There were ten of them round her table, carefully positioned with place cards to stop them from going astray and to help them with their neighbours' names. Sinclair's and Janey's status was of the humblest; they were in the lowly positions in the centre of the board.

Two bearers served the food with admirable speed and efficiency. Sinclair observed that Mrs Lenton, nodding like a doll to her neighbour's conversation, kept her eyes on her servants all the time they were in the room. Tomato soup and rolls, both home-made, bland, were succeeded by chicken in cream with potatoes and peas. Sinclair realised that since arriving in Delhi, apart from his breakfasts, he had not eaten European food. Janey was presumably responsible for ordering the meals and preserving him from Anglo-Indian cooking for which, when crème caramel appeared on the table, he was deeply grateful. The mysteriously named messes that were produced by Barua at Hugo's house were infinitely preferable to a meal which Sinclair regarded as nursery fare.

Sinclair's neighbours at dinner were as lacking in spice as the menu. On his left he had the wife of the guest of honour, a Czech lady; her place card announced her to be Mme Sakal. Noticing her silence while Bryan was speaking about Indian travel to his other neighbour, Sinclair swivelled his head and asked politely, "Have you been living in Delhi long, Mrs Sakal?"

The lady tore her brown roll apart with energy and tossed a quarter of it into her mouth while she watched Sinclair with interest. She did not reply. After a moment, assuming deafness or inattention, Sinclair repeated the question. She regarded him as if introduced for the first time to a talking doll and fascinated by the ingenuity of the toy. Sinclair was thoroughly disconcerted and was only saved from a third try by Bryan's breaking into his own monologue to say, "Mrs Sakal does not speak English. She speaks Czech, Russian and some French, I believe."

Sinclair felt a brief French conversation was not beyond his powers. Until Helena, his fourth child, was born he and Teresa had spent their holidays every summer for six years in Normandy.

"Est-ce que vous aimez habiter Delhi, madame? L'Inde vous plaît?"

Mrs Sakal's face, slavically broad, was enlivened by a smile at a language she recognised. She replied slowly, enunciating with care; her accent was exact and perfectly comprehensible.

"J'ai deux enfants, monsieur, un fils et une fille."

She drank her last mouthful of soup. The conversation with its intriguingly surreal possibilities was ended by Bryan's taking charge of Mrs Sakal and speaking to her in Czech. After this Sinclair left her well alone.

On his other side was the wife of an Indian journalist, plump and shy, who only responded to his conversational overtures when he had run out of subject matter and in despair asked her about her children. Mrs Mehta was an expert on education in Delhi; her boys were at Delhi Public School, she informed Sinclair, which was the best. To enter a good school was very difficult. Registration at the moment of birth if not conception was necessary. A very hard exam was also involved.

Sinclair vowed to himself never during the rest of his stay in Delhi, or his life for that matter, to allow himself to be embroiled in a diplomatic party, an occasion of excruciating boredom and fatuity. Why had he agreed to come? Janey. The single word answer formed in his mind but he did not dwell on its implications. Instead he brooded on that box of gold, its weight and value as yet uncalculated. It was the first flaw in the neat front presented to the world by Hugo, and it was at that chink that he must place a lever to remove the façade and discover the secret life behind.

The ladies withdrew after the cheese while the men remained in the dining-room listening to a monologue on India from Bryan. Eventually they rose to join the ladies in the next room and, released from the preordained patterning of the dinner table, were free to choose whom to talk to.

Sinclair took his coffee and wondered whether to try Mrs Sen Gupta, the other Indian lady of the party, or to sink onto the sofa beside Janey. He knew that to do that would be almost, though perhaps not quite, as grave a solecism as to be seen talking to your own wife, so, rejecting the temptation, he turned towards Mrs Sen Gupta. As he made to move he found himself addressed by Mr Sakal.

"I understand you are here from London to investigate the death of our *cher collègue,* Mr Frencham."

Sinclair nodded agreement.

"I only met him once myself, at the farewell for my predecessor, Mr Muller. I believe he was a most popular, deservedly popular, member of the diplomatic corps accredited to this country." The unwinding of his sentences displayed not only Sakal's command of a foreign language but also that generalising and platitudinising which marks diplomats of all nationalities. "He was a friend of my colleague in the Russian Embassy, Counsellor Dolgov, who has been sincerely moved at his sad death. He and Counsellor Dolgov played chess together, a model of diplomatic friendship in this time of détente."

Sinclair had already noticed the way diplomats told you things that they knew you knew as if they were imparting confidential information. He began to keep a mental list of these diplomatic devices, heading it with acting ability. He wondered whether auditions were part of the Civil Service exams for the Foreign Office.

"Counsellor Frencham's death shows us the dangers we are subjected to living in this country," Sakal continued. "Have you any success in finding the criminals?"

"I am afraid no arrest is imminent."

"I assume that robbery was the motive. This sort of crime must abound in a society displaying the extremes of wealth and poverty such as India."

The temptation to ideological generalisation to which Sakal gave way allowed Sinclair to avoid the probing of his earlier statements.

"Extremes of wealth and poverty undoubtedly increase the temptation to steal, but I think we must agree that the impulse of greed lies deep within man's nature. Indeed, perhaps we can say that the social controls on greed are stronger in a society like India where the hierarchy of wealth and position is felt to have a religious and moral basis than in a more egalitarian society where even quite slight differences in wealth can create envy because no particular right is felt to attach to its owners."

Sakal's brows creased slightly as if in mild pain; he bowed and said, "I can see you are well versed in the theoretics of your subject." He moved off in the direction of the tirelessly smiling Andrea Lenton, while Sinclair, complacent at having neatly evaded the probe of Mr Sakal, turned again towards the beautiful Mrs Sen Gupta.

❀❀❀

The next morning Sinclair was in his office early, drafting telegrams of enquiries for London. At eight thirty he lifted his phone and tried Turnell's number.

Though he knew that his point of reference and consultation in the High Commission should be the acting Head of Chancery, Bryan Lenton was more than he could take. He had decided to bypass him as much as he could. Alan Turnell might look like a tailor's dummy but he had displayed no animosity nor grotesquely distorted judgment. Sinclair hoped that Turnell would co-operate and not turn him back to the proper channels.

Alan was already in his office reading the papers and agreed to Sinclair's coming up at once. He met him at the lift and took him punctiliously up to the Chancery, that holy place of all embassies where the uninitiated can go only with an escort.

"I've come for advice on relations with the Indians," said Sinclair. "The officer in charge on the Indian side is a good bloke called Battacharia. He's friendly and helpful and has shown me all his files. Now, I've just come across something of interest about Hugo and it might lead us to the reasons for his death. However, I need to tell the Indians about it and get them to make some enquiries for me. This may involve some embarrassment for the High Commission, so I wanted to make sure that you're warned and that it's not going to make too much of a diplomatic rumpus."

"That's very—er—considerate of you, Sinclair. Supposing you tell me about this something and then I can tell you my opinion about the advisability of giving this information to the Indians."

"Frencham's safe is stuffed full of gold."

Turnell had been through too many negotiations to reflect in his face anything other than what he considered was fitting: a mild puzzlement in this case.

"Gold," he said reflectively. "Gold objects, perhaps? You are, of course, aware that Hugo was a..."

"No, no," interrupted Sinclair who, rarely impatient, wanted to break down Turnell's discretion. "Not gold objects, or gold rings, or bangles or anything else, just gold, pounds of it, pounds weight I mean, in bars."

"That certainly is something—er—unusual," said Alan cautiously, "I would agree. I am not sure what the legal position is about British citizens holding a stock of gold…"

"Look Alan," said Sinclair slowly, "you're missing the point. I came out here with a brief to investigate Hugo's security. I'm not going to be able to tell if there's been any breach until I know how and why Hugo died. We have no witnesses or leads to Hugo's murderer. So we have to look at it from the other end. Is there anything in Hugo's life that might have led to his death? Up till now, though I've had a few hints, I have been given nothing definite to make me think that Hugo wasn't the respectable senior diplomat he appeared. Until the gold turned up. British law at the moment says that British citizens cannot hold gold bullion. So I want to find out where Hugo got this gold from, why he had it."

During Sinclair's speech Alan's brain had had time to work out some of the implications of the news he had received for he spoke more briskly in reply. "Yes, yes, I'm with you there. You know, discretion is the thing. Don't tell your friend Battacharia yet. Do what you can on your own. If it does look as if Hugo was involved in—er—well—anything the Indians might not like—we may want to keep that part of it veiled as far as possible." His face registered decisiveness and determination to impose his opinion on Sinclair. His expression or his words must have been persuasive for Sinclair simply said, "In that case, I'll need to do some work outside the compound myself. I can assume, therefore, that the High Commission will support me in that?"

"Within reason, within reason, Sinclair. And with discretion, of course. I shouldn't like to have the reputation of obstructing your department, but we're going to have to live and work here long after you're gone, you know."

Smiling, Sinclair went back to his office, where Sue was ready with the list of the day's interviews. He felt that he had shown his own skill at the diplomatic art of making the other side insist on what you want yourself.

The rest of the morning was tedious in the extreme, only enlivened by the suspicion, irritation and hostility which he encountered in more or less overt forms. He was questioning a bachelor from the Consular Department when the phone rang. The consular official was being particularly obdurate, having to be led through the evening of Hugo's death hour by hour. Sinclair guessed that he had spent the night at his girlfriend's flat rather than his own and was debating whether to admit to it or not.

"Mr Sinclair, I have the Czech Embassy for you," the operator called. There was a series of clicks and grunts intervening before the voice of Mr Sakal came on the line.

"Mr Sinclair, it was so interesting to meet you yesterday. We enjoyed the delightful party so much, my wife and I. We have a small reception at our Embassy this evening and I wondered if you would like to come. Mr and Mrs Turnell have also kindly accepted." This was an indication, Sinclair assumed, that he was not being inveigled into a trap unchaperoned. So unlikely an invitation caught him off guard and, in spite of his previous night's vows, he accepted.

"Perhaps the charming Miss Somers would come too?" was Sakal's last question. Sinclair declined to answer for Janey. Promising to pass the message on he put the phone down and turned back to the vice-consul to learn, with suppressed amusement, that his evening had involved skinny-dipping in the Australian High Commission pool, followed by an overnight stay in the Australian compound.

❁❁❁

At lunch Janey agreed with enthusiasm to accompany him that evening saying that she had never been to the Czech Embassy before.

"Do you usually stay this long in Delhi gadding about?" Sinclair asked.

"I don't know what you mean by 'this long'. Yes, I usually need ten days or a fortnight here to get various papers. I've an introduction—it was through Hugo in fact—to a Tibetan Incarnate Lama, a very learned scholar who lives at Uptak, one of the monasteries in the military zone in Ladakh. I have to have special permission to go there and I've almost managed it. First you have to pull strings and visit various people with letters of introduction. Then you have to go down the line and sit in offices and drink tea. I'll be ready in another day or so I should think. I was hoping to be in Ladakh this year for Buddha's birthday, but I'm not going to make it, as the road isn't open yet. There are no civil flights to Leh you see. I shall fly to Kashmir and do some water-skiing until the road opens, then on to Ladakh."

"What's closing the road?"

"Snow and ice. It's a military road so they won't let civilian traffic on it if it's dangerous."

"For goodness' sake, it's May and the temperature is forty-two degrees, according to the paper."

"It isn't when you're at 13,000 feet. And this time of year is the worst. The snow is melting and is constantly avalanching across the road. So as fast as they clear it, another avalanche comes, the road is sixty feet under and they have to dig it out again."

"I hate snow," said Sinclair, "but at forty-two degrees it has an appeal."

"Kashmir is the place," said Janey. "Brilliant sunshine, moderate temperature, hills and lakes. I shall be there in a few days staying on a houseboat on Lake Nageen."

"I promised myself a few days in Kashmir at the end of this."

"You should go. It's the most beautiful place on earth. If you're there before I leave you can share my houseboat."

❀❀❀

As they set off in the evening, Sinclair wondered what the diplomatic guests would make of Janey. Her red hair was always a huge tangle of curls looking unbrushed and beyond control. Round one bare arm she wore a large henna-stained ivory bracelet and on her left leg a heavy silver anklet.

"I bought this today," she explained, extending her foot. "So expensive but I couldn't resist. They said in Sunder Nagar Market that I should wear it as a bracelet. I thought I would try it like this, as the peasant women wear them. If their husbands have any spare money they buy some silver and put it round their wives' necks and ankles. You can see women with dozens of them."

"I'd've thought your feminism would have triumphed over your vanity," commented Sinclair. "Those anklets are symbols of male domination." Janey did not look put out.

"I'm wearing it to express my solidarity," she said loftily.

Since Sakal's telephone call in the morning Sinclair had been pondering the significance of the invitation. Not for a moment did he think that either his charm or even Janey's appearance was responsible for the Czechs' desire to see them again. The Sakals bowed and welcomed them, but made no other gesture towards them. For the first hour of the party it was no clearer why he had been asked to make up one of some eighty diplomats who were circulating and gossiping according to the rules of their game.

The human kaleidoscope had broken up and reformed its patterns several times before Sinclair suddenly recognised the reason for his unlikely presence at the Czech Embassy. The key was a stout balding man in a light-weight grey suit and plain tie. There was something American in his appearance, in the round skull, the short, fluffy hair below his tonsure, the determined, rather arrogant stance. But his accent was not American.

He inserted himself into the group between Sinclair and his neighbour and shook hands all round, murmuring his name to the one or two who did not know him, "Dolgov, Soviet Embassy." The newcomer allowed conversation to restart around him before saying to Sinclair in a voice low enough to make his remark personal rather than general, "My collcaguc, Mr Turnell, tells me that you are here to help the Indians enquire into the death of my friend Hugo Frencham."

Sinclair doubted whether this information had come from Alan; from Sakal more probably.

"I was disturbed to hear of Hugo's death. You know, I called him Hugo, he called me Vasili; he was my good friend. We played chess together. Hugo was moderate chess player, so-so; good enough to play a Russian however. My chess is not so good, for a Russian, so we played together. When I heard Hugo is dead I could not believe it, I could not believe it."

Almost everyone in Delhi had started their conversations with Sinclair with the subject of Hugo. 'Sad death', 'terrible tragedy', the ritual phrases had come with hardly any emotional force behind them. Even Janey, whose affection for Hugo could not be doubted, had described his death with a mixture of flippancy and calm to distance herself from what she had experienced. So Sinclair was astonished to hear the feeling in the Russian's voice; the words were not remarkable, but the phrasing and emphasis given to them produced a strong effect. Sinclair looked at him curiously; either the acting power of Russian diplomats was infinitely greater than those of other nations or Dolgov was genuinely upset by Hugo's death.

"It must have been a shock to all his friends."

"Now you are going to catch these bad men who done this thing. The Indians have good names for such men. Badmash. A good word, no? Dacoit, goonda. Good names, but not so good at catching them. You are bringing the expertise of Scotland Yard to help the Indian Police."

Sinclair was not so easily caught; he neither confirmed nor denied his attribution to Scotland Yard. He was finding his dialogue with Dolgov increasingly difficult; the Russian was searching for something and Sinclair could not guess what it might be. He could not understand what Dolgov needed to know so he could neither judge whether it was advisable to give him the information, nor deny it to him. Dolgov's questions were put in general terms; their thrust was against Sinclair's relations with the Indians and the line of his enquiries. Sinclair decided that expansiveness and an appearance of simplicity were his best tactics for discovering more from Dolgov. He spoke at length about the Indians in terms of highest praise, about

Inspector Battacharia's close co-operation and advice, his personal friendliness. The only negative note he felt it safe to strike was an adverse comment on the quantity of paper work involved in an Indian investigation. Dolgov became more specific in his questions. Whom had Sinclair and Battacharia interviewed, he wanted to know. Sinclair spoke of servants, guards, High Commission staff; he did not mention the Turnells' party. In spite of the efficient air conditioning he could feel cold rivulets of sweat on his back. He wanted to escape from Dolgov before he gave him everything he wanted without knowing how or why. The Russian had carefully wedged him into a corner of the room gradually placing himself between Sinclair and his former group. Looking over Dolgov's shoulder for Maggie Turnell, who he knew would rescue him, Sinclair saw Janey. She was already on her way over to him, her hair sparkling, her voice rather loud.

"There you are, Sinclair. How do you do, Mr—er? Dolgov? Dolgov. I've been drinking some marvellous Czech vodka; it's yellow and really tastes, unlike ordinary vodka. Mr Sakal tells me it's made with flowers. It's wonderful stuff."

Sinclair reckoned Janey had had too much of the wonderful stuff, though he was too grateful for the interruption to feel embarrassed, as he might normally have done in the company of a slightly drunk and talkative woman.

"This vodka we have in my country too. It is made at midsummer from the flowers of a certain yellow plant." As Dolgov gave Janey a detailed account of how to steep the flowers in the spirit Sinclair made good his escape.

Later the vodka-exhilarated Janey insisted on taking him to dinner in a primitive open-air restaurant in Old Delhi. As they climbed into their taxi she said, "I enjoyed that. I think I should make a good diplomat: I love cocktail parties."

"I doubt it," Sinclair said drily. "I expect you'd be wildly indiscreet. Especially if you got drunk on vodka every time."

"Nonsense, I'm not drunk, but I could do with some food, couldn't you?"

Through the trellis of leaves above the bare table and benches at which they sat in the restaurant Sinclair could see the stars. Janey joked in Hindi to the bearers, ate enthusiastically with her fingers, and, when she had finished, went to rinse her hands under the stand pipe which served as a wash place for all the customers. Her enjoyment of everything, vodka, food, people, had a vigour and simplicity that Sinclair envied. Dolgov's questions and the reasons for them hung in his mind, distracting him from the warm night air, the spiced scent of the food, Janey.

She returned to the table and sat down opposite him. She lit a bidi which she had just bought from the paan seller at the door.

"What was that comic Russian talking to you about?" she asked. "You looked desperate when I came up to you."

"Dolgov? He was talking about Hugo. Wanted to know who I thought had done it, who was being interviewed. I wonder why he's so interested."

"He was asking me about Hugo, too," said Janey. "He was absurd."

"Why absurd? Absurd to be asking you?"

"No. Absurd to think anyone'll be able to tell him who did it." Sinclair's brows raised in query. "How can anyone know what happened that evening, or how or why? We're so brainwashed by detective stories and television series and Sherlock Holmes that when a tragedy like Hugo's death happens we expect someone to come with a big magnifying glass and solve it. How can anyone do that? I just don't believe in it. It is quite impossible for someone to go around and from physical clues and people's memories reconstruct someone else's life and death. Hugo was a very complex and secret person and his life was much too intricate to get to the bottom of easily. There was Hugo the diplomat, on the surface. Everyone saw that one. Then there was Hugo the Tibetan scholar. I knew something of that part of him. And there was his family life, his sex life, his friendships. Life's too complicated and various. You can't just open the lid of someone's past and find everything neatly arranged for inspection."

"Do you think that's what I expect to be able to do? I wish it were so easy."

"No, but you believe it's possible, if not easy," Janey retorted. "It's a question of approach, of attitude to life. That's why I like the subcontinent so much. Here they don't see life cut and dried and labelled and laid out for inspection. They know that it is amorphous and indiscriminate and that you can't lay your hands on it like that."

"I can see you think I'm wasting my time here," Sinclair commented.

"I distrust the idea of reconstructing a past event by a two and two makes four method. Any occasion is made up of feelings, thoughts, intentions; how can those be traced by a magnifying glass?"

"But you admit murderers are uncovered? Or do you think the courts usually convict the wrong person?"

"Of course not." Janey breathed smoke from her bidi impatiently. "Plenty of murders are proved satisfactorily but it's not by the Sherlock Holmes method, I am sure. It's because it is quite clear for other reasons that such a person must have done it; very often the murderer reveals himself.

Anyway, you must know quite well that most crimes aren't 'solved' at all."

As they talked, each thought he or she had summed the other up.

Sinclair saw a clever scatty girl whose interest in India and Tibet, Buddhism and Hinduism had undermined her European rationalism. His rejection of what she propounded had no effect at all on the attraction she exerted. His concentration focused on her mobile face and the small gestures of her hands; everything else disappeared into the haze of the night.

To Janey, Sinclair arranged life into pigeonholes. Yet she respected his capacity for debate, unheated and persistent, enough to wonder and care about which pigeonhole she had been sorted into.

Chapter 6

THE NEXT DAY Sinclair turned his attention to the gold, which he had already removed from the house and placed for safe keeping in Registry in the High Commission. He had found no key to fit the boxes so he had sealed them with red tape and sealing wax. The Registry Officer who had taken them from him was a cheerful boy who looked barely fifteen.

"That looks safe enough," he had said, eyeing the seals and strings. "We'll put them here where the boss keeps her precious things." He swung open the door of a large press and winked at Sinclair who saw with amazement that at the bottom was a jumble of old shoes, bottles and carrier bags. "Don't look so worried, mate. No one'll nick them out of here." He picked up one box by its string handle. "Gor, tied up like Houdini and weighs a ton a bricks. What you got in here? Gold?"

"Of course," Sinclair had replied. The boy had looked at his retreating back and pulled a face.

"No sense of humour, these Security blokes."

As he walked to the office Sinclair carried with him, in a large paper bag to avoid stares and questions, a set of scales borrowed from Barua's kitchen. From the covering of dust Sinclair did not think it would be missed. Barua was clearly of the school of cookery that works by eye and imagination rather than by scientific accuracy.

Sinclair recalled the boxes from Registry and in his small office sat down to examine their contents carefully. Laying out the pieces of gold he found that there were thirty-five of them in all. They were roughly of a size with little variation between them. In shape they were rather like fingers, almost cylindrical with one surface flattened, so they sat firmly on the desk at no risk of rolling off. On the flat surface of each was a small circular mark stamped into the metal, its detail difficult to distinguish with the naked eye. Sinclair traced a lens in the library attached to a dictionary and carried it off to his room. It did not help him much, however, as the only addition it made to his observations was that the circle had six spokes. He finished his work by looking in the most recent copy of *The Times* available in the High Commission and learning that the price of gold was $173.87 an ounce. Each finger of gold in front of him weighed something over a kilo. After complicated calculations to translate metric weight to troy ounces he estimated that he was looking at over a quarter of a million dollars' worth of gold.

He put thirty-four of the pieces back in the boxes which he retaped and sealed for return to Registry. The last piece he placed in an envelope and stowed in his briefcase.

He then brought to the forefront of his mind the problem that had been niggling at him all night. He had been reluctant to credit too much of what the spiteful Lenton had said at his first interview with him. The man disliked Hugo, and had been jealous of him, or professionally thwarted by him, to such an extent that Sinclair had felt his judgments were not to be trusted. But there was no doubt that Dolgov was behaving oddly. He was interested in Hugo's death for no reason that Sinclair could understand. He could not decide whether it was the death itself or the enquiry into the death which concerned Dolgov.

Sinclair reached for the phone and at the same moment it shrilled back at him. It was Sue.

"Bryan wants a word, Sinclair. Can you come up?"

"I'm on my way. I was just going to ask to see him."

Bryan behind his desk wrenched off his glasses with an air of nervous self-importance that set Sinclair's teeth on edge.

"I've just had a telegram in about Hugo's estate which is somewhat disturbing. Now, apparently you asked your people to make some investigations into Hugo's finances, yes?" His tone was accusing.

"Yes," said Sinclair calmly. "It was the first signal I sent on the day I arrived. It as a purely routine move and I decided to start with it when I saw the extent of Hugo's collection."

"You didn't tell me you were asking about that aspect."

"No, I didn't."

There was a silence as if Bryan was waiting for him to justify himself. Sinclair had no intention of becoming involved in a wrangle about whom he was working for and how he was to proceed. If Bryan wanted to make an issue of it he could put it into words himself; Sinclair was not going to help him create a quarrel.

Eventually Sinclair said, "What does the telegram from

London say?" Discontentedly Bryan pulled a sheet of paper towards him.

"I'll let you have a copy; the gist is that Hugo had much more money just in terms of cash in deposit and current accounts, as well as in investments, than one would expect. They've compared the picture with when he was last positively vetted which is about six or seven years ago and his assets have increased enormously."

"I suppose they've looked for the straightforward explanations, legacies, playing the stock market, things like that?"

"One must assume they have and have ruled them out as the overall message is that there's something very fishy about Hugo's money. Here, they say that… Where is it? 'Frencham's account'—I quote—'showed very large sums paid in almost every month, in an irregular pattern, with no day or even week of the month as a norm. The sums were also very varied, ranging from a few hundred pounds to thousands at a time.' There were also some hefty outgoing sums which they say they're going to look into in more detail."

"Right. I'd better have a look at his rupee accounts as well and see what they're like. Can that be fixed?"

Bryan made a note on a pad and said, "We all use a branch round the corner. I'll have a word with the manager and see if he can tell us anything. Are you free this afternoon if he can sort something out by then?"

"Any time today. I noticed the lack of bank statements among Hugo's papers at the house. It may well be that the rupee account is as interesting as the sterling ones." He waited while Bryan called Sue to ask her to make an appointment with the bank manager that afternoon. When Bryan turned back to him he began on his own subject. "You mentioned Hugo's relationship with the Russian Counsellor Dolgov when I first spoke to you. I wonder if you can tell me anything more about Hugo's meetings with him. Do you know, for instance, how often they met? And that's another thing—I've found no diary of Hugo's. He kept no personal one at home. Presumably his official one was in the office?"

Bryan was stimulated by this line of enquiry, probably because he felt that he had initiated it. After calling Sue for Hugo's office diary he said, "I don't know exactly how often they met. Maybe once a month or so. Hugo sometimes put in a short report if he was given any gossip worth having or if he thought he was being fed a particular line that was significant. We could look those up for you."

"You wouldn't say Hugo ever brought home any high grade information from Dolgov?"

"No, he never pulled off any coup. Dolgov is used by the Russians as one of a number of channels to test out their ideas on the Western circuit in an informal way."

"Where did they meet, do you know?"

"At times they certainly met in the Russian compound; I don't know whether they always did. The Russians presumably favoured their own ground so they could listen in to make sure Dolgov didn't get into mischief, as well as to hear anything Hugo might let fall."

"I'd like to see someone in SIS about Dolgov. They may have some useful background on him."

"Charlie Croom is your man. He is SIS chief in India. I'm sure he'd be delighted to help. Give him a buzz. On the list he's commercial."

"I'd also like a mug shot of Dolgov to try on Hugo's servants. Do you have one?"

"The personalities file might produce something. Let's see." Sue came in with Hugo's official diary and was sent off again to find a photo of Dolgov. Sinclair was relieved to discover that Bryan had not taken over the diary as well as everything else of Hugo's. The last entries crept ahead of the date of the murder indicating official lunches and meetings which Hugo never attended. Sinclair started to flick back through April and March; he observed meetings with visiting MPs during the Easter recess, lunches with EEC groups, cocktails with Swedes and Norwegians, Thais and Burmese; no chess, no Dolgov mentioned.

Sue returned with a newspaper photograph of Dolgov at an Indo-Russian cultural event. It was blurred but recognisable. Sinclair pocketed it.

"Did Hugo have another diary?" he asked Sue. "A personal one I mean."

"He might have had one at home, most people do, but he didn't have a pocket one if that's what you mean." She thought for a moment and added, "Hugo had a marvellous memory. Things were only put in the diary to stop me double-booking him; he hardly needed one."

To finish the morning Sinclair took himself to meet the SIS Resident at Delhi. Charlie Croom might appear humbly among the first and second secretaries in the Commercial Section on the Diplomatic List, but he had a smart suite of offices to himself and was guarded by the prettiest and debbiest secretary that Sinclair had seen. Croom was fifty, more or less; more in appearance and less in manner, which was of boyish earnestness and keenness, emphasised by the use of out of date slang. He listened to Sinclair's story about Dolgov and said, "Something rum there, old boy, not a doubt of it. Now, as to what we've got on him: not much, I'm afraid, and most given to us by Hugo. What I'll do is send a signal off to London and ask for a trace on him for you. If he's been up to real mischief in any of his postings they'll have it there.

They can probably do a match with the Cousins' material, see if they've anything to add. We'll do it thoroughly. That'll suit you, eh?"

Sinclair agreed it would. He still did not know what he was looking for. Dolgov seemed as promising a lead as any and one easier to follow than, for instance, the gold.

Janey was in for lunch. She took a mango from the fruit bowl and started to roll it between her palms.

"I'm leaving tomorrow," she announced when she had taken her first bite. Sinclair looked up. "If that's all right with you, of course. I was told to stay until you'd seen me. I expect you've seen me enough by now."

"Is your road open yet?"

"Not officially and not even unofficially, I think. I've managed to fix a flight to Kashmir which at this time of year is quite hard to do, so I'm going to take it and wait in Srinagar until I can drive through to Leh."

Janey was munching her mango between sentences; Sinclair pushed away his plate. Jogiram who kept a keen eye on what was happening through a glass panel swung instantly through the kitchen door and removed the plate, putting a glass in front of Sinclair. Janey poured some coffee into it. When Jogiram had gone Sinclair asked, "How long will you be in Kashmir, do you think?"

"Depends. Sometimes the road isn't open until the middle of June. That doesn't bear thinking about; I must be through before then or I'll have lost a whole month's work. Usually the road is passable intermittently before it is completely cleared for the summer and I hope to dash through between avalanches. I'll have to persuade someone in Srinagar to give me a piece of paper allowing me through, so I expect I'll be in Kashmir for a week or so."

There was a pause as if each were waiting for the other to say something more.

It was Janey who said, "Do you think you'll come to Kashmir?"

"It depends how long all this takes me in Delhi. At the present rate of progress it may take for ever. Janey, before you go I need your help: a goldsmith."

"A goldsmith? Oh yes, I see, a goldsmith."

"I can't go to Battacharia for help and I want as few people as possible to know about the gold. Do you know anyone who could help?"

"The dealer I bought the anklet from, I know him quite well; he was a friend of Hugo's too. He's a business man, has a jewellery shop as well as an antiques business and God knows what else. I'll speak to him."

She went out into the hall and Sinclair heard her dialling. "Mr Singh? It's Janey Somers, you know… Yes, yes, I'm well, thank you… No, I don't mind the heat. And how are you? Yes, I love the bracelet and I did wear it as an anklet… Yes." The opening formulae were properly oriental in their length and detail. At last Sinclair heard her say, "Mr Singh, I'm ringing to ask a favour… You're too kind. A friend from England and I, while we're in Delhi, would like to see a goldsmith at work and we wondered whether… Yes… That would be marvellous… You're sure he won't mind? Can you tell me how to find it? No, really? That's so good of you. Many thanks. Yes, goodbye… Goodbye."

She came in again. "He's sending his car to take us to a goldsmith who works for him in Old Delhi. I hope four o'clock is OK. What are we going to do when we're there?"

Sinclair smiled at Janey's self-inclusion in the expedition. He took out the gold bar from his briefcase and handed it to her.

"We'll ask him to look at this, analyse the purity and so on. Have a look at the mark on it for me."

He gave her the lens from Hugo's desk. Janey peered at the slip of gold for a moment and then said, "It's so small and fuzzy. The only thing it makes me think of is the Wheel of Existence; that's probably only because my mind is full of Tibetan images anyway. Look, you can see it there on Hugo's tangka." She pointed to the mysterious cloth painting which Sinclair had noticed the first morning in the house. "There's the central ring; then there are six divisions representing the six different forms of life." She indicated the six sectors on the tangka in turn. "Gods, titans, yiddags, creatures in purgatory, animals, men. And in the inner circle are the causes of rebirth. You can see the same shape in the gold mark." She passed the lens and bar back to Sinclair who re-examined the stamp on the gold.

"Perhaps," he said. "You could be right. So where does that take us?"

❀❀❀

Jogiram looked at the newspaper cutting of Dolgov and others dubiously. "No, Sahib, not know them."

"What about that one. Did he ever come to see Mr Frencham?"

Jogiram concentrated his attention on the one face.

"He is in the High Commission?" he asked, as if it were a game which Sinclair had devised for him.

"No, Jogiram. I wondered if he ever came here to the bungalow to play chess with Mr Frencham. He is Russian."

Jogiram brightened. "One sahib come to play chess two-three times. Was this sahib?"

"I hoped you could tell me Jogiram. Never mind."

❀❀❀

The ramifications of bureaucracy at the bank were not as extensive as at the Police Headquarters. The offices consisted of one large room which served for all the clerical work and for serving customers and a much smaller one where the manager could shut himself off from view. There were no security devices of any kind to prevent a raider from leaping over the counter and seizing the bags of money which lay beside the cashier's desk. A thief who tried this would probably have encountered little resistance as many of the clerks were surreptitiously listening to a cricket commentary on portable radios hidden in their in-trays.

The manager, Mr Prasad was already armed with papers when Sinclair was ushered in and was eager to start.

"We are very happy to be talking about this account to you, Mr Sinclair, because it has been a problem to us for some time."

"In what way has it been a problem?"

"First I must be explaining to you the way the diplomats' and foreigners' accounts work. Usually every month the foreigner pays a cheque in a hard currency to us—in this case it would be pounds sterling—for his use during the month, according to his need. Sometimes £200, sometimes £500, sometimes £1000, depending on what he is wanting to spend in India. But Mr Frencham never paid any hard currency into his account."

"Never? At all?"

"In the first few months he was here, more than three years ago, he did. Then he was ceasing to do this."

"And what money did Mr Frencham use after that?"

"He paid money in to bank himself in cash—rupees, you understand—at different times, not just at the beginning of the month as most foreigners do, coinciding with their pay cheques from their organisations."

"Have you any idea where this cash came from?"

"This is a very embarrassing question, Mr Sinclair. You are asking us to make guesses which could be wrong, and about a valued client. The British High Commission is always banking here and we would not be wanting to lose this custom." Mr Prasad was gently working his hands together. They were supple hands and looked as if they might be made with wire rather than bone as he pushed the fingers of one hand backwards until the palm seemed to be almost turned inside out.

"Mr Prasad," said Sinclair in his most confidence-inspiring voice, "I can understand your reluctance to raise suspicions which may prove unfounded. I must tell you that the High Commission is co-operating fully with the Indian Police in the matter of Mr Frencham's death. We believe there may be some—er—irregularities connected with Mr Frencham's finances, which is why we have come to you. Anything you say will naturally be regarded as only a hypothesis until it is fully confirmed and, if it is not borne out, it will be forgotten."

"Mr Sinclair, are you knowing what black money is?"

"I can guess, but perhaps you had better explain it to me in detail."

"Black money, Mr Sinclair, is the money that is funding and is made out of the secret or unofficial economy. Every business man in India I should say has a little black money;

some have much. Some black money is made in illegal activities; some is made in activities which are legal in themselves but which are not declared to the tax officers. The trouble for people with black money, especially with a lot of it, is what to be doing with it, how to be turning it to use without becoming liable for tax."

"And you think that Mr Frencham's money was off-loaded black money? How would he have got it?"

"Let me be telling one pointer to black money, then I am explaining to you how Mr Frencham might obtain it. Are you seeing in your stay in India any thousand rupee notes, Mr. Sinclair?"

Sinclair had handled very little money in his few days in Delhi, handing over something to Barua for food and paying taxis. The largest note he had seen was Rs 100, which was worth about £6.50.

"No," he replied, "But I don't need such a large amount at one time. Even a hundred rupees seems too much for a taxi driver to change."

Mr Prasad regarded this as a kind of triumph. "Aachhaa, no, you are not seeing them. They have been withdrawn by government. And it is for your reason. Who needs a thousand rupee note? Not for bazaar, not for rickshaw, not for taxi. Thousand rupee notes were being mostly used for black money. Government withdraws notes and so wipes out all those in secret stores. This is clever. Now Mr Frencham. When he was first paying in cash he was always bringing thousand rupee notes. This is not necessarily black money, but it is making us think. Then one day Mr Frencham is paying in ten one thousand rupee notes; two days later government withdraws all thousand rupee notes."

"Where was he getting these thousand rupees from, do you think, Mr Prasad?"

"In my opinion it is a little currency dealing that he is doing. Indians cannot have dollars, sterling, hard currency. If they go abroad they may exchange at the Reserve Bank of India and this is being strictly controlled and at a bad rate. Now many Indians going abroad make arrangements. They are having families in England or the States who help them. Or they are having foreign friends here who are giving them a cheque to cash in England and they are giving rupees in Delhi in return. Everyone is doing this. I think perhaps Mr Frencham has a friend who wants sterling and Mr Frencham is giving him sterling to his account in England and he is taking rupees in India to live off and at a very good rate of exchange. I think the rupees were black. Mr Frencham might not be knowing they are black when he takes them." The bank manager finished on an excusing note as if oriental courtesy demanded he make light of the errors of his guest's compatriot.

"Did you ever speak to Mr Frencham about this?"

Mr Prasad's hand movements, which had ceased as his anxieties were expressed in words, began again. "Yes, once I was obliged... But it was very... Mr Frencham was a burra sahib of the old days... It was very difficult." Sinclair had an unpleasant vision of rank and race being used to subdue the nervous Prasad. It was the first really distasteful, as opposed to simply disreputable thing that he had discovered about Hugo and he was surprised at the feeling of revulsion and disappointment which overcame him.

"Why did you have to speak to him?" he asked gently.

"He said he was going abroad and was needing dollars. For foreigners we may issue dollars in cash or travellers' cheques and we debit their accounts. The rupees are coming from hard currency and can go back to hard currency. Mr Frencham asked for dollars but had given no sterling, so I was obliged to ask him for this. He then presented a large cheque for sterling which he immediately drew out as dollars in cash. This he continued to do every month since." Sinclair leaned forward.

"When did this start?" he asked eagerly.

"The first time was in the summer, yes, it would be June last year."

Sinclair eased his position in his chair in front of Prasad's desk.

"You have been most helpful, Mr Prasad. I have only one or two things left to ask now. Could I have copies of Mr Frencham's bank statements for the whole time he was in India? Thank you. And the other question is: have you any idea who Mr Frencham's colleague was in this laundering of black money which you have described?"

Mr Prasad rose. "I have been taking much of your time, Mr Sinclair. I hope I am helping somewhat. No, no, that I am not knowing. I do not know Mr Frencham's friends. No, I cannot be saying that. Goodbye, Mr Sinclair."

The manager led Sinclair at a brisk trot through the open-plan office, through the flap in the counter to the door where the refrigerated air was suddenly exchanged for heat blazing from the sky and rising from the concrete and tarmac.

In front of the bank was parked an ancient American car, of 1950s vintage, Sinclair reckoned, with the elongated bonnet and boot and sharply peaked tail fins of that era. In a country where imported cars were rare and the Morris Oxford was standard this lovingly maintained period piece was a remarkable sight. Its black and chrome bodywork glowed from incessant polishing, done, no doubt, by the smartly dressed driver in a white uniform who was holding open the rear door for the occupant of the back seat to climb out.

"What a marvellous old car," said Sinclair as he proffered his hand to Mr Prasad.

"Yes, yes," said Prasad, rocking his head on his neck in the peculiarly Indian fashion which combines both nodding and shaking in one movement. "Yes, this is Mr Ranjit Singh's car. Are you knowing him?"

"No," replied Sinclair indifferently. "His car is superbly kept. It'll be a museum piece one day. Goodbye, Mr Prasad, and thank you." He turned away into the heat to meet the car's owner about to enter the bank. He stepped to one side and then walked over to the Cortina waiting for him under the trees. He would be back just in time to go to Old Delhi with Janey.

❀❀❀

At the High Commission Sinclair locked up Hugo's bank statements and set off down the stairs at a run. On the first floor landing he met Sue, laden with papers.

"Oh, Sinclair," she called as he swung round the turn.

"Just out, Sue. Tell me tomorrow."

"It's that Dolgolf."

Sinclair stopped, turned back. "Dolgov. Yes?"

"That bloke whose picture I got for you this morning. I remember seeing him a couple of times with Hugo at the pool at the Chandragupt Hotel."

"The Chandragupt Hotel? Where's that?"

"It's a big new hotel a few blocks over that way. I know the manager there. He allows me to use the pool and I go and swim there sometimes. It's better than this rotten little paddling pool we've got here."

"And what were Hugo and Dolgov doing there?"

"Just sunbathing, I suppose. I never saw them swimming, though they were both wearing trunks and sun glasses. That's why I didn't recognise the photo at first, but now I realise that's who it was."

"Did Hugo see you?"

"Not the first time he didn't. The second time he did because I waved to him. He seemed a bit off really. Never mentioned it to me at the office."

"Do the Russians use that hotel a lot, do you know?"

"No, I don't think so. In fact, I know for entertaining they use the Mandi Hotel on Niti Marg because if you go there to eat there are more Russians than Indians or even tourists."

"Where's the Chandragupt Hotel?"

"On Chandragupt Marg where it meets Sardar Patel Marg."

"Thanks, Sue, you're a clever girl." Sinclair continued down the stairs two steps at a time. He was late.

Chapter 7

THE CAR PARKED in the drive of Hugo's house ready to take Sinclair and Janey to the goldsmith's was not the expected Ambassador, the ubiquitous Indian version of the Morris Oxford; it was a black fin-tailed Dodge, immediately recognisable as the one Sinclair had seen outside the bank half an hour earlier. The driver standing in the shade of a neem tree regarded the arrival of Sinclair rather reproachfully. Janey did not just look her reproaches.

"You're bloody late," she said furiously as she stepped out of the front door.

"I'm sorry," said Sinclair. "I was held up."

Janey hustled him into the back seat and sat tight-lipped as the chauffeur reversed out of the drive and set off slowly to the main gate of the compound.

"Janey, I'm sorry I was a bit late. This is a rather extreme reaction, you know."

"I've been to the trouble to ring a friend who lends his

car, all for the purposes of your peering and prying and you can't arrive at a given place at a set time."

"Janey." Sinclair's voice had a harsh note in it. "Stop behaving like a spoiled brat."

She turned her sulky profile towards him and scanned his face with interest at his display of anger.

"I've a vile temper," she said, though her tone was complacent rather than regretful. "And one thing I can't bear is being kept waiting." Sinclair said nothing, content to forget the whole episode. Janey, her temper over now, reached out her hand to him; he patted it conciliatorily for a moment.

The journey to Old Delhi was long and slow and as they came closer to the Red Fort of Shah Jehan the road filled with the cycle rickshaws and tongas pulled by frail-legged ponies, which were not seen in the modern city. The car turned down Chandni Chowk, the main street of Old Delhi, and slowed to walking pace. Half way along the driver mounted the car onto the pavement and said in Hindi to Janey that they must now walk and he would guide them. He locked the car carefully, as a gang of small boys touching the backs of their hands to their foreheads gathered round him chanting, "Chowkidar, Sahib, chowkidar, Bhai sahib." One was chosen to be watchman for the car's safety and the chauffeur turned down one of the narrow lanes leading off the Chowk. The road was cobbled and carried plenty of traffic; bicycles, cycle rickshaws, pedestrians thronged it. The shops and houses on either side had been built long before motor traffic and no car could start down it without becoming inexorably jammed in the narrowing, winding way. Sinclair looked, fascinated, at the shops on either side of the street, his first sight of an Indian bazaar. Each shop consisted of a single small room, hardly more than a cubby hole, filled to the ceiling with merchandise. Cross-legged amidst his wares sat the banya. Sinclair stopped in front of a stall full of fabrics. Two Indian ladies had climbed the steps up to the shop and had many bales of material unrolled for their inspection. Lapping waves of cloth still lay on the floor though the women had made their purchases. The shopkeeper took the notes they held out and inserted them between his toes while he selected the correct change from the tin box by his side. Handing the coins to his customers he neatly placed the notes in the box with his foot.

The driver led them for some five minutes through the lanes before he turned down a urine-smelling passageway and up a flight of steps. In a lobby they were met by a small elderly man with grey hair, neat features and several teeth missing, dressed in a crisp white kurta, a long Indian shirt, over his loose pajama trousers. He greeted them with a salaam and spoke in Urdu to them.

Janey said to Sinclair, "Mr Saleem says that though he speaks a little English he prefers to talk Urdu. I can translate for you, OK? We must take our shoes off now." They discarded their shoes and walked across the cotton-covered floor to the next room. This also was carpeted in white cotton and round the edge of the room were white bolsters and pillows. In response to Mr Saleem's gestures they seated themselves on the floor, Janey crossed her long legs, clad in her Indian chundars, with ease; Sinclair pulled up his trousers to accommodate his knees with less grace. As they were arranging themselves Janey said to Sinclair, "I'll make some general chat first about his work and then towards the end you can bring out your piece of gold. Is that all right?"

Mr Saleem had been warned to expect guests for

tea and Indian sweets were brought in by a teenager, his grandson, who was learning the craft of goldsmith work from his grandfather. The sweets clung softly to fingers and tongue and were to Sinclair almost nauseatingly glutinous. Janey, however, expressed delight, exclaiming, "Oh luddoos, how delicious!" Sinclair was almost sure that her enjoyment was genuine.

The elderly goldsmith had equipped himself with his tools and various examples of his work which he spoke of at length and with enthusiasm to Janey. His desire to explain his beloved craft even made him break into English for Sinclair's benefit if he felt that Janey's translations were too cursory. The patience needed in any investigation enabled Sinclair to sit through the examination of a gold bracelet made of strands of gold wire, of a gold box, filigreed, with an intricate clasp, to endure the numbing of his buttocks and aching of his knee joints without any outward sign of discomfort. Janey needed no patience. Her questions, her detailed study of each article, charmed the little jeweller, whose gappy smile was frequently and flirtatiously directed at her.

Eventually the balance of talk shifted in Janey's favour. She was explaining something to the goldsmith. Sinclair took out the gold which had been weighing down his pocket and placed it on the cotton beside Janey's hand. She took it up smoothly without breaking off what she was saying and handed it to the jeweller. She was talking about the stamp, for Mr Saleem took from the pocket of his kurta a lens and fitted it into his right eye to examine the mark. Janey waited for his reply and translated for Sinclair.

"Mr Saleem does not know the mark. He has not seen gold like this before. Apparently in India it does not normally come in this shape." The jeweller interrupted her with his next comment and their exchanges continued for some time. For Sinclair it was like watching a mime in which the expressions and gestures interpreted the music of the incomprehensible language. Mr Saleem's excitement and astonishment were expressed in a series of rapid questions to which Janey replied with some signs of embarrassment. The goldsmith weighed the finger of gold in his palm, stroking the surface, seemingly assessing its density and purity. After further conversation he carefully placed the gold on the cotton-covered floor and went out. Janey turned to Sinclair and said, "He says it's very valuable, worth over half a lakh of rupees and that you are mad to walk around with it in your pocket. I had a hard time to defend that one. He spoke a good deal about its weight and its lustre. By its colour he thinks that it is very pure and he will do an acid test for us. Analysis is much more complicated and he will not do that, but he will tell us the carat value."

The jeweller came back carrying a square ceramic slab on which was balanced a small bottle. In his palm he held a ring from which dangled a number of matchsticks of gold, like keys on a key ring. He put all these on the floor, arranging them in a meticulous row, the sticks of gold to the right, the bottle to the left, the slab in the centre. He settled himself cross-legged in front of them and picked out one of the needles of gold. Speaking in Urdu he made gestures over the slab.

"He is going to make two marks along the touchstone," Janey translated, "with two of the pieces of gold and in the centre he will make a...a stroke—sorry this vocabulary is a bit strange to me—with our gold. Then he takes some acid from the bottle and puts a dab on each mark. After a time he compares the colour of our gold with the others and if it matches one of them it is of the same purity as that one." While she had been speaking Mr Saleem was already at work and they both watched the deft movements of his fingers. When he had finished he again examined the stamp with his lens and spoke to Janey. She questioned him and listened to his reply.

"This is very interesting," she reported. "Mr Saleem has heard that a month or six weeks ago some gold something like this was acquired by a Bombay jeweller whom he knows. He heard about it from him when this man was in Delhi recently to give Mr Saleem some work. Mr Saleem, you see, does not buy or own the gold he works; he is the craftsman. The jeweller from Bombay was in Delhi and gave a commission to Saleem and while he was here he told him about some unusual gold he had bought in this shape."

"What's the Bombay man's name?"

"It's Hamid. I'll find out where his shop is."

Mr Saleem was now looking carefully at the touchstone and starting to comment on it to Janey. They all leaned forward to look at the marks on the slab.

"Mr Saleem says that this gold is nearly twenty-four carat but not quite. This streak is twenty-four carat, this is ours. He says that there is a little difference in the colour, they don't match completely. I can't see any difference, can you? The other streak is twenty-two carat gold and there is a clear difference between the colours there. Ours is the purer." She questioned the goldsmith for a moment. "This gold is nearly pure, but not absolutely so and he thinks this is because it was not refined using modern methods and so a little impurity is left in it. Our gold is ready for use by a goldsmith who would mix it with alloy of silver and copper to make it hard enough to use and of course to make it go further."

"What about its shape?" asked Sinclair. "What does he say about that?" After a brief patter of Urdu from Janey Mr Saleem drew two small bars of gold from his kurta pocket.

"These two are the shapes usually seen in India," Janey translated. The Indian held out one, slim as a book of matches, surprisingly heavy in the hand for its size.

"This is a ten tola bar," Janey recounted. "It is the traditional bar of gold for India, but nowadays apparently this other is also becoming popular." The other was fatter and rounder in shape. "This mark shows it is a Johnson Matthey. Does it come from London or New York with a name like that?" she asked. The jeweller's reply was long.

Sinclair was becoming attuned to the way in which Indians incorporated English words into their speech and caught 'smuggler' and 'import' before Janey produced her translation.

"Perhaps you know all this," she said, "I didn't. I am told that India forbade the import of gold at Independence in 1947. Gold is very much in demand here. People hoard it against bad times, or use it for their daughters' dowries or just show off with it. So to meet that demand a lot of smuggling goes on. Gold comes in dhows from Dubai to Bombay and is paid for in silver. That's how most of the Johnson Mattheys arrive here. The price of gold is higher in India than on the world market so there is a good incentive for the smugglers. Mr Saleem is hinting politely that his contact in Bombay, Mr Hamid, may have had dealings with the smugglers."

"Does he think this is smuggled gold?"

Saleem's reply was uncertain. He did not think it was Indian gold as the weight, shape and stamp were so strange, but on the other hand the smugglers were careful to provide what people wanted. A Johnson bar was acceptable even in the villages, its purity recognised. An unfamiliar shape and mark made people reluctant to buy. Janey finished, "He says perhaps it is some old gold we have found."

❀❀❀

The Dodge delicately nosed its way at no more than walking pace along the Chowk, hemmed in by cycle rickshaws whose drivers' stringy legs pumped like slow steam pistons as they passed the car.

Their departure from the goldsmith's house had been prolonged, involving thanks, compliments, salaams and the putting on of shoes. Their waiting driver had led them back to the car and in the weird orange glare of the old city at dusk they had begun their return journey to New Delhi.

Janey half-opened her window to allow the thick air to blow on her face.

"I hope you didn't mind my taking over," she said.

"I could hardly have spoken to him in Urdu myself and I have no one else to help me. I'm very grateful."

"Do you think Hugo had already disposed of some of the gold and that's how the man in Bombay had some? Or did Hugo buy his gold from Hamid in the first place?"

"It's hard to say. We don't know what Hugo was doing with the gold, bringing it in or taking it out. It is possible that both Hamid in Bombay and Hugo got it from a third person."

"But where oh where would Hugo ever find the money to buy so much gold?"

"My dear Janey, Hugo wasn't short of money, even of the hundreds of thousands we're talking about. Anyway it's quite possible he didn't pay for it."

"You mean he robbed some gold vaults or was a receiver

of stolen goods? Hugo? You have a very lively imagination, Sinclair." Janey laughed at her own satire. Sinclair did not respond. After a moment she went on, "I hope you will be coming to Kashmir so that I can hear how you decide to end the story." When Sinclair again made no reply she leaned back on the white cotton-covered seat and stared out of the window.

Sinclair covertly watched Janey's face, turned away from him in quarter profile, alternately lighten and darken as the beams of oncoming cars shone and passed, shone and passed. He could sense the way her response to him wavered from moments of intense interest and involvement as they talked to Mr Saleem to the mocking disengagement once they were on their own again in the car.

In his own feelings he recognised a similar ambivalence, not to his work but to Janey herself. He realised that she was playing a larger role in his investigation than he had ever allowed any outsider before. There was, of course, the language problem; he needed an interpreter and she fulfilled the part admirably. But he scrutinised the motives of others, ostensible and concealed, too often to allow himself to evade the question so easily. The truth was, or so it seemed to him, that living for a few days in close proximity to Janey, energetic, talkative, physically attractive, had reopened an area of existence which he had shut off since his separation from Teresa. Though he acknowledged his own state of mind he could not bring himself to think either about what Janey herself might feel or of the implications for the future.

The Dodge took them to the drive of Hugo's house. The front door was unlocked but no lights were on. Looking through the drawing-room, Sinclair could see that the sliding doors onto the verandah were open. He walked through to shut them, before turning on the air conditioning and enclosing himself again in a cooled limited world in which he might be able to think clearly.

In the darkness at the edge of the lawn a shadow moved on the ground and then the shadow's shadow. There was something so eerie and so unexpected in that rolling, uncoiling movement on the spot where Hugo's body had lain that Sinclair jerked one door towards him more sharply than he intended.

"Who's there? Jogiram?"

The twin movements hardened into shapes and he saw two men just risen from squatting positions, their blurred moon-like faces turned towards him. Janey snapped on a light and in the intensified blackness outside the figures disappeared.

"Who are you? Come here please." Sinclair's voice was loud in his own ears.

"Sahib."

"Good evening, Sahib."

Jogiram entered from behind at a trot, at the same time as the two men from the garden stumbled, blinking, into the room. Explanations in several languages washed round the room. Janey, Jogiram, the strangers, were all speaking.

"...Frencham Sahib dealer. Come often before, now come to see Sahib..."

Janey's clear voice cut through Jogiram's tangled explanations and the murmurs of the strangers. "This is apparently Kalsang Lhawang who deals in Tibetan objects and this is Tashi Gangshar, a monk."

The flat round faces of the two men placed them unmistakably as Tibetans. One of them, the monk, had a close cropped bullet head and wore a sleeveless crossover gown of thick dark red material, out of which dangled thin arms ending in large shovel-like workman's hands. There was about him a strange and touching combination of frailty and strength which sat oddly with his monkish robes. The other wore his straight black hair long, flopping over his forehead so that he peered askew at Sinclair and Janey. His clothes were roughly Western in style, soiled and stained with sweat and dust.

The initial moments of confusion were quickly resolved into order by Jogiram who switched on lights and air conditioning and brought tea. The Tibetans had arrived some half an hour earlier and had settled down to wait for Sinclair's return, Jogiram told them.

Sinclair had read Battacharia's account of the police interview with the Tibetan dealer and had decided no further action was necessary on his part. He wondered what the reason was for the Tibetan's visit in the unlikely company of a monk.

Kalsang Lhawang began by explaining that he used to visit Mr Frencham frequently, bringing him pieces of Tibetan silver.

"The pieces I brought him last time..." He paused and glanced at his companion. The monk appeared to be taking no notice at all of what was going on. His eyes were dreamily fixed on Hugo's tangka.

"Yes," Sinclair prompted. "The Buddha and the knife?"

No response.

"What were they like?"

Kalsang Lhawang suddenly broke into fast speech. "The knife was very fine, very old. You know what it was used for? In Tibet where we come from we do not burn bodies of the dead like Hindus; we lack wood for the pyre. We do not bury the bodies in the earth like the Moslems and

Christians; earth in Tibet is too hard very often. So we cut up bodies for the birds to eat. First they are…" His language gave out and he made sharp, chopping signs with the edge of his hands.

"Dismembered," Sinclair supplied.

"Yes. And then placed outside, far away. Special tools are used. Sacred knives to cut."

"And the one you brought was one of those?"

"Yes."

"And the Buddha?"

"Buddha very fine piece also, silver work very old. Come from Lhasa that piece. Buddha in earth-touching pose…"

The echo of Battacharia's words, themselves undoubtedly an echo of Kalsang Lhawang, caught Sinclair's ear. "What's that?" he asked.

"Important story of Buddha. Buddha sits beneath the Bodhi tree for he is about to reach moment of enlightenment. He is attacked by demons. They come to test him. They bring storms and fire and wind and earthquake, but Buddha is not moved. Then Mara the Evil One denies Buddha's goodness and Buddha calls the earth to bear witness for him. He touches the earth with right hand and earth replies, 'I am his witness.'"

The dealer was sitting in a chair; as he spoke he twisted his right leg under him and reached down towards the floor with fingers outstretched. His gesture attracted the attention of the monk who shifted his rapt gaze from the tangka and began to speak in Tibetan to his companion. Kalsang Lhawang interrupted him by saying to Sinclair, "We came to know about Buddha and knife."

"To know what happened to them? I am afraid I can't help you. Neither has been found as far as I know."

Sinclair's negative tone was understood by the monk who spoke again to the dealer.

"Mr Frencham said that Tibetan things go for special Tibetan place," the dealer remarked.

Sinclair glanced in query at Janey who had sat uncharacteristically silent throughout the meeting. She shook her head.

"I'm afraid we know nothing about that."

Kalsang Lhawang shrugged. Before letting him go, Sinclair took the opportunity to question the Tibetan about his last visit to Hugo. The two men eventually left, the dealer leading the way, the monk behind, again wrapped in his silent dream.

"What was that about?" Sinclair asked Janey in bewilderment. "What did they want—apart from casing the joint. A shiftier rogue than that dealer I've rarely seen."

Janey stretched thoughtfully. "No, you're wrong. Not about his being shifty, but about casing the joint. They came because they want to know where the Buddha and knife are."

"But why? They sold them to Hugo. They can hardly care what's happened to them since."

"They do. Or at least the monk does. I couldn't understand all he said; his accent was strange. I think the monk supplies the dealer with holy objects for sale. You can see why: he was completely zonked."

"On drugs?"

"Oh yes. It's not only western hippies that are cast up and dropped out in India."

"And why is the monk concerned about the knife and the Buddha?"

"It's the Buddha in particular. He seemed upset that it had been involved in a murder. He said something to the effect that the earth bears witness to Buddha's goodness and the statue bears witness to taking of a life."

"Curious. It is a witness in a way. If we could only find it we would be nearer knowing who killed Hugo than we are now."

❀❀❀

Janey went out in the evening to a party with some of her Indian friends. Sinclair saw her go off with a young Sikh, incongruously named Bunny Singh, who was well over six feet tall not including his elegant pale blue turban. He dined at home, served by Jogiram to whom he chatted in a desultory way, mostly about Hugo, while he ate. Jogiram instead of peering through the glass panel from the kitchen stationed himself on the dining-room side of the door and elaborated his late master's character.

"Frencham Sahib very strong, Sahib."

"Strong, Jogiram?" From other descriptions Hugo appeared to have been slight, thin, unathletic."Yes, Sahib." Jogiram tightened every muscle in his face to indicate the kind of strength he meant. "Sahib angry, Barua and me frightened."

"Was he often angry?"

"No, Sahib, but sometimes. Frencham Sahib also very good. Give me five hundred rupees for my daughter's wedding. Two times give."

After dinner with the house quiet except for the soft roar of the air conditioning Sinclair slouched in an armchair in the sitting room, feet on the coffee table, staring at the fragile silk tangka sandwiched between glass hanging on the wall opposite him. Janey had explained the Wheel of Existence which was depicted there: each of the six segments of the wheel represented one of the forms of existence. The aim of a Buddhist's life is to be removed from the cycle of rebirth by reaching true understanding, but this is not easily achieved, and for most men death inevitably means rebirth. Tibetans believe, Janey had told him, that the dead man is reincarnated according to the merits of his life. A good man might hope for a better life next time, might even hope to be taken out of the category of man to those of Gods or Titans. For the evil man there was the fear of reincarnation as an animal, without thought or speech; or as a yiddag, a creature condemned to an existence of unquenchable greed and desire.

Sinclair wondered about Hugo's passionate interest in the artefacts of the Buddhists. Had he also concerned himself with their beliefs? Had he never feared that the acquisitiveness that consumed him might cause him to be reincarnated in a less favoured status next time round? His accumulation of possessions, the money revealed in his bank accounts, the gold, spoke of a yiddag-like craving in his last life. Sinclair rose to ease the stiffness in his legs and went to gaze at the Buddhist images of desire. They fascinated him, with their tiny bee-mouths which could never take in enough, their swollen stomachs which had consumed too much already.

He wondered if he would have liked Hugo. A lot of what he had heard of him was unattractive: Hugo had been bullying, pedantic, obsessed with things and almost certainly a swindler of some kind. But his friends and enemies spoke well for him; Janey had been his friend, Bryan Lenton his enemy.

Sinclair discarded thoughts of his own feelings about Hugo and tried to put together what he knew and what he could guess of Hugo's life and death. He had been an undoubted security risk; his financial dealings, illegal as far as the gold went, were of a kind that made a servant of Her Majesty's Government eminently blackmailable. Could that be the connection with Dolgov? Had there been a security leak there? As Head of Chancery Hugo saw almost all confidential papers in the mission. He oversaw the work of the political officers and would have known of most of the commercial, the aid and consular business as well. There was plenty to worry about if Hugo had been blackmailed.

Then the gold. What had he been doing with it? One possibility was that he was using his diplomatic immunity for smuggling operations. If he had been bringing gold into India he could sell it at a profit. The question remained of where he could have got the gold from. He had not left India for a year so he could not have imported it himself since then. Could he have brought it in a year ago? It was a long time to keep gold in your safe if you were planning to make money out of it.

And finally Hugo's death. Sinclair went over all that he knew about the murder in his mind. It had the feel of an unplanned killing. The murderer had been lucky. It had been late at night and no one had seen or heard anything. But to risk a killing in a compound with police outside, Gurkhas on duty, a party next door. No one would plan that. Would they?

Where, he wondered, was the murder weapon? In all likelihood it was the knife that Hugo had bought that evening. Where also was the silver Buddha that was Hugo's witness?

He turned off the air conditioning, poured himself a long whisky and soda and went outside onto the verandah. The night was thick and still; heavy scents filled the air.

Sinclair sat looking through the frame of the bougainvillea at the garden where Hugo died. When at one o'clock Janey came back he had made two decisions: he must go to Bombay and he must see Dolgov again.

"Sinclair you're still up." He rose, stretching wearily.

"I was wondering what time your flight is tomorrow."

"Nine, I think. I'll leave here at about a quarter to eight. I've arranged with Jogiram for a taxi to call for me."

"I'll come to see you off."

"There's no need. I can just dash in to say goodbye before I go."

"I'd like to. I'll come."

"All right. If you really want to."

"I do. Goodnight, Janey. Until tomorrow."

Chapter 8

IN AIRPORTS Sinclair met one of the many Indias he was sheltered from in the cooled air of Hugo's house. Crowds of people filled them, standing, squatting by their bundles and suitcases, even stretched out fast asleep on the floor. They did not push nor jostle, but waited, waited with a perpetual patience and stoicism. Only Europeans shouted and raged, driven beyond their slender endurance by the heat, noise and squalor. The time spent queuing for tickets, check-in, body searches, seat allocation, at one place or another merged as all the same in Sinclair's memory, so he could barely distinguish one airport from the next, nor one journey from another.

He had begun by seeing Janey off on her flight to Kashmir. She had seemed depressed and their ride to the airport had been a silent one. Not until she had checked in and was about to go into the departure lounge did Sinclair say, "How can I get in touch with you if I'm in Kashmir?"

Janey took a notebook out of her bag and began to scribble in it.

"I'm staying on a houseboat on Lake Nageen called 'Nightingale'. It's even on the telephone so you could ring before you come if it's in the next couple of weeks. After that you could write care of Mr Jigme Namgyal whom I stay with in Leh; this is his address. Even if I'm in Ladakh, do come. It'll be worth it."

They stared at one another for a moment, both at a loss, then with simultaneous, unplanned movements they embraced. Janey went into the departure lounge without looking back.

❀❀❀

Sinclair was not quite sure how he managed to find himself on the shuttle to Bombay and he suspected uncomfortably that someone had been left off in order to accommodate him. The journey to and from Bombay flashed images of India before his eyes that were surreal in their juxtapositions. He felt as if he were being pulled at high speed past a procession moving in the opposite direction in slow motion, so each image his eye fell on was held for a moment like a still picture before he was swept on and a new picture clicked into place. His taxi swerved and he saw in the fast lane of the dual carriageway a cow lying down, her calf beside her, calmly chewing. Then a man on a bicycle, his wife between his arms on the crossbar, a baby on her shoulder and a toddler holding onto the handlebars. He looked up at towering film posters, showing plump, pink-faced stars, their lips pouting moistly at the mannikins beneath them. He looked down at a soft cry from below and met the eyes of a beggar with neither arms nor legs who was lying on the pavement beside his bowl gazing at the titans striding around him. The only moments of the day he could recollect with ease were when, in the plane, lifted and protected from the earth, breathing the purified air, he managed to think of his own activities, saying goodbye to Janey, his conversation with Hamid the jeweller.

Hamid was fat, his pudgy softness confined and shaped by his western bush suit of pale pink. He was also wily and suspicious and saw no reason why he should give something for nothing. He at first took Sinclair for a client and his welcome was effusive as he ushered him into his large modern office in which the hushing air conditioning shut out the noises of the city. Cold drinks were called for and an array of various Indian forms of Coca Cola were lined up on the desk before specific enquiries were made into the nature of Sinclair's business. Sinclair began with a tentative question about the gold with a reference to Mr Saleem of Old Delhi. This was no good; it was enough to put Hamid on his guard. His reply was voluble but vague. He could not say if he had or had not had such gold. Did Sinclair know the quantities of gold that his firm dealt in each year? The sums involved were amazingly large. Lakhs, no crores, of rupees were laid out to acquire the best gold, the finest gemstones in India. Why, Sita the famous star of the film *Jehan* had come to him to buy her jewellery when she had decided to marry her co-star, though that had now been called off, but not the order for the jewels, no. Jewels and gold remained though marriages failed and engagements were broken.

Sinclair cursed himself silently for a fool and began on another tack. He remembered the lengthy and elaborate openings used by Janey, usually so direct, with Mr

Singh and Mr Saleem, and sought to emulate them. He had come, he said, to Mr Hamid because not only had Mr Saleem of Old Delhi mentioned him as the finest jeweller in Bombay, but his name had also been mentioned to him as an outstanding expert in the field of precious metals by an old friend, Mr Hugo Frencham, of the British High Commission in New Delhi. The fulsome compliments which Sinclair felt no one could listen to without regarding their perpetrator as insincere and sycophantic had some effect. They did not make Mr Hamid any more eager to answer Sinclair's questions without good reason for doing so. They indicated, however, that Sinclair himself was not the fool he had seemed at first and did, in fact, know the proper way to conduct a business interview.

Sinclair went on, "I believe that Mr Frencham was in touch with you about some gold and was able to come to a mutually agreeable arrangement with you some time before his death."

Hamid's little eyes in his large fleshy face did not convey any emotion, not even surprise, as he said, "Mr Frencham is dead?"

Sinclair let his breath out slowly and evenly. Hamid had implicitly admitted at least knowing Hugo.

"Yes, he died in most tragic circumstances two weeks ago."

"The circumstances were tragic you are saying?"

"It seems that he was the victim of a dacoity. The Delhi Police are working on the case."

Hamid looked unimpressed by the mention of the Delhi Police and began a forcible monologue about dacoits and the danger to prosperous and law-abiding citizens that they represented. Finally he discoursed on the unfair reputation attaching to Bombay of being a city of crime and vice when in fact, as could be seen from this incident, Delhi's record was probably worse.

As he spoke both men were planning their next moves in the conversation; Hamid's generalisations allowed both of them to reassess the situation and Sinclair found that he had gained a small initiative. Although Hamid had not admitted he had had recent dealings with Hugo he seemed very slightly put out by hearing of his death and there was an air of expectation about him, as though he now was prepared to listen to what Sinclair had to say, if it was what he wanted to hear. Sinclair read these signs in Hamid's adjustment of his body in his chair, the slight forward tilt of the huge torso, the tension that entered the jelly-like folds of flesh round the face.

"I represent certain interests of Mr Frencham's," Sinclair informed him. "When a man dies suddenly his affairs are not always in order and a careful man like Mr Frencham does not commit all his dealings to paper. In this way it is sometimes hard for his, shall we say colleagues, to pick up the threads and to continue the arrangements already made without a break." Hamid's eyes, dull currants in his doughy face, expressed cautious understanding. Sinclair thought that his words, misleading to the jeweller, were nonetheless all too true.

"You are wishing to continue previously made undertakings of Mr Frencham?"

"I feel that this would be a sensible way of clearing up Mr Frencham's affairs."

"When I last was speaking to Mr Frencham he was uncertain whether there would be any future business to be done."

"That was obviously before his unexpected death. I cannot say what were his plans at that stage."

"You are having some sample perhaps?"

Sinclair opened his briefcase and took out the envelope containing the roll of gold. He handed it over to Hamid with an expressionless face; he had had no idea until Hamid's last remark whether he was appearing as buyer or seller. Hamid's pale-palmed hand grasped the gold and weighed it, the thumbs caressing the smooth surface.

"Yes, yes," he murmured, the sight and feel of the gold suddenly making him co-operative. "Yes, from Mr Frencham I have bought ten of these already, a total of 417 troy ounces," he stated, his vagueness vanishing into detailed accuracy. "And we were negotiating a very favourable rate, favourable to both parties I must say."

Under the spell of the gold Hamid told Sinclair that Hugo had arranged the deal some six weeks earlier; the gold had been handed over and Hugo had been paid so many lakhs of rupees, a sum which had been transferred into a Bombay bank account.

Sinclair's brows puckered on hearing of this new strand in the tangle of Hugo's financial affairs. He encouraged Hamid to go on. He wanted above all to know where the gold had come from, but Hamid seemed genuinely not to know. Sinclair decided Hamid had not cared to find out and Hugo's evasiveness had enabled the Indian to obtain the 'favourable rate' he spoke of. Hamid then began to discourse about business methods and discretion and Sinclair reckoned that all that could usefully be gleaned from him had been taken by now. He prepared for departure in the next break in the monologue.

"I am reluctant to be talking about this at first," Hamid was saying. "I am not a man for talking, no. Besides, I have been having too many enquiries about this matter, which is not good. It is not proper business practice to be talking of a deal with another person. Such enquiries are only made..."

"Enquiries? Many enquiries, Mr Hamid? Has someone else been asking about Mr Frencham's—er—business connections with you? The police, for instance?"

"Police—puh!" Hamid's contempt for the forces of order and justice in his society was underlined by a slurping swig from a Campa Cola bottle. "What would police be knowing?"

Sinclair could only be thankful he had followed his instinct to pose as a business man rather than as an investigator. "No, they are not concerning me. No, it is Ranjit Singh. You are knowing Ranjit Singh in Delhi?"

"I have heard of him I think," said Sinclair slowly.

"He was also doing some business with Mr Frencham, he said. But I was suspecting his story and he had no sample. He came to me then nosing, sniffing. These princely Hindus," he exclaimed with anger, "thinking they can influence in Bombay as they frighten everyone in Delhi. But he is not frightening me."

Sinclair jumped up from his chair, seized the gold from the desk and rapidly snapped it into his briefcase. He took Hamid's plump hand and shook it heartily.

"What? What?"

"Mr Hamid, you have helped tremendously. I must go back to Delhi at once."

"But we have not... We must be making..."

"Yes, at another time, perhaps. Now I am most urgently returning to Delhi. Many thanks for your hospitality."

Leaving Hamid still struggling from his chair, he strode rapidly out of the office, through the huge carpeted showroom in which customers were bent over the glass counters whispering as if they were in church, out into the sweltering humidity of the street.

❀❀❀

For this forty minute conversation Sinclair had gone to Bombay and when he was once again enfolded in the cool envelope of the plane sliding through the hot air back to Delhi he tried to assess whether he had learned anything that could weigh in the scales against the physical discomfort to which he had subjected himself in order to achieve the interview. From the top pocket of his bush shirt he drew a scrap of paper and pencil. He rolled the pencil between thumb and forefinger, occasionally making as if to put the lead to paper, then drawing back as he considered the implications of what he had discovered from the wily jeweller. His thoughts seemed to give him little pleasure and no certainty. Only after a long time, just before the plane began to descend towards the burning levels below it, did he slowly write on his slip of paper:

Battacharia—R. Singh
Alan T. Charlie C.—Dolgov

and below that:

Ruth Quinton.

He folded it once and replaced it in his breast pocket, leaned his head back against the seat and closed his eyes. If he hoped that to his idling brain some spark would come to illuminate and interpret the patchy facts he had uncovered he was disappointed. For the only image to appear behind his lids was the red-gold mass of Janey's retreating head which seemed to pervade him with a generalised aching discontent as if there was something wrong with his life, something he would act on if only he could identify what it was.

The feeling persisted when he arrived home: discontent, irritation with himself, a restless desire for action without any clear idea what action to take. Janey was very absent and Hugo very present in the quiet rooms. The neatness which must have characterised the place when Hugo had lived there had reappeared. The books and papers which Janey had scattered on coffee tables, book shelves, chairs and floors were no longer there; her sandals and sunglasses formerly to be found under the cane furniture or discarded by the glass doors had gone with her to Kashmir; their absence was a positive quality. Instead, Hugo's possessions reasserted their claims to attention as they had that first morning before he had met Janey. The tangka of the Wheel of Existence exercised a dominating fascination. He stood in front of the mantelpiece and examined the cloth painting once again and Janey's voice spoke in his memory as he looked at the top right hand segment of the circle.

"Titans are creatures of envy and ambition. They are supermen, with many advantages and blessings that man does not have, but at the same time they are discontented. They are passionate and warlike. Can you see their coats of armour and their weapons? The fate of the Titans is to die in battle with the Gods whom they envy. And their women…"

She had pointed to the lower part of the section in which could be seen a pool around which was gathered a group of women who were bending over and gazing into the waters. "They are horribly punished for their attachment to life. They must look into the Reflecting Lake of Perfect Clearness and see the defeat of their lovers and their own ultimate fate of rebirth as a punishment for their lives of passion."

"You would have to be very Buddhist or very Christian," Sinclair had remarked, "to accept such a terrible view of life. Endless punishment for the sins of this world."

Looking at them now Sinclair could see that some of the women of the Titans were weeping, their tiny figures bent with their grief. The minute scale of the scenes made him feel as though he were watching, godlike, from far above, the activities of puppets for whom he felt sorrow and compassion, but whom he could not help.

As he moved from the tangka with a sigh, restlessness, for a moment subdued, returned. To give activity to his mind rather than to his limbs, he went to the phone in the hall and called the next-door house.

"Maggie, this is Sinclair. Could I have a word with Alan? Alan… Yes, I've been to Bombay…. Quite tiring and only moderately fruitful. I want to ask for your help. I need to meet friend Dolgov in an unofficial way. I wondered if you could suggest something."

"You want to meet socially and, as it were, accidentally? Let me look in the diary." There was the sound of pages being turned close to the receiver. "Tomorrow. Tomorrow is the Cameroon National Day reception. I'm sure he'll be at that. I can smuggle you in without causing too great offence to the Ambassador and you can do your best there." Turnell paused portentously. "I'd like a briefing in the morning, Sinclair. Am I to understand that you think Hugo's relationship with Dolgov was—ah—seriously worrying?"

"I think there was something going on, more than just the odd game of chess. How much more I've yet to find out. I'll tell you what I've found so far in the morning."

❀❀❀

Just before Sinclair left for the Police Headquarters the following day Charlie Croom dropped into his office carrying a double enveloped report, stamped head and foot, sides and back, SECRET.

"This is what you were wanting, eh, old boy?" Croom perched himself on the edge of the desk, swinging one stick-like leg as Sinclair extracted the single sheet of flimsy from its layers of protection. "From that lot you'd think he was the genuine article, a straight Russian diplomat. But there ain't no such crittur that I've met. Even if they're not mainstream KGB they can be put under pressure to do whatever is wanted. Your boy wants a place at a university, your sister wants a promotion: you do as we say or else. That's how it is. I admit he looks clean enough but don't you believe it."

Sinclair half-listened to Charlie's commentary as he examined the brief report from London.

> VASILI ALEXEIVITCH DOLGOV. Summary. b. 1930 Moscow. Married; divorced 1965. 1 son b. 1957. Main line Foreign Service, joined MFA 1955. First posting Berlin 1957–61, political officer. 1961–64 Moscow MFA First European Department. 1964–68 London. 1968–72 SALT I in Geneva. During SALT I he made a number of contacts with Americans, French, British, Germans in Geneva. Described as

> personable, lively, attuned to western modes of behaviour. Languages are good: English excellent, French and German fluent. 1972 returned to Moscow and during at least part of his home posting 1972–76 worked in the Third Department of the MFA in the Arms Control Bureau. His posting to Delhi 1976 was out of line with previous record. He must have been considered for the post of First Counsellor, Washington, which fell due in that year. Job went to Vladmir Ostrovski (file ref.) a known KGB officer. In Delhi cultural work and western contacts.

Sinclair studied the sheet carefully pausing particularly on the penultimate sentence. He remembered Dolgov's voice. "He is my good friend." Had he recognised in Hugo a man whose career had also gone indefinably wrong at some point? Perhaps Dolgov was a disappointed man missing the bright lights of Geneva, cheated of Washington, who looked to Delhi to put his career back on its tracks. He re-enveloped the paper and locked it in his desk.

❀❀❀

Battacharia amid his papers at the Police Headquarters was as cheerful as ever, a specific against the depression which had filled Sinclair the previous night.

"Sinclair, what can we be doing for you, ji? Be seated, be seated."

"Pratap, on the guest list of the party given by Mr Turnell on the night of Mr Frencham's death there were the names of Mr and Mrs Ranjit Singh. I've come across his name again in connection with Frencham and I want to know more about him. What can you tell me of him?"

Sinclair had decided to come to Battacharia for information about Ranjit Singh and avoid High Commission sources. Ranjit Singh turned up at the Turnells' party, was a friend of Hugo's, lent a car to Janey; he was closely tied into the diplomatic nexus. Sinclair could imagine the hostility that would bristle at the questioning of Ranjit Singh's antecedents among British officials. To them Dolgov was an acceptable target for suspicion. If a pet Indian, a favoured contact, were spotlighted it would threaten their own judgments.

Battacharia was calling for the inevitable tea and only when it had come did he address himself to Sinclair's request.

"Ranjit Singh," he said, stressing the three syllables of the name evenly and strongly. "Ranjit Singh is business man now. He comes from Rajasthan. He is of princely family, cousin to the Maharaja of Chhotrapur." The name was famous from the past for wealth, for displays of hospitality to Viceroys and visiting Princes of Wales. Today it meant polo, even to Sinclair. "So you can imagine he has plenty of contacts, plenty of friends in high-up places. He was in the Army before Independence and he resigned from that fifteen years ago. You know what was in 1962?" he asked abruptly.

Sinclair's mind skated over the early sixties. Profumo? Kennedy? His orientation was entirely western.

"War with China," Battacharia went on without a pause, for there was no doubt for him about the significance of the date to anyone who heard it. "At that time Ranjit Singh was brigadier in the Army. His brigade was in

Ladakh which was the western front against the Chinese. Most of the fighting was in Assam in the east, but there was also much going on in Ladakh where the Chinese had taken Aksai Chin from us. There was one very well-known action in which many Chinese were killed and also many Indians; so many that only three, all wounded, were returning to the Battalion HQ and one was Ranjit Singh. This action was mentioned by Pandit-ji in Lok Sabha and became famous for bravery shown. After the end of the China war there was a big reorganisation in the Army and it seemed that Ranjit Singh would gain promotion after his courage and praise he had received. But, very strange, he left the Army in 1963 to go into business. It was said he had quarrelled with one general and would not serve under him." Battacharia took his tea, cooled by the softly beating fan, and drank it in gulps. "After leaving the army he went into business: import-export, antiques, jewellery, precious things. It was said he was going into politics; he did stand for Parliament in 1968 election but did not get in and never tried again. Does not need to, I say. He is knowing so many in government that to get permit, licence, this, that, he picks up phone to speak to whoever and he is having it."

"Did you interview him about the Turnells' party?" Sinclair asked, looking up from the notes he was making on a scrumpled piece of paper.

"Yes, now we have seen all the guests at that party. You want to see what he is saying? I will call for papers. Chuprassy!" A messenger took his orders and while they waited for the file Sinclair asked, "How old is he, Ranjit Singh?"

"About fifty-five or fifty-six he must be," Battacharia replied. "A very powerful man he is. An angry man."

Sinclair pondered. Public displays of anger, irritation, frustration are often visible in the west, but in India he had seen nothing of this; passivity or stoicism, depending on your own attitude to the phenomenon, was the characteristic reaction to difficulties. Ranjit Singh was an angry man, brave, warlike, ambitious, a Titan.

The chuprassy returned with a folder tied neatly length-ways and across with tape. Battacharia extracted the papers.

"First thing. On the list it is saying Mr and Mrs R. Singh but Mrs Singh did not come to party. Ranjit Singh came alone. His driver brought him and waited the evening. They both agreed that he left about 12.30."

From the typescript it was evident that the interview with Singh had been conducted in English and had been brief. The answers, as reported, were short to the point of brusqueness. Sinclair's eyes jumped down the page, sampling the questions and answers.

> What time did you arrive at Mr Turnell's house?
> About a quarter to nine.
> Where did your driver park the car?
> He dropped me at the door and then, as the Turnells' drive was full of cars, he went and parked on the perimeter road inside the High Commission.
> Did you speak to Mr Hugo Frencham during the course of the evening?
> I said hello to him some time during the party but I did not speak to him at any length that I remember.
> Did you see Mr Frencham leave the party?

> No. He must have left before I did because he was not there when I said goodbye.

"Pratap, I have been asking about Ranjit Singh because it is possible from some—er—papers that I've come across that Frencham had some business dealings with him. Do you think you might be able to find out for me something about Singh's business affairs? Any hint of a connection with Frencham. I have no idea what their dealings were, I am afraid, so I can't give you much help."

Battacharia expressed his willingness to have some research done into the nature of Singh's companies, though he was reluctant to re-interview the man himself.

"This would be very embarrassing. The first time all were interviewed who were at the party. Some were annoyed but there was nothing particular about it. To be going a second time and without very good reason. This I am not wanting to do."

Sinclair said, "No harm if I go, though."

Battacharia considered. "No, you from the High Commission could go. That would not be looking so bad."

"Where does he live then?"

"A big house in the Prithviraj Road. Better to find him in his offices on the Barakhamba Road, near Connaught Circus."

Chapter 9

THE TREELESS STREET glared in the rising temperature of midmorning. The light shimmered on the plates of glass of the western-style high-rise blocks and on the roofs of the cars lining the pavements, and crawling bad temperedly towards Connaught Circus. The painful, shifting effect of the light was repeated for another sense in the cacophony of horns blaring up and down the street, varying in strength and setting the nerves on edge with the expectation of the next blast of sound.

Sinclair's taxi was shunted slowly along the desolate street until it stopped outside a modern glass and concrete construction which soared up into the heat. He climbed out grimly, the back of his shirt and trousers dark with sweat from sitting on the torn plastic seat of the old car. Sinclair paused and took in his surroundings for a moment, the light and sound producing an instant tightening of the skull around the brain. There were signs that this street had once been like others in central New Delhi, broad-verged, tree-lined, with low verandahed buildings sheltering under foliage from the destroying sun. Now the verges had been rolled under a carpet of tarmac, leaving an untidy car-strewn parking bay in front of the towers of glass which proclaimed no fear of the climate.

Inside the doors the cooled artificial atmosphere closed behind Sinclair and his soaking clothes took on a pleasant chill. He studied the board at the entrance to the lift: Ramnagar Engineering; Jay Gee Exports; Ashoke Mills. Significantly at the top was Ranjit Singh.

When Sinclair stepped out of the lift on the eleventh floor he found himself in a large reception area dominated by a view over the centre of the city and noticed only a fraction of a second later a beautiful girl. To her Sinclair gave his attention first, walking over to her desk which was placed well back in the room away from the windows. She had the fine classical profile of many Indian women and a great quantity of glossy hair coiled at the back of her head. She was slim and fine-boned, her wrists so thin that it seemed they might snap if she unwisely lifted a heavy weight. Her sari was brilliantly coloured in pinks and oranges and she wore a good deal of jewellery, more than the puritanical Sinclair felt was appropriate before six in the evening. He had sufficient time to study these details and to make his judgments on them as the receptionist was in no hurry to ask him his business. He stood above her while she composedly moved papers about, making piles, pausing to read a title or a note, opening drawers, her fingers flashing with diamonds and nail polish.

At length without looking up, still gazing abstractedly at a paper she said, “You have an appointment?” on a faintly sceptical note.

"Yes," said Sinclair, firmly. "I phoned an hour ago to ask if I could see Mr Singh and someone—you perhaps—told me I could come at eleven."

"Oh, yes?" This time the voice conveyed mild astonishment.

"Is Mr Singh here?"

"No, he has not arrived yet." She still had not looked up.

"Then I'll wait, if you think he will come."

"He will be coming." Her tone was negligent and not encouraging.

Sinclair moved over to the windows and seated himself in an armchair where he could look out at the spectacular view. To the left were massed clumps of trees, their textures silky, woolly, curly or smooth, like heads of hair or coats of animals, and amid them, glimpses of roofs, domes, walls. Beyond the groove of the railway line which demarcates Old Delhi from New, buildings dominated vegetation and geometric lines like a cubist painting built up the pattern of the city to the hazy horizon.

Sinclair spent an hour and a half with the surly girl in Ranjit Singh's reception area before admitting defeat and leaving. His patience and stubbornness were great enough to wait on even longer, but he was driven away eventually by a power cut. He had sat near the window flicking at a magazine for some time before he was forced to move away from the view. Through the sheets of glass the sun burned with a power against which air conditioning was impotent. He wondered at the folly that had led Indian architects and builders to abandon their traditional low, dark, shaded houses for these high, exposed towers dependent on electricity and air conditioning and quite uninhabitable without them. Sinclair understood why the disdainful girl had huddled herself and her desk as far from the light as possible. He shuffled his chair further into the centre of the room to be met by the repellent stare of the receptionist. Sinclair was not a natural chatter-up of girls and this one's basilisk eye deterred him from any enquiries to pass the time. What went on behind the doors of the top floor he could only guess. No sound came from them and no one went in or out.

After forty-five minutes he said, "Is Mr Singh likely to be much longer?"

"He will be coming," was the reply; but he didn't.

Later still, the humming electrical and cooling systems gave a sigh, a croak, and died away, leaving an ear-numbing silence for a moment. Like water seeping through a crumbling dam and filling up the empty levels in a swift flowing movement, hot air surged into the building overpowering the frail cool which had been kept in place by so many support systems. Sinclair could feel sweat start to ooze from his body. He rose.

"This is power cut," said the girl with a note of satisfaction in her voice. "It is lasting three hours every afternoon."

"Will Mr Singh come now?"

"He may be coming this afternoon."

"Can I make another appointment which you can assure me will be kept?"

"You can come at two thirty."

"Very well. Until two thirty."

He turned away and moved automatically towards the lift doors.

"Lift is not working." Sinclair wondered how the indifference of the voice could at the same time convey pleasure at his discomfort. He started towards the stairs, eleven flights, but at least it was down. He was round the second bend when he heard the trill of the telephone. He swiftly took off his shoes and raced silently up the concrete steps in his sock-clad feet; just below the first turn he stopped, the sweat prickling his scalp.

"Yes." The voice was as languid as ever. "Yes... Very well. No, Mr Singh is at airport all afternoon seeing to cargo. Aachhaa, tomorrow morning then... Yes... Yes...Goodbye."

❀❀❀

The phone was ringing as he entered Hugo's house. It was Alan Turnell telling him that the reception that night was from seven to nine and they could share a car; he also wanted his briefing on Dolgov.

"Can we make it over here in half an hour?" Sinclair suggested. "I want to go out this afternoon if I can have an airport pass."

"There should be no problem about that. All the international flights at Delhi come in during the night so I don't suppose anyone'll be using the passes until this evening. I'll be over after lunch."

Jogiram and the others had already gone when Sinclair let Alan in. They both took some iced coffee and carried it into the sitting room.

Alan crossed his neatly creased trouser legs and said, "Now, what's all this about Dolgov. Are we to understand that we've a major security scandal on our hands?"

Sinclair stared up at the tangka above him; within the central boss of the wheel a cock, a pig and a snake circled endlessly chasing one another's tails. They represented the causes of rebirth, desire, anger and ignorance.

"That's hard to say. It's possible. It could on the other hand have nothing or little to do with Dolgov."

"When you say 'it' what do you mean?" Alan asked with bureaucratic exactitude.

"I suppose I mean first Hugo's murder. That is a fact which cannot be explained away, however much we misinterpret or misunderstand the circumstances surrounding it." As he spoke, gazing at the tangka he felt as if he were addressing the absent, skeptical Janey, as much as Alan Turnell. "And then along with that I mean the fact that Hugo had been handling a quarter of a million dollars worth of gold and had assets worth God knows how much in England. I cannot believe his murder was unconnected with his financial affairs. It is statistically fairly rare for a Head of Chancery to be murdered, though not unknown, and it's usually for political reasons. It is also eccentric—not to mention illegal—to have so much gold lying around the house and two such oddities in the life—or death—of one man are more than likely to be connected."

Alan was turning his highly polished ox-blood shoe to and fro to admire the sheen on the leather as he listened.

"All right," he said at last as though it were an immense concession in a difficult negotiation. "I'll accept that. We are now at the position that we think Hugo's death was not a random accident of fate. But why Dolgov? Are you saying that Hugo's ill-gotten (we assume they are ill-gotten) gains came from slipping off down the road to the Russkies with all the goodies in Chancery?"

"It's possible. You can't pretend it hasn't happened before."

"But why would Hugo do it? Why? It's so unlike him. He was really the least political political officer you could imagine."

"That is an easily assumed front," said Sinclair gently, amused to point out this obvious fact to a master of the deceitful art of diplomacy. "But I agree. I doubt very much if politics was a part of this. Everything smacks of money rather than ideology." He paused a moment to swirl the cold beige liquid in his glass. "What about blackmail?"

"I don't know what you could blackmail Hugo for."

"Don't you?" Sinclair's voice expressed mild disbelief.

"He's got no wife so girls could hardly matter. Oh, I suppose..." Alan was too delicate to fill out his supposition.

"Come, Alan, you can't be as obtuse as you make out. It must have occurred to you that Hugo might be queer. Divorced for years, no girlfriend in sight."

Alan remained silent, not to be drawn on his speculations on a colleague's sex life. Then he said, "If it was blackmail, why was Hugo making so much out of it?"

"These things can work two ways. Stick and carrot."

Alan's grunt was unconvinced. Sinclair watched him and seemed pleased at the response to his suggestions.

"I have no evidence that Hugo was homosexual. Nothing. But I wonder whether Hugo would do anything just for money."

Alan contemplated the moral alternatives: Hugo was a man blackmailed for his minority sexual tastes; Hugo was a man who sold confidential secrets for money alone.

"Hugo needed money for his collection," he said at length. "He lived modestly; no extravagances; no exotic holidays; no big car. But this lot," his hand embraced the watching Tibetan idols, the static wheels of cloth and silver, "must have cost him all he had and more."

Sinclair was never sure whether Alan had chosen

money rather than sex as Hugo's weakness because he felt it was more respectable and in a way less discreditable to his old friend, or because he honestly thought it was so. The depths, or otherwise of a diplomat are hard to plumb even for an experienced investigator.

"We need to consider what Hugo had to give," Sinclair said after a moment. "What would you regard as the most sensitive material he would see?"

"Hugo's role was, as you know, supervisory, so he had access to all areas of High Commission work but some of the things that are most important to us could scarcely be much use to the Russians."

"Their information gathering is done on a squirreling basis. Picking it up whatever it is and keeping it just in case it may be useful one day."

"The greatest immediate benefit they might derive from Hugo would probably be commercial, particularly arms sales or big development contracts."

"And have there been any unexpected upsets in this area in the last few years while Hugo has been here? Have we lost contracts to the Russians?"

Alan brooded on this for some time. "We have missed some contracts, of course, though it's not been to the Russians. But then, it's rarely a two horse race, so it's hard to tell. The trouble with all this speculation about treachery is Hugo's and Dolgov's relationship." Sinclair nodded encouragingly as if to an intelligent student. "Would they really have met regularly to play chess if Hugo was spying for them?"

"It would certainly be most unusual and would focus attention on Hugo the moment any suspicions were aroused. And another oddity is Dolgov's behaviour since Hugo's death. It's either deliberately attention seeking or caused by desperate need for some particular information he wants from us."

"So, on balance...?"

"On balance, I don't know. I think by seeing Dolgov, by giving him opportunities to do or say something we may learn more."

"So am I to prepare the High Commissioner for the deluge or shall we hang on a little longer?"

"Prepare him, by all means," Sinclair rejoined promptly. "As a dedicated pessimist I believe in people expecting the worst. It cheers them up when it doesn't happen."

"And redounds to your credit that you succeeded in averting it," finished Alan shrewdly. "That's not being a pessimist. It's simply being a sensible civil servant."

Chapter 10

SINCLAIR AFTERWARDS ACKNOWLEDGED that he made a number of misjudgments in the matter of Hugo's death and perhaps the most significant was the mistake he made at this point. He knew that his strengths in doing his job were his patience, his persistence and the careful psychological interest he bestowed on his subject. It was at this stage that his persistence overrode his other qualities.

"It's hard to see what I should have done instead," he justified himself to Janey later, in Kashmir, when he was recovering from the results of his error. "I had to see Ranjit Singh in order to make any progress at all and he was obviously stalling on me. The mistake was to go to the airport. I should have waited, but a morning wasted in that pretentious office with his supercilious bitch of a receptionist made me determined to push ahead. So I went."

"And lived to regret it," Janey remarked drily.

"Lived, yes, thank God, but regret it, no. I'll stand by my mistakes."

❀❀❀

The weather, Sinclair noticed as he chugged out to the airport in a creaking taxi, had thickened since the morning. The sky was no longer the scalding blue of the earlier part of the day; it had filmed over in a grey haze that added weight to the air and pressed everything closer to the face of the earth, slowing everything with the burden of the atmosphere. All movement had a labouring futility about it as though nothing could reach completion but was fixed in perpetual striving. Passing the cantonments Sinclair saw soldiers on guard duty as still and neat as the sharply painted white stones that edged the entrance. The air that slowed down all other life seemed to have petrified them.

The taxi dropped him at the departure building. Sinclair saw it off before trying to find his way to the Cargo Area. He had no very clear idea what he intended to do there. He wanted to find Ranjit Singh at the airport when a meeting at the Barakhamba Road offices had been arranged; to catch him off guard; to see him at work; to assess and judge him; to make an inescapable appointment.

Although he carried with him one of the official High Commission passes allowing him to go through Customs and Immigration to the airside, he found he did not need to use it. He enquired for the Cargo offices and received directions which brought him eventually to a low building hiding behind the crates and bundles stacked around it. Inside was a large open area with a number of small offices leading off it. The main building had no cooling system but in one or two of the offices air conditioning units roared. In the doorway a few men in shabby khaki uniforms squatted, puffing on bidis, not talking. Sinclair expected to be accosted and had prepared a story about a mythical suitcase to be airfreighted to London; no one took the least notice of him.

In the first room a white-clothed Indian sat behind the piles of paper which Sinclair now knew characterised all Indian offices. Standing in front of him were two exasperated men talking in English about a lost consignment. Sinclair skulked past the door and moved towards the next. The offices were separated from the main hall by glass partitions and he could glance through these in order to see what and who was within. The next compartment was empty; a hollow had been made in the piles of papers in front of the vacant chair and a cup of tea stood in the cleared space, a scab of milk forming on its surface. The occupants of the third office were speaking in Hindi. Sinclair could see the clerk's face, quite young, made melancholy by the drooping lines of his moustache. He was holding a sheaf of papers, flicking backwards and forwards through it as he spoke. Facing him, with their backs to Sinclair, were two other men. They were both seated and it was through the frame made by their shoulders and heads that he could see the clerk behind his desk. He had no opportunity to study this group nor to try his hand at guessing their status and business from the backs of their heads, for at that moment all three pushed their chairs away from the desk as if it had suddenly become electrically alive and shocked them. The two visitors led the way out of the office, followed by the clerk.

By now Sinclair was becoming accustomed to styles of Indian dress and in the subtle adaptations of western clothing could sense the messages about status and role that were conveyed. The Customs official wore a short-sleeved shirt, long, hanging outside his wide trousers to make a tighter, less comfortable version of the India kurta pajama. The next man wore trousers; instead of a shirt he had on a fine cotton kurta embroidered on the chest and hanging to his thighs. The third man, the one who led the way out of the office, made no concessions to Indian taste. His white cotton shirt was tucked inside his belted narrow trousers. Though he had only seen him briefly as he emerged from the bank a few days earlier, Sinclair recognised the man.

Ranjit Singh was a striking figure. He was clearly the superior in the group, the deference of the other two implicit in their bearing and gestures. He was not tall, under six foot, and had a muscular strength that stood out in comparison to the physical slightness of so many Indians. As he walked past the unnoticed Sinclair he turned back to talk to the two following him. His face was square, very light skinned, with a nose of an Arabic curve and thin slanting nostrils. His moustache, unlike his flawlessly dark head, was grizzled.

The three crossed the floor of the hall, the older man at a smart march, swinging a stick though he showed no sign of lameness, the other two more languidly, with the characteristic unhurried Indian stroll. At the indication of the clerk they converged on one of the piles of cargo stacked against the walls. The pile was made up partly of crates of raw wood, white and roughly splintering, and partly of bundles covered in creamy unbleached cotton, the seams neatly sewn. A reconciliation between list and crates was taking place.

While this went on Sinclair completed his tour of the

offices. In one was a group of five or six men standing listlessly around a desk. Not much seemed to be happening and it was hard to tell whether they were a delegation or a queue. In the last room a clerk bent over his work, raising his grey head only at Sinclair's second "Excuse me", his ears filled with the piercing creak and snap of the turning fan above his head.

"I am looking for Mr Ranjit Singh. Can you tell me..."

The clerk jerked his head, butting it forward to indicate the direction of the hall.

"He's there," he said.

His recognition confirmed, Sinclair settled on the rim of a crate waiting for a suitable moment to present himself. He was half shielded from view by two boxes, one on top of the other, between him and the three men. He could hear their voices and could see their profiles as they bent over an opened crate. Ranjit Singh stood with his back to him.

Discussion and examination went on for some time, then the contents of the crate were laboriously repacked and the lid hammered on again. The clerk started back towards his office and as Ranjit Singh turned Sinclair pushed himself off his seat and started to stride towards him.

"Mr Ranjit Singh." His voice made it a statement not a question. He put out his hand. "My name's Sinclair. I'm from the British High Commission."

There could be no doubt of Ranjit Singh's surprise. It showed clearly in the twitching together of his brows, the tremor of his aquiline nose. It lasted only a second; his palm came out smoothly, without hesitation, to grasp Sinclair's hand powerfully. This was not the limp Indian clasp which flinches from contact with the casteless, but the hearty military grip denoting honesty and virility.

"How d'you do, my dear chap. What a place to meet, what?"

Sinclair had not yet heard him speak in English and his first sentence sounded almost parodic. The democratisation of English accent had left those colonial tones preserved only on the sound tracks of wartime films like shards in medieval layers of earth. Ranjit Singh did not notice his hesitation. "Demmed hot," he went on. "Looking for me, were you, in this demmed heat?"

"Yes," said Sinclair, "I was," and his voice was nearly a drawl in comparison with the sharply clipped tones of the Indian. "I heard you might be here so I decided to come to try to have a brief word with you."

"Heard I was here, eh? Well, now you've tracked me down what d'you want? What d'you want to see me for, eh?"

"I should say," said Sinclair with the formality of a police man giving the statutory warning, "that I am here from London in order to investigate the death of Hugo Frencham of the British High Commission and I am working closely with Inspector Battacharia of the Indian Police. I understand you were an old friend of Mr Frencham's and I was anxious to hear about him from you."

They sat down, Singh on the edge of a wooden box, propping his stick against its side, Sinclair on the softer, lower seat made by several of the cotton-covered bundles. Very small things can affect the course of a conversation and the relationship between two people that develops in even a short dialogue. It is possible that the way they sat, Sinclair marginally below Singh so that he had to tip his chin up while the Indian's lids were lowered to see his companion, had a powerful effect on their understanding of one another, or of Ranjit Singh's reading of Sinclair. In any case, his higher position, or something else, put Ranjit Singh in a good humour. He slapped his thigh, a gesture Sinclair had never seen made in life, and said, "Hugo's old friend, yes. You're right there. Hugo's oldest friend in India I should say. No one knew him better; you've come to the right man for that."

Sinclair's phrase had been a formality; he had no idea how long the two men had been friends so he was forced to ask, "How long exactly had you known Mr Frencham?"

"A long time. Thirty years ago and more we met. We were subalterns together in the Army in the old days; before Independence that was." He leaned a hand on each knee, muscular arms akimbo and his smile gleamed down at Sinclair. "A long time ago. Young people now think Independence part of history. Our tryst with destiny has come and gone and we cope with the morning after now earning a living in the hard world. People of Independence time have been and gone, Gandhiji, Panditji, Patel, where are they? In the history book. But we saw it; Hugo and I did, and we remember. And not such old men either."

Hugo was gone too, though not to any history books; that too was forgotten in the oration. Unimpressed by rhetoric, Sinclair registered Ranjit Singh's message.

"And you kept in touch with Hugo all these years?"

"Yes, yes," said Ranjit Singh expansively. "Many times Hugo has come to stay between his postings, on his leaves, and we have been shooting together. We took a tiger once in the old days in the Kumaon hills; now it's birds only, on the jheels in Rajasthan, no more tigers. And Hugo and his Tibetans since 1960. Collecting, collecting. Tangkas, bronzes, books for publication. Who will read such stuff? It became an obsession with him, always bringing him back to India."

"And I believe you and Hugo had some business connections as well as your long friendship."

The thick brows met above the fine nose which seemed to curve more fiercely into the bristling moustache.

"Who tells you this?"

Sinclair leaned forward resting his forearms on his legs, gazing at the dusty, slightly ribbed concrete of the floor to allow Ranjit Singh to recover himself from his squall of anger, to appear as if he had not seen it and it had never been.

"Now Mr Frencham is dead," Sinclair said formally, "all his affairs are to be cleared up. It has fallen to me to deal with his papers and notes in India." He spoke lightly with no pointed emphasis. His words could be taken to answer Ranjit Singh's angry question, if he had heard it; as a warning of the extent of his knowledge; as a non sequitur. The quiet between them, into which his words dropped, spread out and seemed to muffle the voices in the offices, the whirr of the fans, the roar of the air conditioners.

Sinclair waited dangling his long whitish hands between his knees. There was no tension visible in the slack lines of his body, though he knew that if Singh ignored the implicit questions and refused to answer them, or quite simply denied what Sinclair had stated as an assumption, this round would have been lost. He would either have to mention Hamid's name, which he did not want to do at any price, or, acknowledging that he had got no further with Singh than had the police, he would have to go back to Battacharia to see what less direct approaches he could come up with.

The silence, filled for Sinclair by the sense of balance,

scales tipping one way—which way?—in Ranjit Singh's head, lasted in reality very little time. The Indian gave a shout of laughter.

"So you found that out, did you?" He took out a folded handkerchief and blotted the sweat that his laughter had induced in the close air of the Customs Hall.

"Hugo always said you chaps would find out in the end. Used to be as jumpy as a cricket about it. I would not have believed he had left anything in writing about it, it made him so nervous. But you chaps nowadays, modern methods, eh? You can find out anything, what?"

Sinclair began to feel that the admission which had swamped him in relief when it was first made was going to tell him nothing. More like the stereotype of the politician than the military man, Ranjit Singh was adept at using words to say little.

Suddenly the Indian added sharply, "But what had he got to be afraid of, man? That's what I was saying to him. Nothing illegal about it, so why worry? And he used to say 'Rules of the Service, my dear Ranji.' So you tell me what had he to worry about, eh?"

Sinclair leaned back on his pile of bundles. He had bluffed this far, he must bluff his way to the end. "I would really need to know more about the details of your business arrangements to be able to comment authoritatively. There are certain general guidelines: a diplomat's activities must not contravene the laws either of Britain or the host country and the Civil Service does not look favourably on its members involving themselves in private enterprises, especially if they have anything to do with official contracts."

When he heard Sinclair acknowledge the limitations of his information about Hugo's business affairs, Ranjit

Singh must have felt a relief similar to Sinclair's own a few moments earlier. It was relief, perhaps, that made him respond with such contemptuous energy.

"Official contracts? You think Hugo Frencham and Ranjit Singh were involved with supplying chairs and tables, carpets and curtains, like some banya from Sarder Bazaar?"

"I was speaking theoretically." Sinclair's quiet voice was swept away, trampled in the Indian's burst of speech.

"We were involved in export, man." He slapped the crate he was sitting on. "Fine things, rugs, papier mâché, silver, brass, bronzes, wood carvings. Finest craftsmanship. No Jan Path trash for boutiques, but contracts with the biggest stores in America, in London, Bloomingdales, Harrods, Selfridges." He seemed to be invoking the high gods of thc retail world, and at the same time stoking his anger. "So now Hugo is dead, what can you do to him? You come here to question me, you read his papers, you examine his bank accounts." Sinclair realised that their first brief meeting on the steps of the bank, when he had been admiring the old Dodge, had not been missed by Ranjit Singh. "For what? What good will it do to say this or this was against 'Rules of bloody Service'? Can you prosecute Hugo posthumously?"

"Mr Singh, there is no question of prosecuting Hugo posthumously, as you put it. It is a matter of clearing up some puzzling, not to say astonishing, details that have come to light as a result of Mr Frencham's death. They may well be irrelevant, but until they are satisfactorily explained I must pursue them. You have done much today to help me put some things in perspective."

Sinclair's voice was that of countless officials soothing irate members of the public. The technique is to speak in long and general terms, to imply all is well and there is nothing more to worry about. The desired result is to remove the angry man in front of you. It only works as long as he is ignorant of the circumstances and the ways of officials. If he is, he may well go away soothed, thinking no more of the matter. But if he knows as much or more than the official he is complaining to he can interpret correctly the vague references in the generalised phrases.

Ranjit Singh seemed to behave like a reassured member of the public. His anger died away and he began to talk to Sinclair about the export side of his business. He rose, gestured to packing cases with his stick, described the folding and sewing up of rugs in the cotton bundles, complained about the bureaucracy of the lost packages. He grumbled at the clerk with his clip full of documents, but without heat; he seemed preoccupied.

"You're going back to the British High Commission now? I will give you a ride. Come, Ajay." He waved to the man in the embroidered kurta, who joined them. "The car is parked round here, in the shade I hope." They turned the corner of the building and through the bars of the gate that enclosed the Cargo Area Sinclair saw the old Dodge under a tree, the driver gently polishing one wing as he waited. For something to say, to reinforce the unthreatening atmosphere he had been trying to create he said, "I have already enjoyed one ride in your car. It's a superbly kept machine." Ranjit Singh ignored the compliment.

"You have, eh? When was that?"

"You lent your car to Janey Somers to go to Old Delhi."

"And you went too, eh? You were Janey's friend who wanted to go to..." Saleem the goldsmith.

Sinclair's mind had recognised his mistake, had raced to Saleem and the gold long before Ranjit Singh reached the end of his sentence. But the Indian was never able to finish his phrase, aloud at least, for suddenly, as they approached the shade, the driver standing quietly on the far side of the car executed a strange skipping sidestep and at the same time shouted, "Sahib, look out!" Ranjit Singh stopped short, Sinclair and Ajay a pace or so behind him.

Dragging itself out of the dimness of the tree's circle of shadow came a naked pink creature, its teeth bared. It took Sinclair seconds to realise that this beast was a dog running on three legs, one hind leg raised and useless. It was making for the group of three men.

Sinclair was conscious of his empty hands; he had nothing to fend it off with, but he could outstrip it, for the ghastly creature could hardly make much speed on three legs. He hesitated waiting to see what the animal would do. It continued its dislocated course towards them and when it was a few paces away Ajay gave a sudden yelp and swung to the left, running for a line of low buildings which formed a guard house for the Customs Area gate. Sinclair sprang after him. The dog, distracted by the abrupt movement, swerved in the same direction. Before it could start on its new course Ranjit Singh had made two steps forwards. Sinclair did not see what happened; he heard a cracking blow, a scream, a second blow. When he turned the dog was sprawling in the dust. Its neck was broken.

The four of them walked towards it, gathered round to look at the fallen enemy. It was quite hairless, its hide eaten away by mange; its injured leg was broken, the lower part showing bone through its skin. Its mouth was set, snarling. Ranjit Singh leaned on his stick.

"Rabid," he said dismissively.

They all climbed into the car, Ajay with the driver in front, Sinclair and Ranjit Singh in the back. Sinclair was filled with an obscure shame and disgust. No one spoke and he was glad to sit back to think of what he had learned and what he had given away.

He placed too much reliance himself on the unspoken signals not to realise the significance to Ranjit Singh of his flight from the dog, instinctive as it had been. And the damned car—he cursed himself for mentioning it. Why had he done so? To make conversation, to fill a space in time, to think of Janey.

He roused himself at the High Commission gates to make his thanks for the lift. As he walked away he felt Ranjit Singh might well have thanked him for all the information he had received.

Chapter 11

THE LAWN WAS WELL FILLED with knots of guests, white-coated bearers moving between them, as Sinclair and the Turnells emerged from the receiving line at the reception that evening.

"Do you want to be introduced to anyone?" asked Alan, poised like a diver about to launch himself into water. Maggie had already thrust off from the bank and was rapidly engulfed in the group nearest the house.

"No, thanks," Sinclair replied. "I'll just circulate."

"We're going to a dinner, so we'll have to leave in about an hour. We can drop you home if you've finished by then."

"Thanks, I'll look out for you in an hour's time."

They were approached by a procession of bearers; the first carried a tray of drinks from which they both took glasses of whisky; the second offered jugs of water and soda; the third carried a bowl of ice; the fourth a tray of cigarettes and matches. The little line trudged on, Sinclair's eyes following it.

"I'd never have believed it if I had been told," he said.

"What? Oh, that." Alan shrugged. "Your duty as a foreigner in India is to employ as many people as possible and that's one way of doing it." He raised his hand in a kind of salute. "Good luck," he said and strolled across the grass in the direction of a large cluster of guests.

Sinclair remained where he was for a time, thoughtfully sipping his drink and surveying the party. He could see no sign of Dolgov yet. A chattering flock came out of the house and threatened to enfold him; he moved off, slowly circling the lawn clockwise. The light was fading from the sky and candles under latticed covers flickered around the edge of the grass. It was hot, but the open sky and garden made it preferable to the cramped cold of the Czech reception a few nights earlier. This evening he could see a greater range of nationalities and races as well as greater numbers; every continent was represented. No one addressed him or made any move to check his perambulations.

At last he saw the stocky form of Dolgov. Though he had been watching the doors from the house he had not noticed his arrival. The Russian's solid figure was now paunch to paunch with a tall African who was laughing down at some remark of Dolgov's, displaying huge white teeth between his plum-purple lips. Beside these two were three others chatting to one another, eyes flicking predatorily for more interesting companions as they half-listened to the conversation.

Sinclair moved slowly upon his prey, coming in from Dolgov's rear. He did not know whether the Russian would welcome his approach and he was giving him no chance to escape. He imitated Dolgov's own technique of the previous meeting, inserting himself gently into the group on Dolgov's left between him and the four others. Dolgov appeared not to notice him for his conversation with the African went on without interruption. On Sinclair's left was a Greek or Turk who was talking about polo to a scrawny blond man, a Scandinavian of some kind.

"Up at five," he was saying, "and out to the Parade Ground to practise stick and ball..." Sinclair did not concentrate on the words. He assumed an expression of interest, turning his head from speaker to speaker as the conversation moved on.

"...expensive..." the Swede objected.

"No, no... Good polo pony for a few hundred dollars... wonderful sport." The Swede looked unconvinced and said nothing. The proselytising Turk (or Greek—Sinclair could not make up his mind about accent or appearance) looking for a convert, turned to Sinclair.

"Do you play polo?" he asked.

"No, no I don't, I'm afraid." Sinclair's voice, not loud and with its characteristically apologetic phrasing brought Dolgov's head round like a slammed door, his body following it seconds later as he seized Sinclair's hand enthusiastically, interrupting the African in mid-flow to introduce Sinclair to the rest. Sinclair began to sense success in this welcome. Dolgov still needed him, or some information which he hoped Sinclair would give him.

The introduction reintegrated the group for a time. The Greek (or Turk) was quickest off the mark to start up his topic of conversation, inevitably polo, and for a few minutes he had an audience of five to hear of the rigours and excitement of early rising, stick and ball, chukkas, and handicaps. But polo is notoriously a clique enthusiasm not shared by Russians, Nigerians or Swedes, so quite soon everyone except Dolgov and Sinclair had quietly backed away and the Turk (or Greek) himself went off to find representatives of more sporting nations to talk to.

Sinclair made as if to move off too, swilling the remains of the whisky round his glass, his eyes surveying the busily eating, drinking, gossiping humanity in front of him.

"Tomorrow," he said casually. "Chandragupt Hotel, three thirty. Can you be there?" He was not looking at Dolgov and so did not see the almost comical expression of sullen acquiescence, the pouting baby appearance of the thrust-out lower lip. The silence lengthened and neither moved. Dolgov said harshly, "I will meet you." He strode off purposefully and Sinclair allowed his gaze to follow him for a time before he moved towards the house, glancing at his watch as he went.

❀❀❀

"Did you have any success?" asked Alan as he manoeuvred the Cortina out of the line of parked cars, avoiding a bicycle which was wavering along the road laden with an improbable quantity of people and goods. From the back Sinclair replied, "Yes, I did what I went to do."

"And have you learned anything useful?"

"No, but I didn't expect to. Ask me this time tomorrow and I may have an answer for you."

"I wouldn't have your job. Endless searching, very often without finding, and without even being sure you're on the right track. A recipe for frustration."

"I'm a patient man. I don't mind waiting and taking my time. And I couldn't do yours. A party like that every night."

"Not quite every night." This was Maggie from the passenger seat. "But they are fair hell, aren't they? You grow used to them though, like everything, I suppose."

"Do you mind if I drop you at the gate rather than coming in?" Alan asked as they ran down the slip road parallel to the perimeter wall.

"Lucky you, with a quiet evening in front of you," said Maggie enviously. "What'll you do?"

"Jogiram was leaving me something in the fridge. I'll listen to Hugo's records and try to think some sense into what I know."

"So tranquil, even if it is work of a kind." Sinclair climbed out of the car and waved his thanks. "Enjoy your evening," Maggie called as they moved off.

❀❀❀

"A tranquil evening you had of it," Maggie's voice was sarcastic as she stepped through the door Sinclair opened for her. "I heard what happened and I wondered if you needed anything."

Sinclair closed the front door and followed her into the sitting room.

"I hardly know," he said vaguely. "Oh yes, a couple of glasses might be useful."

Maggie had found a space in which to plant her large, sensibly shod feet and from her vantage point she looked round the room.

"What," she demanded briskly, "are you going to do about it?"

Sinclair regarded the scene. It was not substantially different from the sight that had met him when he had unlocked the door the previous night after the Turnells had dropped him with wishes for an enjoyable and quiet evening. As he had pushed the door inward then, dismay and unpleasant anticipation had risen at the resistance to his pressure, as though the door's movement was sweeping back objects piled in front of it. He had forced it wide enough to step in and found that he was right though things were not piled in front of the door, simply flung at random. Everything in the house was on the floor it seemed, except the rugs which had been rolled up and were standing in a corner. Instead of them, pictures, tangkas, silver, brasses, coins, carpeted the floor. He had walked over the lot as if it were a rug and into the next room. The shelves had been emptied, nothing remained on the walls. Books were heaped up, their pages gaping silently; a prayer wheel had come apart and the leaves of the prayers within were exposed. Bronze figures linked their many arms. The silver-bound wooden lid of a food bowl was broken in two. On the top of the pile lay a painted wooden mask, eyes bulging, mouth snarling impotently up at him. The glass that had clamped the tangka of the Wheel of Existence was smashed. Sinclair's first action had been to take the cloth by the brocade edging and gently lift it clear of its broken frame. The glass had pierced the fabric in several places and the splinters that adhered he had carefully removed. He had placed it flat on the dining-room table, noting that, though holed, it was not seriously torn. The pig, cock and snake, ignorance, lust and anger, circled untouched at the heart of the painting.

The dining-room had been treated in the same way as the sitting room though here it was glass flung from the sideboard cupboards which crunched under foot. Sinclair had made a rapid tour of the house, through kitchen, study, utility room, bedrooms, and bathrooms. In each the walls were denuded, cupboards emptied the contents flung carelessly into the centre of the room. He only paused in Hugo's room to look at the exposed safe door. The plaster surrounding the metal door showed evidence of attack with an iron bar; less crude methods had eventually opened it. The safe door was open and its contents, several bundles of papers, had been thrown out.

He walked down the stairs, extracted the phone and the High Commission directory from the rubble and sat with them on the bottom step of the stairs, rubbing one hand over his face for a minute or two, before flicking through the booklet and dialling.

Hipkin had not at first taken kindly to being ordered round to the Head of Chancery's house at 9.30 at night. Sinclair had tracked him down to the bar where he was playing darts against the Australians. Hipkin had suggested that Sinclair could wait until the following morning, or at least until 10.30 when the darts match and subsequent booze-up would be more or less over. Sinclair had not given any reasons over the phone for his request to see the Chief Security Officer; Hipkin's breezy excuses had been met with a cold, "I'll expect you in five minutes, Bill," and the line had been dead before Hipkin could riposte.

Sinclair was still sitting on the stairs when a couple of minutes late Hipkin knocked.

"Come in," he shouted without moving and Hipkin thrust back the door, meeting the same resistance as Sinclair, as he had to force it wider to admit his greater bulk. Sinclair heard his, "Oh my Gawd," and called, "I'm over here, Bill. You see why I called you."

Hipkin was upset, outraged. "Oh, my Gawd," alternated with "Wha' a bleeding mess," and "Here's a fine fuck-up." With rusty efficiency he went into action immediately, going from room to room, surveying the damage, examining doors and windows. He passed Sinclair on the stairs without a direct word and could be heard in the bedrooms chuntering expletives to himself. Eventually he called to Sinclair, "Best to sit down in here. It's the clearest room." Sinclair joined him in Hugo's bedroom and sat on the edge of the double bed. Hipkin was assessing the damage to the wall round the safe.

"Anything in there, was there?" he grunted.

"No," Sinclair said, "not now."

"Not now?" Hipkin's mind was quicker than his lumbering body. "But there had been? You know what they were looking for?"

"I can guess."

"And did they get it, huh?"

"Not if it's what I think it is. They could have taken anything from Hugo's collection and I'd not know. But I doubt it. They don't seem to have had a delicate touch with fine things, do they?"

"They were looking for something particular, you can see that. They could have done much more smashing if that's what they were about. You going to tell me what they was after?"

"No."

"Right, so we're straight there. Now what can I do about this lot? You want the bloody Indians in on this? We'll have to go to them for finger-printing and all the technical stuff."

Sinclair pondered for a moment; Hipkin picked up the seascape which had covered the safe door. The frame was broken but the canvas seemed impervious to its ill treatment. Hipkin fidgeted with the damaged frame and then laid it reverently on the bed next to Sinclair.

"Let's leave the Indians out of this for the time being. How far can you go on who did it and how?"

Hipkin went over to the easy chair in the corner and sank into it, sitting forward, hands linked between his open thighs.

"Well, I can make a start. It's not a hard thing to guess the servants were involved somewhere."

Sinclair felt a stab of distaste. He had come to like Jogiram's personality, his swift mind, and this savoured of picking the easy victim, the already vulnerable.

"Come Bill," he said sharply. "You're not suggesting..."

"I'm not suggesting they did it," said Hipkin impatiently. "You can see this is a professional job by that safe. But you look here. No windows broken, no doors down. How did they get in? You tell me. The back door is what I say. It's locked now all right but I'll bet that back door key went missing from someone's pocket for an hour or so this evening. How long have you been out?"

Sinclair looked at his watch; though it was only ten o'clock he felt as if it were the dead hours of the early morning.

"I was away a couple of hours I should say."

"And did they know you were out and when you'd be back?"

"Yes, they did. I asked the bearer this morning to tell the cook to put some ham and salad or something in the fridge for me as I was going to a reception and didn't know what time I'd be back. I said there was no need to wait for me and sent them off."

Hipkin almost exploded at this recital. "There you are. Bleeding servants. Half our security worries boil down to servants. If everyone would only look after themselves...I do. No servants. My wife does the lot. Cleaners in the offices are always a problem, sticking bugs all over the place given half a chance. I could tell you a thing or two about my time in East Berlin."

Sinclair was familiar with the paranoia of the security officer who sees threats in everything, especially after a breach. He let Hipkin bluster on while he tried to fit what had just happened into some pattern in his mind.

"What people don't understand is these soft posts like Delhi are much more dangerous from the security point of view than Moscow and places like that. If I was the Russians I'd spend a few rupees on getting servants' gossip in India and have a better return than on thousands of hours of bugging time behind the Iron Curtain where people are on their guard. Here you can buy anything for a few hundred rupees. Servants are all over people's houses, listening to all the conversation, with all their perks of the empty bottles and waste paper. There's nothing they don't know and give 'em a few rupees a month and there's nothing they wouldn't report…"

He was stopped short by Sinclair who suddenly looked up from the bed.

"What's that? About their perks? What are servants' perks here?"

Hipkin seemed momentarily bewildered, not recognising his own words. He had been allowing his grumbles to slide on while Sinclair was sunk in thought, as he waited for the signal to notify the police or to bring in the servants. Suddenly Sinclair, who had seemed partially paralysed with thought, was striding about the bedroom, kicking books and pictures from his path.

"Servants' perks," repeated Hipkin. "Well, it's like I said. They're used to taking the rubbish to recycle, you know. They sell the bottles. We tried once to collect them for the Club for some charity but the servants almost went on strike as they'd always been allowed to have the bottles. Same with waste paper, newspapers and so on. They take that to sell. Have you never bought anything in the market here? Don't suppose you would have. Well, you go to Khan Market and buy a pound of mangoes or some sewing thread and as like as not it's given you in a paper bag with writing all over it, made out of waste paper not even repulped."

He stopped and looked at Sinclair who had sat down on the bed again and seemed hardly to be listening.

"Read a funny thing about that in the paper," he went on. "A boy went to buy some sweets, was reading the bag on the way home. Says to himself, 'Funny that looks like my sister's writing.' Shows bag to sis who says, 'My Gawd, that's my university finals paper.' Rings up university. Finds servant has taken exam papers and sold them and—this is the best part—before they had been marked." Hipkin guffawed at the thought of the students retaking their exams because their scripts had been made into paper bags.

Sinclair took no notice. He stood up again and said, "Yes, yes, yes. Right, Bill, if you think it's the servants let's have them in and see what they have to say about it. Where'll they be?"

A Club bearer was despatched to the servants' quarters to find Barua, Jogiram and Babu Lal. While they waited, Hipkin and Sinclair cleared some space in the dining-room and sat down at the table. Hipkin seemed unexpectedly cheerful, perhaps in anticipation of bullying the servants. Sinclair remained silent and thoughtful. He might or might not have been listening to Hipkin's stories about the wiles of Indian staff in comparison with the cunning of East German cleaning ladies. He certainly heard the rattle of the back door key before Hipkin and broke in on him to call out, "I'm in the dining-room, Jogiram. Come on through."

They could hear exclamations and conversation in the kitchen and Jogiram's face appeared in the glass panel of the swing door. He could not open it wide enough and Sinclair gestured to him to come round through the hall and sitting room. Eventually two figures arrived both dressed in their own clothes, rather than their usual white uniforms. Jogiram wore pajama trousers and a singlet; Barua's more portly frame was clothed in grubby western trousers and a huge kurta.

"Jogiram, where is Babu Lal?" Sinclair asked.

"Babu Lal out, Sahib."

At this Hipkin let out a satisfied "Ha!" emitted on a rising note. Both the Indians clearly felt at a disadvantage at being suddenly summoned from their rooms and families and both looked shocked and frightened. A first glance at the place told them what the break-in would mean to them. Jogiram's eyes shifted uneasily, darting from the broken glass to the torn books. Sinclair looked at Barua and saw with amazement and embarrassment that tears were running down his fat cheeks. Hipkin had seen the same phenomenon and said, "Right, you two, we want a word with you buggers and you can see why. I'll take the fat chap—Barua are you?—and Mr Sinclair'll take the other and we'll see what you have to say for yourselves. Stop 'em concocting stories to back one another up. OK?" His last sentence was addressed to Sinclair, who rose and said, "We'll go into the study, Jogiram."

Sinclair listened to Jogiram's account of his evening first and then asked about the back door and its key.

"How many keys are there? Do you have one each?" he asked. It appeared that there was only one key. A long time ago there had been two but one had been lost and never replaced.

"So who has charge of the one key? Who looks after it?"

"No one, Sahib. Key is kept in jhallee outside kitchen door." The jhallee had to be explained to Sinclair. It was, Jogiram told him, a screen of pierced bricks, built outside the kitchen wing of the house to hide it from the garden. The key was placed high up in one of the spaces in the screen and thus it was available to any of the three servants. Whoever was last to leave the kitchen at night locked up and put the key into its slot; whoever was first in the morning found it in its customary position and opened up. It looked to Sinclair as though Hipkin's faith in the servants' being the route to the criminals was not going to be borne out. Jogiram's nervous movements and rolling eyes had become calmer under the quiet questioning and so when Sinclair said, "What's the matter with Barua? Why was he so upset?" Jogiram's reply was full and informative.

"Barua Buddhist, Sahib, come from Assam. Barua very much like Frencham Sahib things and sometimes do little puja in house." He made a gesture with his work hardened, immensely supple fingers as if plucking a flower and placing it reverently in front of an image. "So Barua very angry to see his gods thrown down on ground."

Sinclair sighed. Never the simple explanation. Rage at impiety rather than guilt caused those astonishing tears to roll down the plump brown cheeks. He wondered whether Hipkin had managed to establish the difference.

"You may as well leave the clearing up for the morning," Sinclair said as they went out. "There's nothing to gain by trying to do it now." Jogiram turned to go. "And, by the way, no one else has asked you where the key was kept, have they, Jogiram? No stranger, other servants, even friends or relations?" Jogiram's face was quite clear as he said, "No, Sahib."

From the hall they could hear banging in the kitchen and a high pitched angry muttering. Jogiram hesitated at the kitchen door.

"Barua very angry," he said in explanation. "Talk in Bengali now." He seemed reluctant to enter and when he did a moment or so later Sinclair heard the mutter change volume and language as the cook's bad temper found immediate vent on the bearer. Although Jogiram had more direct contact with his employers Sinclair had come to understand that in prestige he was only second to the khansamah who ruled the kitchen, often despotically, and in Barua's case temperamentally.

In the dining-room Hipkin looked gloomy. "Stroppy bugger, that cook of Hugo's. Wouldn't have 'im in the house myself," he grumbled. Sinclair ignored this remark.

"If what we've heard about the key is the same the servants aren't going to help us much, Bill."

Hipkin grunted. "There's still the sweeper fellow. Funny they couldn't find him."

Though Sinclair had wanted to see Babu Lal particularly he merely commented mildly, "No, it'll only be funny if we can't get hold of him in the morning."

Hipkin yawned massively. "So what we going to do about this shambles?"

"I'll phone Battacharia who's in charge of Hugo's case on the Indian side in the morning. You can spend tomorrow grilling the Gurkhas about people coming into the compound, and finding anybody jogging past this bit during the evening. OK? Give me a call before lunch to let me know how you're doing. I'll be out in the afternoon."

Hipkin gave another of his grunts and said, "Right you are," as he rose. Sinclair watched him making elephantine ballet leaps, tip-toe, through the chaos of the sitting room and hall. From the front door he called, "Night!" and slammed it behind him.

❀❀❀

It was not to be expected that Sinclair would sleep well; the break-in, Babu Lal, and how much to tell Battacharia revolved in his mind. Then the even greater worry of his gamble on Dolgov rose to torment him. The meeting with the Russian which he had arranged was not just for the benefit of his own investigation.

Sinclair had told Charlie Croom of SIS of his suspicions of Dolgov and what he planned to do about him merely to cover his own back, as all good civil servants know well how to do. He knew prolonged departmental bickering would result if SIS did not hear about Dolgov until it was all over. Poaching would have been the least of the accusations he would have had to face. Croom, bored with his routine liaison work, had fallen on the idea with enthusiasm.

"You don't understand, old chap," he kept saying to Sinclair. "This isn't just a question of clearing up Hugo's mess. We've a potential defector here. Once these guys go in for private enterprise they're half way over. The stuff he'll have to tell!"

Sinclair suspected that Croom saw Dolgov as revivification of his career and when he heard of London's response, he reckoned that Croom was going to be lucky.

"It's a do-it-yourself job, but we've got the go-ahead," Charlie had reported. "Really this is a case for a Fireman, but there's no one available at such short notice. All these cuts, nothing left of us. And since you've set it up they'll let you go through with it. They'll look at the sample and decide what to do next. I'm not really supposed to do any operational work here, you understand," he confided. "If the Indians catch us there'll be hell to pay and I'll be out on my arse and on to my pension. But there's no risk of that. The van'll be unmarked, Delhi number plate. Leave Rodge in the back. He'll swelter but no one'll see him. No one in the front. Can't have a white face sitting in a parked van for an hour—attract attention—and can't take an Indian driver. Once we have the goods I'll have London eating out of my hand."

Sinclair was sure that the whole operation would suit SIS in London down to the ground. If all went well they would have a defector with a lot of interesting European and SALT experience; if anything slipped up Security Department would get all the blame and Croom would be quietly given his cards. They couldn't lose.

What would happen to Sinclair himself was another matter. He had been sent out with a brief to smoothe everything over and he looked like stirring a good deal up. If it went wrong there would be little support for him from Anderson.

At last he did fall asleep and in the early hours he dreamed vividly of Janey and woke just before six, sweating and surprised. Quite soon he heard voices below and went down on to the verandah.

Babu Lal was there sweeping the floor with a bundle of twigs. He giggled anxiously when Sinclair said he would like to talk to him, and stared in surprise at the first question.

"You were angry when Mr Frencham started to burn his own waste paper, weren't you, Babu Lal?"

"Sweeper has waste paper," Babu Lal replied as though stating a fact as incontrovertible as the sun's rising in the east.

"But you still had the newspapers, didn't you?" The sweeper conceded that point. "So if you still had the newspapers to sell why did the loss of the waste paper mean so much to you? So much that you could tell exactly how long it was since Mr Frencham started burning his own waste. June it was, wasn't it?"

Babu Lal stood shifting on his bare feet, wrinkling his face nervously. It was not clear how much he had understood. After a pause he repeated stubbornly, "Sweeper has waste paper."

At that moment Jogiram came out with a tray of tea. Sinclair poured himself a cup, saying, "No, Babu Lal, don't go yet." He waited to allow himself to drink and to provide a sense of a fresh start. Speaking slowly and patiently he said, "What do you do with the waste paper, Babu Lal?"

"Sell it, Sahib." The answer was so self-evident as to define the questioner as a man of gross stupidity.

"Who do you sell it to?"

"Jai Dutt, Sahib. Come to compound, every week."

"And the waste paper as well as newspaper went to Jai Dutt?"

"Yes, Sahib."

"All waste paper?"

"Waste paper to Jai Dutt."

It was hard for Sinclair to tell whether Babu Lal understood the subtleties of the difference of phrasing between question and answer or not. Sinclair studied the thin worried face and could come to no conclusion. He called Jogiram and went through his questions again with the bearer translating them into Hindi for the sweeper, with no clearer result. He sent Jogiram away and asked Babu Lal about the previous night, about the key, about anyone whom he had told of the key's hiding place. Some of Babu Lal's habitual giggles returned but he was not going to admit to any involvement. Old, uneducated, an untouchable he might be, but he was not so foolish as to incriminate himself. There was a large question mark in Sinclair's mind about Babu Lal and he had to admit that if he was suspicious of the sweeper for knowing less English, being less co-operative, there was all the more reason to suspect the greater fluency and helpfulness of Jogiram.

The problem of Battacharia loomed larger. He had anyway to decide how much he could avoid telling the Indian police about what he suspected was the reason for the break in. A more worrying decision was whether to try to protect the servants from Battacharia's boys and their methods. Did he even have enough influence with Battacharia to do it? He felt in dealing with the three servants that, though they were to an extent dependent on him as their current master, without them he would be helpless. They had firm roots here and were adaptable and clever enough to mediate between the world of urban India and the sheltered Europeans in their diplomatic compounds. They no doubt took what they could from their masters both materially and in status. They were in touch with the reality of Indian life which Sinclair knew he was not, nor, he judged, were any of the Europeans he had met. So perhaps Battacharia would know how to handle these mysterious creatures with their elaborate codes and prestige of which he knew so little.

Battacharia's men would beat them up; the inspector

had almost said as much. To Sinclair physical violence was abhorrent. His chosen role as investigator or interrogator was the kindly, patient one. If necessary he would bully, blackmail or threaten using jobs, promotion, finances, infidelities; never violence. It wasn't his style; he prided himself on his results without force. He sighed and put the problem on one side unresolved, as he so often did. He would let events decide. It might be negotiable; he would see how Battacharia played it.

Chapter 12

SQUARING UP TO MORE SWEET TEA, Sinclair's first gesture on reaching his office was to lift the receiver to make an appointment with Battacharia.

The phone rang for a long time and he was just about to redial when he heard a sing-song voice chanting, "Delhi Police Headquarters."

"Inspector Battacharia, please." He waited for the clicks and renewed dialling tone and impatiently shouted, "Pratap?" over the intervening static as soon as he heard the receiver lifted at the other end. The next few minutes were ones of confusion and annoyance.

"This is not Inspector Battacharia speaking."

"I'm sorry. I must have been put through to the wrong extension. Could you transfer me, or return me to the switchboard?"

"Who is this speaking?"

"My name is Sinclair and I'm trying to reach Inspector Battacharia."

"Inspector Battacharia is being posted to new duties. I am taking over his cases now."

"Posted? Why is he being posted?" Sinclair was completely taken aback.

"For operational reasons he is being transferred."

"In the middle of a case?"

"In the middle of several cases, Mr Sinclair. Yours is not the only one on Inspector Battacharia's desk."

"And who am I speaking to now?"

"I am Inspector Verma."

"I have one or two points to discuss, Inspector Verma. Would it be possible for me to see you some time today?"

"Today? Today is not very convenient for me. Can you say over the phone?"

Sinclair silently grimaced at his end of the line, clenching his teeth in an expression of fury. "One matter I can report on the phone. There was a break-in at Bungalow 2 in the British High Commission compound last night with a fair amount of damage."

"Is anything of value missing?"

"Not as far as I can tell."

"I will send constables as soon as operationally possible."

"One last thing, Inspector Verma. Inspector Battacharia was undertaking some enquiries for me." Sinclair listened to the rhythms of Indian English taking over his own speech. "Do you have any reports for me?"

"No," Verma spoke without hesitation. "There are no reports for you."

"And never will be," Sinclair finished for himself as he slammed the receiver into its cradle. He smoothed his hair for a moment as if suppressed rage had made it stand on end, then seized the phone again.

"Bill, listen. Some Indian police'll be round some time in the next month to see about the break-in. Keep an eye on them, will you, and don't allow them to beat up the servants. What? Yes, I am bloody angry. My guy Battacharia has been removed from Hugo's case and I've had some pompous little prick called Verma yapping at me and being as obstructive as he can."

A second call in more controlled vein was made to Turnell.

"Alan, are you having a row with the Indians at present? Why do I ask? Because they've frozen up on Hugo's case. Almost quit on it. So it's either because they want to get at HMG or... Well, in that case it's something or someone else and I can guess who... Yes, some diplomatic representations would be useful. Pressure from both sides could burst the boil... I mean someone is trying to slow it down if not stop it completely."

A third call gave him an airport pass with strict instructions to bring it back by 1.30 when a car was going to meet a Bag from Kathmandu.

Looking up at the sky as he walked to the taxi rank Sinclair shuddered slightly, easing his shoulders inside his shirt. The sky was grey, though there were no clouds, grey because filled with heavy invisible particles which produced the impression of a lowering, threatening malevolence.

He was coming to know the route to the airport quite well. He watched the diplomatic quarter pass, the crowded government flats, the spacious outer suburbs, the tattered cotton shelters of the Rajasthani road workers at the very edge of the city, perched on the rim of the rough scrub which the Indians call the jungle.

At the airport this time he knew where to go and walked without asking directions into the Cargo Area. The stencilled crates of raw wood stacked inside and out of the building could have been the same as yesterday. Perhaps they were; perhaps nothing ever moved here, the crates standing as symbols of trade and merchandise to a people who acknowledge the unreality of externals. Sinclair's trade was in information, almost entirely in the world of the unreal, only occasionally substantiated with scraps of paper, microfilm or bars of gold. To trade in information required mainly a recognition of the currency needed to obtain it: flattery, interest, reasoning, threats. Cash was the crudest payment, non-negotiable with a Hamid, a Saleem, a Battacharia. He hoped it would be acceptable exchange for a Customs clerk.

The row of glass-partitioned offices also looked much as they had done the previous day, some empty, some filled with exasperated exporters, arguing with the clerks. Sinclair glanced into each one, scanning the occupants, and continued to the end of the line. There, as before, the grey-haired clerk bent over his papers under the creak of his punkah. Sinclair took in the white letters on the card on the door and entered saying, "Mr Aggarwal?"

The clerk betrayed no recognition, welcomed him politely and indicated the chair on the other side of the desk. He listened, head cocked like an intelligent bird, to Sinclair's story of his desire to export a large carved wooden elephant. He recommended a Chinese packing firm and made a detailed explanation of the forms to be submitted with the package. He suggested an agent who would see to the whole business of export. Sinclair solemnly noted down names and addresses.

"There's just one thing I am worried about, Mr Aggarwal. My elephant is quite old. Now, should there be any problem about that?"

There was a pause before the clerk said, "How old is 'quite old'?"

"Oh, a hundred years, at least."

"There could be problem here. Export of works of art more than one hundred years old is prohibited."

"Even if it is not actually an Indian piece? Supposing just for the sake of argument, it were—er—Tibetan?"

Mr Aggarwal absorbed the surprising concept of a Tibetan elephant without blinking. "This is making no difference. We have many old cars, for instance, Rolls Royces, which were not made in India. Nevertheless they cannot be exported."

"And this rule is never waived?"

"No, never."

A silence prolonged itself, during which Sinclair theatrically slapped his thighs and chest, reaching into a pocket to draw out wallet and sunglasses. These he placed on the desk and then dug out a handkerchief with which to polish the lenses of the spectacles.

"But..." It was the longest drawn out short vowel Sinclair had ever heard. "With Indian things made in traditional way it is often hard to say whether they are made ten years, twenty years, fifty years ago."

"Ah well," Sinclair sighed. "I never like to break a law. I may give up on my elephant."

"I did not believe much in your elephant—from Tibet," said Mr Aggarwal calmly.

"You didn't? So you know I don't want to smuggle out an elephant. What I want is some information. You've been very helpful so far; I need a little more, something a bit more specific. I need to know if this uncertainty about the dating of objects operates in favour..."

"No names are necessary," Mr Aggarwal interrupted him. "I know your interest. I can give," a slight stress on this word, "you what knowledge I have. This case is not one I am handling. I know my colleague who is dealing with this is moving into a larger flat; he is buying new moped. This is requiring money. I am thinking there are some things leaving India which perhaps should not be. I am looking at papers and consignments and I am seeing one very busy man, always coming to airport to check through consignments. It is the one you are interested in; he is doing something. You are knowing more than I, perhaps, what it is."

Sinclair matched Aggarwal's factual approach. "I need the addresses of consignees. The most usual ones'll do if there are a lot. Can you get them?"

Aggarwal went out of the room and was gone about ten minutes while Sinclair in boredom read a blurred typescript declaring lists of cotton skirts, dresses, blouses, jackets. Aggarwal came back with a sheet of paper which he handed to Sinclair who folded it and placed it in his wallet, taking out a number of hundred rupee notes. He passed them over, saying, "I hope I may call on you again if necessary."

Impassively, Aggarwal counted the notes under the desk, closing a drawer on them with no sign of guilt as the door opened and a melancholy moustached young man entered. He was the clerk Sinclair had seen with Ranjit Singh the previous day.

"I need file V E R oblique four oh seven nine X, Mr Aggarwal. Are you having this file?" He eyed Sinclair curiously as Aggarwal flipped through the papers on his desk.

"No, I am not having that file, Mr Sen."

"I am sorry for disturbing you, Mr Aggarwal. I will ask Mr Pai."

Sinclair followed him out soon after. As he passed the third office he noticed that Mr Sen had not gone in search of Mr Pai and the lost file. He was talking on the telephone.

❀❀❀

The pool of the Chandragupt Hotel was a lozenge of chlorinated blue. Around it a broad pavement was arranged with padded cane lounging chairs facing in towards the water, in a neat line, like patients at a Swiss nursing home. On two sides was the hotel itself, its glass façade tinted black-coffee colour to shield the inmates from the sun as they sat in the cool restaurant which overlooked the pool.

Sinclair arrived at three and already knew exactly where he was to position himself. Sue had drawn a diagram for him showing where Hugo and Dolgov had been sitting the times she had seen them there. The poolside was one of the most exposed places possible for a meeting, but edging the paved area were two lines of trees repeating the angles of the lozenge and beyond lay a large patch of lawn encircled with shrubs and here was shade and a screen from the hotel's windows.

The pool was busy when Sinclair strolled out on to the hot paving stones, his feet protected with chappals. He wore swimming trunks and carried a towel; apart from his wristwatch and a coin medallion about his neck everything else had been left in his locker.

Children and their mothers splashed in the shallow V of the lozenge, calling in high voices in several languages. Bearers dressed as if for a high budget movie in blue and yellow tunics and churidars moved among the tables and lounging chairs, adjusting umbrellas in time to the movement of the sun, carrying soft drinks and ice-creams.

Sinclair walked slowly towards the grassy area. Only Europeans lay exposed to the roasting air; the Indians spread themselves in groups under the trees or huddled under the shade of the parasols. He looked down with distaste at his own greyish white flesh revealed to the sun for the first time for at least a year. He could do with half an hour or so to give some colour to his skin; no chance of that. The position indicated by Sue was shaded by a huge tree, flanked by low flower beds and commanded a clear view of the poolside area and the entrance from the hotel.

Sinclair selected two folding chairs, positioned them to his satisfaction and settled down to watch and wait. At 3.23 he saw Dolgov's round and hirsute belly precede him through the glass doors from the building. The Russian carried his towel across one shoulder and his walk and manner were relaxed and unhurried. Sinclair checked his watch, pleased. He had not thought Dolgov would be late; he had anticipated a rigid exactness in timing. An early arrival by even a few minutes spoke of anxiety, a haste to meet the worst. That anxiety, a probing uncertainty which he had sensed in Dolgov from the first, was his only weapon to extract from him the story of his relationship with Hugo.

Sinclair had read nervousness into Dolgov's early arrival; nothing else showed it. Without his clothes the Russian looked like a large hairy baby. The impression of bulk and force which he produced clothed was softened, dispersed. The bulk was now flab, the force relaxed. He moved, slowly unhesitatingly, towards Sinclair, raising his hand in greeting as he came near.

Seating himself in the empty chair he said, "I have asked for juice and cakes. Beer," he added virtuously, "I do not drink in the afternoon." Sinclair saw in his wake a bearer carrying a tray with glasses, jug and a plate of sweet things. Dolgov took his first cake with the care of a very greedy man.

"Doughnuts are very good here and also Black Forest gâteau. I hope you will not let me eat alone. Hugo would never eat. So thin, Hugo, not healthy." He bit into his doughnut and a large gob of red jam oozed from the side of his mouth.

"Look," he said with his mouth full, "look, full of jelly. Now, in Russia I am sorry to say it, the doughnuts are not so full of jelly." Though Sinclair was not a cake eater, he took what looked like a shortbread biscuit to show willing.

"Indian sweets," Dolgov continued as if making a political dissertation, "are good in that they are sweet. But they do not have…"—he made biting motions with one hand—"firmness. They are just milk and sugar, nothing else. No, a good cake must have flour, grain, to give body." Almost without pause, he chose his next cake and went on, "My father was a pastry cook. Such cakes he made once! He told me as a child. He worked as a boy in the kitchens of the Hotel Imperial in Moskva. But when I was a boy he no longer made cakes. I remember the days in the forties when sugar in our sandwiches was the nearest we came to a cake."

The Russian stopped talking and started picking cake crumbs out of the hairs on his chest, popping them into his mouth with monkey-like movements. Sinclair roused himself to take the initiative.

"And you, Counsellor, decided to put some jam back into the doughnut, for yourself at least, with Hugo's help."

Dolgov brushed down his pelt with no sign of agitation.

"Mr Sinclair," he said confidingly, "you are a security man. I could not find you in our records but I recognise you at once. You call me here today because you suspect something and you want me to confirm it. Why should I do that for you? What have you to offer if I do?"

"I've nothing to offer if you do. If you do not, I shall see that your friends come to hear of your—enterprise. You are not a peasant with a private plot, Counsellor, and buying and selling on the open market in your line of business is not permitted on either side of the Iron Curtain. You could have handed a senior British diplomat on a plate to the KGB and all the jam would have gone to them, but you kept it for yourself. They won't like that at all."

Dolgov looked annoyed as though Sinclair had misunderstood or misrepresented something deliberately. "It would not have worked for them. Hugo would not have given them what they wanted. They would have wasted the opportunity. I only asked what he was content to give."

"They won't see it like that."

"That is true," said Dolgov sadly, "which is why I came here today. I hoped also to make a little bargain."

❀❀❀

Charlie Croom sniggered, shaking his head. "He never gives up this one, does he? A rum un." His eyes were fixed on the spool slowly reeling out Dolgov's story.

The room was small, box-like, windowless. Charlie sat chin on fists, staring at the banks of tapes, knobs and buttons; Sinclair had his feet up on the edge of the table and was gazing at the ceiling and reliving the afternoon. Rather upright on a chair to his left sat Roger, a red-headed boy in his mid-twenties, who had claimed to work for Admin: Properties and Furnishing when Sinclair had interviewed him earlier. Roger had been the one who had sat in the back of the brown Tata van all afternoon, headphones on, enduring the temperature of a hundred and twenty degrees as the sun beat down on the tin roof above him, as he wound in Dolgov's words.

On tape Dolgov's voice was thicker, harder to follow.

"Who is Babu Lal?" it was saying.

"Babu Lal is Hugo's sweeper; the one who emptied the waste paper baskets."

"That was just the starting point of how I learned of what Hugo was doing. Hugo was also going in for private enterprise, yes? We were alike in that, Hugo and I. He was my good friend. So. Yes. You want to know about this Babu Lal. This business with waste paper is not my affair. It is routine work by one section of the KGB operation here, and I always read copies of anything significant if any of my contacts is targeted. We cannot do this for all Embassies, you see; this would be too much, even for us. So for one month some are targeted, next month others. Routine search for items of interest. It seems a lot of work to you, yes? I assure you some very good things can be found in this way, as I found about Hugo."

Once he had started on his story, Dolgov showed himself a lively raconteur, filled with enthusiasm and admiration for his own memory, intelligence and enterprise.

To fulfil his social commitments in the western diplomatic community adequately, he explained, he read the western press extensively. *The New York Times, Le Monde, Frankfurter Allgemeine Zeitung* were all carefully analysed for current attitudes to various problems. In what he called the *London Times* he happened one day to see a sale-room report of an Indian miniature of Akbar on ivory, exceptionally fine, which reached a record price at auction. The fuzzy black and white illustration had shown the Emperor seated with musicians playing to him while birds gathered to listen. The beauty and delicacy evident even in a bad reproduction had not impressed Dolgov who had little interest in the arts of any country. But, on seeing the article, his mind had jumped back to a photocopy of a letter from Hugo's waste paper basket recycled for Russian use by Babu Lal, which he had seen some weeks earlier. The paper had been torn up into several pieces by Hugo and meticulously reassembled by the KGB. The copy and file contained no comment that this item was regarded as in any way significant or useful. Only Dolgov who read the western press noticed the similarity between the subject of the letter and the sale report. The letter had been a rough draft in Hugo's hand addressed to the Indian section of a famous London auction house about an Indian miniature which he had offered for sale. The sale report had sent Dolgov hastily and excitedly back to the letter to compare Hugo's written description with the photograph and account in the paper.

The *Times* report had said the miniature had come from an old private collection. Dolgov had not allowed this to put him off once he had seized the idea that Hugo was smuggling treasures out of India and selling them in London. It confirmed his impression that Hugo knew what he was doing was illegal and was providing a false provenance for what he sold. Perhaps similarity or sympathy between the two of them gave Dolgov the conviction, the instinctive understanding, of what Hugo was doing, allowing him to reach his conclusion intuitively before he had hard evidence. It took him several months of patient watching and enquiring and at first, he claimed, he did not have any idea of profiting by his discovery. Sinclair doubted this; the secrecy of Dolgov's exploration, hidden from his own masters, indicated that from the start he intended that, if anything came of his scrutiny, he alone would benefit. He denied this when it was put to him, saying that he had nothing definite to show for a long time and when at last he was certain, certain enough to challenge Hugo and break down his denials, he realised that Hugo was only blackmailable on certain terms. As Sinclair had surmised, Dolgov had confronted Hugo in June of the previous year, when Hugo, shutting the stable door too late, had started to use the mali's bin to dispose of his waste paper.

Hugo had submitted quite meekly, Dolgov explained, once he understood what was wanted: not the keys of the Registry, not the contents of the Top Secret files, not even gossip or personal information. Dolgov made it quite clear he was going it alone. He wanted money; dollars were the only kind he found acceptable and he wanted them in cash. These he could use on the black market in the Soviet Union, he explained.

"You see," said Dolgov, as though in justifying himself to Sinclair he was also speaking to the KGB, "I knew Hugo would not give up secrets to us. This would be too much risk for him. If we threatened to let you people know what he was doing what would he care? He would lose his job, yes, but in four years he would retire anyway. What he did was illegal in India but not in Britain. Once he was out of India, he had his money, he would be happy. He did not have enough to lose to co-operate with the KGB. But with me he would do business. I only ask for money and this he would give because he wanted more time, to do more. I do not know what more, but something more, and that time he could buy from me."

From this Sinclair realised that Dolgov had only stumbled across Hugo's enterprise with Ranjit Singh of exporting Indian antiquities. The gold had remained unknown to the Russian. Perhaps it was for the gold that Hugo had needed time: more time to get it, or more time to dispose of it.

"How did Hugo react when you confronted him?" Sinclair asked with real curiosity, not just feeding the microphone he was wearing.

Dolgov laughed reminiscently. "It was like a movie," he said. "We are playing chess. With each move I make suggestion, drop idea of what I want. Hugo's face never moves. He looks always at the board. He says nothing, nothing." Dolgov shrugged. "I thought I lost. Then he says, 'I'll need six months, or more. A year. You've got a year, Vasili. After that to hell with you.' So I knew it would come to an end. Sad."

Charlie Croom pressed a button and cut off the Russian's voice.

"That was a very nice little operation," he said. "The microphone worked a treat. Beautiful what they can do now, isn't it?" He picked up the medallion and examined it. "You can't believe what they can cram in there. Picked out just what we wanted and eliminated all the garbage. When I think of what things were like when I first started in this business. You walked around with a rucksack on your back to contain it all. I'll have a transcript made for you and send this little lot flash to London. They'll be working round the clock on our friend Vasili. Psychologists listening to every squeak to tell us whether he was a bedwetter as a boy and what that means we should do with him now. If they take my advice they won't let him sit here long. He's too much of a rogue, that one, to leave in place. Lift him out pronto and they'll have a first rate packet about the Ministry in Moscow and background on SALT I. Not what they might choose if they could go shopping round the Soviet Foreign Service but not to be sniffed at all the same." Charlie rubbed his hands together leaning back now, relaxing. "You don't expect to be doing this sort of thing with the Soviets in Delhi. Quite takes me back to my old days. In Berlin, that was, in the real Cold War time. Five years I had before I was blown, best five years of my life. Since then it's been jobs like this for me." He turned to Sinclair. "This isn't your line at all is it? How do you like it?"

"It's not for me," said Sinclair. "I've had what I wanted from him. I'm happy to leave him to you lot now."

"It won't be us," Croom said sadly. "They'll send out a recovery team from London for him." He looked glumly at the tapes for a moment thinking of the fun others were going to have. Then he cheered up. "Come and have supper tonight, Sinclair, old boy. Everything's going flash to London and I might have a signal back late tonight. Keep those duty boys busy, hey? About eight, Vasant Vihar E49/6."

Chapter 13

THE SUCCESS of the afternoon's project which had filled Charlie Croom with euphoria left Sinclair feeling gloomy and depressed. He agreed to dine with him and went off to the bungalow to shower and change. The house was quiet as he let himself in; instead of going straight upstairs he walked into the study and sat down. On the desk was the crumpled scrap of paper with the phone number of 'Nightingale' on it in Janey's angular writing. He smoothed it absently, trying to plan what to do next.

Most of the security work on Hugo's death was now done, or at least the lines of enquiry were laid bare. More work could be done on Hugo's finances in England, tracing sales and payments, following up the list of consignees obtained from Mr Aggarwal at the airport. But to what end? Hugo couldn't be sacked or prosecuted. He had certainly been in breach of Diplomatic Service Regulations; he had been eminently blackmailable. But, when threatened, he had paid up with his own money, not British papers. Sinclair felt that Dolgov's judgment had been sound. Hugo had not much to lose and if he had been seriously blackmailed for secrets he would have refused to co-operate. The Foreign Office could not have done much more than sack him for exporting Indian antiques. He had bought off Dolgov saying he needed a year, meaning, presumably, his last year in India for money-making before he was reposted.

Sinclair could now write his report on Hugo's activities; Whitehall would read the final line which would say 'no breach of security in fact took place', sigh with relief to be saved from a scandal and mark the paper to be put away in the Registry. He could leave for Kashmir with the job neatly tidied away behind him. If he phoned the houseboat tonight, he thought, he could find out if she was still there. He would take the next seat on a flight to Srinagar and have two weeks in Kashmir.

He did his best to think rationally about Janey. If he went to Kashmir he would have to tell her about his marriage, his children, his separation from his wife, his age. All painful subjects he usually avoided. Especially his age. Janey couldn't be more than twenty-eight or so; he was forty-five, almost forty-six. She had said, 'Come to Kashmir,' but what did she mean by it? He felt as unsure as an adolescent; more so, as unsure as a man in middle age. As a teenager he had not known what he was doing, but he had thought he did, so it had not mattered. Now, he knew he did not know.

Sinclair's imagination took him as far as the airport, no further. There was too much left behind undone and unexplained to leave comfortably and with an easy conscience. He might tell himself that there was nothing left for him to do and that he was free to pursue his own private enterprises now; but he could not believe it.

Hugo's murder remained unsolved. He heard Janey laughing at the term. Murder investigation was not his job; it was for the Indian police to find the killer. The break-in and vandalising of Hugo's possessions were undealt with. That again was a matter for the Indian authorities. Yet it was clear that they were in no haste to find either the killer or the vandals and the removal of Battacharia was almost certainly a sign of a withdrawal of interest and sincerity on their part. Sinclair put that down to Ranjit Singh, the man of influence. No doubt, like Dolgov, Ranjit Singh was nervous of what might be stirred up by the investigations into Hugo's death. But Dolgov, Sinclair was sure, had half-wanted his activities to be noticed. Ranjit Singh wanted no one to know of his partnership with Hugo. Perhaps because he had plans to continue even without Hugo.

The gold remained an unsolved problem. If Ranjit Singh had been Hugo's partner, why had Hugo sold the gold to Hamid and why had Ranjit Singh needed to make the enquiries which offended the Bombay jeweller so much? The break-in at the bungalow had surely been to look for the gold. But who was responsible for it? Ranjit Singh, Hamid or someone else with whom Hugo had had dealings?

Finally there were all the loose ends which Sinclair's bureaucratically tidy mind wanted woven into his reconstructed tapestry of events. He had not yet seen Ruth Quinton again as he had been meaning to do since he first saw her excessively tearful reaction to his questioning. Hugo's finances both in England and in India needed unravelling. For some reason London was being unusually slow in establishing who was Hugo's heir.

Sinclair pushed away Janey's phone number and drew out of his pocket five postcards which he had bought in the lobby of the Chandragupt Hotel. Not only was there still much about Hugo's death which he could not leave, he had to remember he was a family man with responsibilities. He wrote one postcard to each of his children. The cards showed sights of Delhi which he had not visited: The Qutb Minar, Humayun's Tomb, the Jama Masjid, Lodi Gardens, Tugluqabad. The children would not be interested; he should have bought ones with elephants or monkeys on. He could hear his wife's contemptuous sigh at his inappropriate choice. He addressed the cards and put them out for posting. In any case Simon would like the stamps.

There was one taxi parked on the verge opposite the High Commission gates when Sinclair walked out of them just before eight on his way to hear an evening of Charlie Croom's reminiscences. Usually he had to walk to the rank where the taxi drivers lived, lying beside their cars on charpoys, or playing cards at this time of evening. He went to the driver's door, to ask if it were free or waiting for someone. The driver had a dirty white cloth round his head, rather like an illustration of someone with toothache in a Victorian picture book. He grunted and nodded his head at the back as Sinclair said, "Vasant Vihar?" Beside the driver was another man, his face also muffled in his pugree. He had his legs doubled up and his bare feet were braced against the dash board.

Sinclair leaned back, letting the dusty evening air blow on his face through the half open window. He suddenly came out of his thoughts to the realisation that he had been travelling for some time. The taxi was slow, but the five miles to Vasant Vihar must have been covered by now. He looked around him and saw small flat-roofed villas huddling close together, their front gardens bare and dry without trees or shrubs. He imagined them by day, harshly unshaded and exposed to the sun. He tapped the driver's mate on the shoulder.

"Vasant Vihar E49 by 6," he said.

The mate did not look round; "Tik, tik hai ji," he said, which Sinclair knew meant 'all right'. Perhaps they were lost or had simply taken a longer route than necessary, like taxis the world over. They passed through a bazaar, still lively even after eight at night, the stalls brilliantly lit by pressure lamps which shone on the mountains of mangoes, the pyramids of tomatoes, the beds of chillies. At the end of the market were the meat shops, the scrawny carcasses of goats hanging whole by the legs, flesh and fat making a pattern of red and cream stripes. As the taxi slowed to let a lorry pass, Sinclair saw the flies swarming over the impassive face of the butcher as he squatted on his slab beside the row of knives gleaming silver like slender fish. Sinclair turned away his eyes. It would be easy to become vegetarian here.

Beyond the bazaar the taxi speeded up. On one side of the road rough scrubland dotted with boulders opened out; on the other shacks roofed with tin or thatch clung to the line of the road. Sinclair was now sure that they were lost. He glanced at his watch; he had been travelling for about thirty-five minutes.

Leaning forward, he said with the clear articulation of the English speaking to foreigners, "We have gone wrong. This is too far for Vasant Vihar. We must stop and ask directions." Neither man turned; one grunted to show he had heard, though whether he had understood was another matter. Sinclair began to find the pugree-swathed heads sinister. He knew the whole thing was absurd. It was the kind of incident that occurred when you didn't speak the language. You panicked, accidents happened; afterwards a completely innocent explanation was given for the whole episode. You heard of such stories and thought with superiority of innocents abroad, seeing muggings and danger everywhere. Even so, he decided he would get out the next time the car slowed down. These men didn't understand a word he said. Probably there was a village with a similar name forty miles out of Delhi. The decision taken gave him a moment's relief until, feeling the door panel so as to be ready at a sharp corner or when a lorry forced them almost to a standstill, he found there was no handle. Nor on the other side. He could not get out unless released from without.

A kind of fury made the next bit easy, though hearing his own voice he could recognise the frustration and impotence. He sat forward and shouted, "Look here. Where the bloody hell do you think you're going? This is miles out of Delhi. I want to go to Vasant Vihar. Now stop. Turn round and go back towards town."

The driver turned his head from the road and shouted back at him in Hindi. He glared at him furiously, only jerking his head round in time to correct the car out of a tight bend. Sinclair had not understood anything he said, but the import was clear and his mind leapt to Hugo. It could not be a random dacoity; it must have something to do with Hugo.

He took his wallet from his breast pocket. It contained

four hundred rupee notes, some fives and ones. He held it over the front seat.

"Take my wallet if that's what you want. Then just stop and let me out."

The ploy gained him nothing, taught him nothing. The driver's mate seized the wallet, extracted the notes and threw the empty leather fold into the back seat without a word.

At this Sinclair had to recognise that money was not the primary object of his kidnappers. He had no further doubts that it was his person rather than his property they were interested in. Threats, torture, killing; his fears escalated. His abhorrence of violence was entirely theoretical; he had never experienced any to speak of. In one investigation a cornered fraudulent employee of the Ministry of Defence had made a rush at him, throwing him against a metal filing cabinet, causing a deep triangular cut on the corner of the jaw extending into the hollow of the cheek; seven stitches had been needed. He could imagine that this was going to be worse, even though no help from office furniture was available to his assailants. He breathed shallowly and nervously, trying to think of ways of protecting himself. If information were demanded would he give it, or lie, or remain silent?

Suddenly, at speed, the taxi left the road, bouncing on its high suspension along a rutted track. In the bounding headlights Sinclair caught a glimpse of a group of shade trees, a long low building, windows above, the open doors of a garage below. The Ambassador stopped and the headlamps were flicked off. With a growl of Hindi the two men opened their doors. Sinclair was sitting behind the passenger seat. As the driver's mate climbed out, he edged forward facing the door, shoulder against the window. His offer of the wallet may have made them think he would come out co-operatively or even reluctantly. They did not anticipate eagerness and so the mate opened Sinclair's door before the driver had circled the bonnet to reach the nearside of the car. As he heard the catch released Sinclair put his shoulder to the door hard and launched himself from his bent knees. The door swung back against the mate, knocking him off balance. Sinclair leapt out of the car and ran.

❀❀❀

He had run, it seemed, for hours, in fact about twelve or fifteen minutes, he calculated, before he pushed his way into a field of maize and stood among the stalks which rose comfortingly above his head, allowing his screaming breath and kicking heart to subside sufficiently to listen. He had been carried by the impetus of his leap from the car down a rough slope and his fear of what was behind almost prevented him from seeing in time the large reed-fringed pond in the darkness in front of him. He bore right, away from it, up the slope this time, hearing yells behind him, and doors banging, seeing a beam of light leaping into the trees. He struck a rough track and used the high central ridge as his running path. Though all the time he wanted to turn to see what was being done behind him he forced himself to look ahead as he ran on and on. He came to a crossroads. The main track continued ahead; to right and left ran paths separating crops. He chose the right-hand path almost without halting and went on running. After crossing two more field paths he came to an impenetrable hedge. He did not want to turn again, afraid he might make a circle and return to the farm house from which he had come. So this time he veered left, running awkwardly, parallel to the hedge. There was no path here and he had to skirt the crop and duck to avoid the stinging overhanging branches.

Then the nullah. In May in Delhi all the ditches had been empty of water, filled only with a tangle of thorns and sun-scorched weeds. This one was an irrigation canal and was full, feeding its subsidiary brooks, the arteries and capillaries of the life of the fields. It was too broad to jump. He lowered himself to a sitting position and tested the surface of the bank just below the water level, hastily withdrawing his moccasin with an unpleasant gulp of released suction. He stood up. Somewhere on his left he could hear noises. He broke into a run again, all the time conscious that if he kept on he must strike the main track from the farm. He suddenly plunged into the maize to try to assess his position.

He had an excellent sense of direction and though he had twisted and turned a good deal since he escaped from the car he knew that, blocked by the hedge and the nullah, he was heading for the original farm track. Beyond that must be the metalled road, so after all, though back-tracking, the direction he was now going in was the most sensible one. He listened intently. He had not heard footsteps running after him through the fields and could hear none now. Dogs were barking agitatedly, presumably from the farm, but he could hear no human sounds. He squatted among the canes trying not to rustle them too much in case someone was listening for him. He rested. He must be some twenty miles outside Delhi, judging by the speed and time of their journey. If he could find a village he could get safely back to Delhi tonight. In what direction? The last huddle of houses he remembered seeing on the road was several miles back. He must first escape from this neighbourhood before he decided what to do next. Was it best to sit still for an hour or so, hoping they would give up? Or to press on and get as far away as possible as quickly as he could? In the end he waited about half an hour to recover, then stiffly rose and started to move cautiously along the nullah.

Afterwards he could never decide whether he had stayed too long or not long enough among the maize stalks. Perhaps, earlier or later, they would have caught him anyway, for with a military sense of country a man had been stationed on the bridge by which the track crossed the nullah. Sinclair, creeping along between the bank and the crop neither saw him, crouched below the level of the parapet, nor heard him. He only felt the heavy blow across the shoulders, striking the cervical vertebrae, which felled him like a villain in a farce, and two or maybe three of the blows to his head before he lost consciousness.

❀❀❀

Pain. It is surprising how much you can bear, and how unimaginably it hurts, something the mind cannot recall or recreate once past, but simply instinctively shies away from. For Sinclair, even in moments of semi-consciousness when nothing else was clearly distinguishable by the individual sense, pain asserted itself in enveloping nausea and in localised agonies. The smaller hurts in some way overrode the major ones. In the first attack he had bitten his tongue which had swelled, constantly rasping the open skin against the edge of his teeth, filling his mouth with the sharp taste of blood. He was tied face down to a charpoy and the pattern of the woven string stamped itself onto one cheek. He was beaten with lathis by three men for a long time. They spoke together sometimes in Hindi as they rested, but he was never questioned, never given an opportunity to buy out of the pain. He realised they spoke no English, were probably chosen for that reason so they could have no pity for pleas, resist all bribes.

The beating was systematic and passionless; there was no anger or spontaneity in it at all. The skin of his back felt as if it were being torn to ribbons and the image of the goat carcasses flayed and hanging in the butchers' shops of the bazaar was printed on his mind to represent what he could not see, only feel.

Later he couldn't make up his mind how long it had lasted. Could it have gone on through most of the night until the early hours when he remembered hearing the first tentative calls of the birds in the darkness? Or did it only last a matter of an hour or so? He could only patch together fragments of memory and was never as successful as the KGB in producing a complete page from the many torn pieces, never being certain where one remembered scrap came in the sequence of the whole. There was movement, as he lay wedged on the floor between front and rear seat of the taxi: that must have been after the first blow on the bridge over the nullah. Or was that the second journey when it was all over, though he did not know it then, before he was bundled out of the car onto the rough verge and the whirring of the taxi's engine ebbed away into silence.

It was there that he made his first voluntary motions since the original blow. The muscles of his shoulders seemed to have locked his arms above his head. The pain of moving his arms in order to try to raise his torso from the ground seemed to shriek through his whole body. After many excruciating minutes he had reached something like a sitting posture. To achieve a fully upright position without something to lean on appeared a hopeless ambition. Nevertheless he put one foot flat on the ground, knee bent. That knee he leaned on to lever out his other leg and so raise himself. He felt he was doing quite well until the moment that his weight was transferred from one to both legs, when his right ankle buckled under him. Pain seared up his right leg and as he lost consciousness again the ground swung up to meet him.

Chapter 14

JANEY LAY SPREADEAGLED on the roof of the houseboat 'Nightingale', eyes closed, the tips of the outstretched fingers of her right hand just touching the pile of Tibetan grammar books. The arch of the sky above her was a Madonna blue and a mild golden sun filled the air with warmth. She felt as if she were floating in the air. On either side on a level with her head hung branches from the trees on the bank and into them birds flew as if she were not there. A kingfisher perched for a minute on the rail by her feet before disappearing in a gleaming flash of blue. Beyond her toes was more blue, the silvered blue of the waters of the lake.

She loved Kashmir, regarded it as a paradise of moderation balanced between the extremes of India, the cruel hot fertility of the plains and the equally cruel cold barrenness of the high mountains. Every year she had come to India she had allowed herself some time on the Lakes in Srinagar as an escape and preparation. Preparation. Her fingers scratched lightly at the surface of the Tibetan books, but she made no attempt to pick them up.

A scrabbling could be heard at the bottom of the ladder which led down from a trap in the roof.

"Miss Sahib. Miss Sahib."

Janey hastily and awkwardly retied the scarf which was her only covering above the waist and seized a towel from the floor beside her.

"Ahmed?"

His presence announced and time allowed for decency to be assumed, Ahmed climbed the ladder and poked his head through the trap.

"Telegram, Miss Sahib." He held it out, signifying he was coming no further. Janey went over to collect it from him.

Ahmed was surly and difficult. He loathed all the rich Hindus and Christians who stayed on the houseboat and made little effort at courtesy to them, an unusual trait in a Kashmiri. Indians returned his dislike; Europeans and Americans regarded him as a character and recommended the boat to one another, not only for its delightful situation but also for the charming eccentricity of the bearer. Though Ahmed despised women, and shameless Europeans in particular, he seemed after three years to have come to terms with Janey. Her travelling alone, her Urdu, even her emaciated figure had produced in Ahmed's mind the concept of an almost-man. But he still would not come all the way onto the roof to give her a telegram.

Janey opened the envelope and looked at the strips of paper gummed onto the form, smiling with amusement and pleasure as she read:

Jananane Somomomers. Sinclclair in hospal
stop suggests convalalalessense Kashmir stop
please phone Tunel stop

❀ ❀ ❀

Janey stood on the steps of Srinagar's small airport building and watched the plane easing itself down through the silver sky. As it came closer it seemed to accelerate until the moment it dropped out of sight behind the hedge that hid the runway when a scream of fury went up as if the plane were protesting at coming down to earth again.

Janey waited amid the crowd of eager Kashmiris all about to fall upon the arriving tourists and fill their hands with cards recommending their taxis, shikaras, houseboats, guest-houses, treks, papier mâché, embroidery, wood carving, before they could so much as collect their luggage. She leaned against the sun-warmed wall and watched the long Kashmiri heads with their finely curved noses and deceptive expressions of innocence and good will. A wheel-chair was being pushed towards the runway by a khaki-clad official. Quite soon a small crowd began to bunch through the opening in the hedge. They all had the expectant and uncertain air of people arriving in a place for the first time. The advance party reached the airport building, walked inside, came out again, stood waiting, while the Kashmiris tripped round them handing out cards, promising the best of everything in Kashmir.

The slower passengers and those furthest from the doors in the plane straggled in. The first trolley of baggage was driven up to the steps and a mêlee, half-heartedly supervised by an official checking the ticket numbers, ensued. Janey looked at her watch impatiently, glanced again at the path from the runway. With a painful slowness came the wheel-chair, loaded with a brief-case; beside it walked Sinclair assisted by a stick. She went out to meet him, deliberately strolling to conceal her impatience, not to hurry him. As she approached she saw a greening bruise on his left cheek shading out from the dark core on the bone, towards the eye, scalp and jaw. Apart from this, and the halting walk, he seemed the same Sinclair as in Delhi, skin paler perhaps beneath the sleek blond hair.

"Sinclair."

"Janey."

Hesitation.

"I've kept you waiting again. I hope you're not as annoyed as last time."

"Not at all," she replied politely. Then: "But why not ride in the wheel-chair? You'd be much quicker."

"Because I prefer to do it slowly, myself." Janey laughed, turning and falling into step with him.

"Sheer affectation anyway," she said, "this stick. You look perfectly healthy to me." Glancing sideways she immediately saw what had not been visible from the front, the fair hair cut away, the thin crusted red line running down the back of the skull towards the left ear.

"You see through me at once," he said. "It's a ploy to come to Kashmir, to have your attention."

"You'll have to do better than a sprained ankle to win sympathy from me. I'm very hard-hearted." She wondered why she was speaking in this way, archly sparring with him.

"There's much more than that to see," said Sinclair

calmly. "I can promise you a new aspect of my injuries every day for weeks."

The suppressed impatience and irritation which had filled Janey from the moment she had seen Sinclair painstakingly hobbling towards her at the airport dominated her for the rest of the day. They had driven along the willow-lined lanes from the airport to the Nageen Club and then transferred to the shikara, a narrow, canopied boat propelled by a heart-shaped oar. It took some time and some assistance for Sinclair to reach a reclining position on the cushions and even more time and the help of Ahmed as well as Janey and the shikarawallah, to manoeuvre him up the steps onto the houseboat.

After lunch Sinclair was looking grey, as though the colour had been bleached out of him by pain. He lay down on a daybed in the sitting room with glass panels open on to a view of the lake and the Shankar Acharya Hill. Janey left him to rest and spent the afternoon sunbathing on the roof and wondering what to do about Ladakh. An amusing and fit companion was one thing, but could Sinclair stand the journey and if he couldn't would she have to stay until he was ready to go back to Delhi, she wondered.

As she went out to water-ski at about five she saw he was asleep and his colour looked better. When she returned he was awake sitting on the verandah and had evidently been watching her performance. After changing into jeans and a sweater she came to join him.

"Alan sent some whisky for emergencies," he said. "Shall we have some now?" Janey poured the whisky into glasses and diluted it with sterilised water.

"Hardly seems much point using sterilising tablets after I have just been wallowing in the polluted waters of the lake," she remarked. "I caught hepatitis a couple of years ago so I try to be careful about the water now. And you can do without anything more going wrong with you. Suppose you tell me the list of damages. The cut on your head I can see, and the injured leg. Is it a sprained ankle?"

"No, I've cracked a small bone somewhere in the foot. It's only strapped, doesn't need plaster. It'll be mended in a day or so."

"Sounds optimistic to me. What else?"

"A few cracked ribs and some bruises."

"You're very stoical. How did it happen?"

"I was beaten up."

"Beaten up? From what Alan said on the phone I imagined an accident."

"No accident. Alan was being diplomatic and discreet."

"But who did it and why?"

"The academic intelligence seizes on the crucial questions with a devastating speed. Who? Three or maybe four Hindi-speaking thugs. Why? Now, there's a question which does not seem important to the Indian mind. No one in Delhi wants to address themselves to that one."

"Sinclair, begin at the beginning and tell me what happened."

"I was going out to dinner with Charlie Croom who lives in Vasant Vihar, a suburb beyond the Ring Road. I got into a taxi which took me out to a farm to the south of Delhi where I was beaten up."

"A taxi? Who knew you were going out?"

"No one except Charlie and I don't think he arranged it. It must have been waiting for me on spec I suppose. I'd used a lot of taxis in the previous few days. According to the Gurkhas at the High Commission gate the taxi was there for some time and had actually turned away some would-be passengers."

"What happened next?"

Sinclair recounted the story of his gradually roused alarm, his attempted escape, his beating.

"How did you get home? Who found you?"

"I was dumped on a roadside before dawn and found by some village women. They were extraordinarily kind. They spoke no English and I was not in much of a state to explain anything in any language. They bathed my head and seemed to understand when I kept saying, 'Delhi, Delhi'. A man drove a tractor with me lying in the trailer to a larger village on the main road where he found a car to take me back to the High Commission. I arrived in Delhi around seven I think. Charlie Croom had already raised the alarm, and Jogiram must have been expecting another body under the bougainvillea when he found my bed unslept in."

"And what did the police say about all this?"

"As little as possible. The inspector who was originally in charge of Hugo's case has been removed and the new guy called Verma is stalling. His display of uninterest was monumental, one huge yawn. They didn't quite accuse me of knocking myself on the back of the head, but they implied I had asked for it at the very least."

"How does all this fit in with Hugo? Does this mean that you're about to uncover the murderer and he tried to kill you in order to prevent your naming him?" Janey's voice was filled with satirical excitement as she used the detective story phrases. Sinclair's tone was light, without sarcasm.

"I think it was a warning to me to go away and stop

meddling. I am a long way from knowing who killed Hugo. But I am sure you're right that it was connected with him."

"So are you warned off? What are you going to do?"

Sinclair paused before replying. "I could give up if I wanted to," he said. "I've ruled out various things in my investigation and those negatives are what the Foreign Office wanted to hear so, as far as they're concerned, I've about finished. I'm not here to find out who killed Hugo or even why he was killed. The Indians are supposed to do that and, if they don't, no one is going to worry too much. They'll just draw a veil over it and there are so many veils draping the past of diplomacy that a murdered head of Chancery isn't going to matter."

"What about the gold we found? Did you discover anything more about that? Or perhaps you're not allowed to say."

"Probably not, but it's hardly fair to say 'nothing to do with you' after all your help. Unfortunately I don't know any more about it than when you left. I don't know what'll happen to it—it may go to swell Hugo's estate, HMG might have a claim on it. We don't even know who inherits yet."

"And the knife and the little Buddha that disappeared when Hugo died? No sign of them either?"

"No, none. The police searched the compound and the surroundings, cleared out the ditch and created a fearful smell, but nothing turned up. I don't suppose they'll be found now. Unless they're spotted in some antique dealer's window, having passed through hundreds of hands."

They sat on as the light dimmed and the air grew chill. Janey watched the horizon darken and the stars appear. Sinclair watched Janey.

"How's your road?" he asked at last. "Is it open yet?"

"Not officially. They cleared the Zoji La, which is the big pass out of Kashmir into Ladakh, last week and a convoy of lorries went through. It was closed again two days ago because of an avalanche. I am hoping to try next week. I've booked the jeep and when I've been given a piece of paper with an official stamp on it I'll set off."

"Will you have room for a passenger?"

"There's room all right. But, Sinclair, can you stand the journey? It's a two day drive to Leh where I'm based. The first day there's the climb over the Zoji La which is eleven thousand feet, and I'll only get as far as Kargil. Then another hard day's driving to reach Leh. You're still suffering from concussion and you have cracked ribs and whatever else you won't admit to. It's very rough, you know. You'll be shaken around like a dry martini."

"If you'll have me, I'll come."

So it seemed to be agreed that Sinclair would go, though Janey remained inwardly doubtful whether he would be able to bear the journey. She also pondered on why he wanted to go. His coming to Kashmir was easily explicable by his need for convalescence and the houseboat provided what he wanted. He spent most of the time in the following days dozing or reading, looking out over the waters of the lake with its silver-green fringe of willows and parallel slats of houseboats parked at an angle along the banks. Janey saw him at meals, otherwise he was content for her to continue her own pursuits and made no demands on her. Her offers to include him in whatever activity she undertook were usually turned down, until their last day in Srinagar.

At breakfast Janey suggested a visit to the Shalimar Bagh and to her surprise Sinclair agreed quite readily.

"The gardens aren't all that good when you get there but the journey is worth it," Janey explained.

"Is it where pale hands were loved?" He started to sing in a pleasant tenor. "Pale hands I loved beside the Shalimar!" Janey laughed, always responsive to happiness.

The shikara slipped across the lake and into one of the winding waterways that entangle the valley in a net of streams. They passed old carved houses on the banks that seemed to be natural forms, strange Kashmiri trees. They wound among the floating islands, on which melons, pumpkins, strawberries were ripening, and watched one island being punted to a new position, the whole fabric of the earth, bound to a solid mass by the roots of vegetation, sliding over the water.

Sinclair lay on the cushions, legs stretched out in front of him, while Janey crouched in the stern occasionally persuading the shikarawallah to let her take charge. As she handed back the paddle after her second turn Sinclair patted the padded seat beside him and said, "Come and lie here for a bit. Learn to be a passenger and let someone else do the work." Janey crawled onto the long seat and sprawled out, lying still only for a moment before allowing her arm to dangle over the side to swish her fingers through the water.

"I can see why you normally travel alone. You can't bear anyone else to do anything while you're there. You always want to row your own boat, don't you?"

Janey watched her hand furrowing the water with the movement of the boat. "It's odd," she said. "My parents are old fashioned socialists and I was brought up on co-operation rather than competition. But as I have three brothers I soon learned that co-operation meant that in any division of labour, as a girl, I always had the least interesting and least demanding part. So at the age of ten I decided to give up co-operating, at any rate with my brothers, and do everything myself so that I wasn't always the one who cast off and tied up, but never had the tiller, who collected the worms and baited the hooks but never had a line." She started plunging her hand in and out of the water, raising small fountains of spray. "I thought as I grew older it would improve, that part of what was wrong was that I was the youngest. Not at all. At university I lived for a time in a house with five others. There were three men and three girls and we were all supposed to muck in and do everything. Of course, it didn't work like that. It was so boring always doing the cooking, the shopping and the washing up because our three males never thought of doing it for themselves. We never did any cleaning, of course, but we all had to eat, and the work that went into that was done by the girls." She paused. "Do you look after yourself?" she asked.

Sinclair thought guiltily of Teresa caring for the five children and said virtuously, "Yes, I do." He paused and then made his explanation. "That's because I'm separated from my wife. I live alone and do everything for myself, shopping, cooking, cleaning. She has to do it for the children though, even though she doesn't do it for me."

Janey listened to his confession gravely and then said, "Children muddle the issue. I admit they do have to be looked after. But if they don't enter the case, everyone should look after themselves. It's the only way. You take responsibility for yourself and there is no ill feeling." She hesitated and then went on, "When I first moved to London and started my post-graduate work I shared a flat with a boyfriend. That was even worse than sharing with five others. I thought he'd be better, because I thought we were in love. I was filled with illusions about sharing everything, even the routine chores. He was no better. His mother had waited on him from the moment he could say 'I want', served him and his father first, given them the best of everything. It was absolutely corrosive. He made me feel like a nagging harpy because he never lifted a finger and I couldn't in the end live with anyone so selfish. So gradually I have come to do everything myself."

❀❀❀

At the gardens which required historical imagination rather than any appreciation of natural beauty to enjoy them, Janey observed that Sinclair moved more easily and began to feel that he might cope with the journey to Leh. Though he still used his stick, he walked freely, with only a slight limp. He held his body less stiffly as though he were no longer expecting a blow inside his skull or rib cage every time he moved.

They climbed up the slope to the top of the gardens and looked out across the formal fall of water and terraces, the sketchy outline of the rich gardens loved by the Moghuls, and on the furthest horizon a tiny line of silver could be distinguished.

"Tomorrow," Janey said in anticipation. "Tomorrow we'll be in Ladakh."

Chapter 15

THEY STARTED VERY EARLY, Ahmed grudgingly giving them breakfast at four in the morning and wishing them good journey.

"Until September, Ahmed."

"Insh'allah, Miss Sahib."

The early start was necessitated by the piece of paper which Janey had wheedled out of someone in the Kashmiri bureaucracy that dealt with Ladakhi affairs.

'Permit to pass,' it read portentously, 'Miss J. Somers in jeep KM 4045 to rendezvous with fruit lorries at Sonamarg 0600 to travel in convoy over Zoji La.'

The jeep had been loaded the previous night and guarded by one of Ahmed's small sons. In the back were piled Janey's rucksack, books, camera, tape recorder and Sinclair's bag and brief-case. Janey had bought stores of tinned food in Srinagar and a camping gaz and kettle were wedged by the flap to be easily accessible.

The first hour of their drive was dark and silent; gradually the light grew, the road started to climb and conversation developed. At last just before six the road, tracing the course of a river up a narrow valley, breasted a rise and the huge meadow of Sonamarg opened out on either side. Ponies grazed in the dawn light and under the trees in the bazaar men were sitting up on their charpoys, cleaning their teeth with twigs, sipping tea from clay beakers. The jeep rattled through the defile made by the shacks on the left and the lines of parked lorries on the right.

"I wonder if those are the fruit lorries," Sinclair remarked. "They seem to be in no hurry to make their rendezvous."

"I have no faith in the fruit lorries," said Janey. "No one in Srinagar can say that a lorry will be at a point on the road at any particular time. In the offices they play with a pretend world in which lorries make rendezvous and proceed over passes in due time and order. It keeps them happy, feeling they're in control. In fact life goes on, with lorries late, breaking down, stopping for chats or lifts or whatever, taking no notice of the bureaucrats' schemes. The official stamp on the pass will be useful, though."

Crossing the meadow, no longer hemmed in by the valley sides, Sinclair could see the mountains rising ahead, forming a wall in front of them. He had to lean forward and peer under the upper rim of the windscreen to see their tops. Janey, driving, was concentrating on the road. They rounded a bend and before them they saw a check point, barrier raised, a soldier on duty.

"It's clear," said Janey. "That's a relief" The soldier read no English but studied the stamp and responded to Janey's chatter. There was plenty of snow above, he reported, but there had been no avalanches yesterday afternoon so all was safe.

"Don't wait," he warned them. "Go through as fast as you can. The avalanches start in mid-morning, when the sun has softened the snow. Go now and all will be well."

The road lifted ahead of them and Janey worked the gears as they plodded up.

"Look up," she said at one point. The mountain-side rose sheer in front with the black zigzag of the road ripping the green, leaving grey trails of rock slips at the turns. "You can just see the snow line at the top."

"My god, what a climb. Will this poor jeep make it?"

"This is nothing," said Janey with the boastfulness of the experienced traveller. "The Zoji La is a mere eleven thousand feet at its highest point. It's the easiest pass in the Western Himalaya. Armies have gone over here with all their baggage. Jesuit priests in the seventeenth century on their way to look for Nestorian Christians in central Asia walked over this pass. We have a military road and we'll be over in a few hours. There's no real romance and adventure left in travel."

The next hour was spent in a gruelling climb, jolting over the rough gravelled surface of the road, swinging through nearly a hundred and eighty degrees on the bends, the rear wheels showering stones a thousand feet down through the trees to the valley below. They could see snow above them creeping nearer to the road with every turn until they suddenly ran into a tunnel of ice. Dwarfing the jeep, walls of snow rose twenty feet on either side. Only a narrow line of the deepest blue sky roofed them. Janey stopped, allowing the engine to tick over.

"We're lucky to get through," she said. "That lot'll be down soon." The road was a river of melting snow bearing out her words. "It's eerie, isn't it? Like a magic entrance to a new land. I've not been through with as much snow as this on the mountain."

Gradually the snow fell back from the road once they had emerged from the ice tunnel. The precipitous climb was over and they were now running between low, lumpy hills, vividly green where the snow had melted. It was hard to tell whether they were still going up.

"When do we know we've reached the top of the pass?" asked Sinclair. "I was hoping for a dramatic watershed with the ground falling away on either side and stupendous views."

"Nothing like that. The Army has put up a board marking the highest spot and commemorating all the soldiers who died building the road, otherwise you'd miss it. It doesn't even feel very high as there are hills all round, and there aren't any views at all. We'll soon be there."

Janey was right. There was a disconcerting gentleness about the place on the road marked by the Army as the high point of the pass. They drove on and soon noticed a snow-fed stream running away from them. They had passed the watershed.

"Second breakfast," said Janey. "I'm starving." A little further on they rounded a corner and tucked the jeep off the road. On a sheltered patch of grass surrounded by snow but warmed by the sun Janey set up the stove.

"You light it," she commanded, "while I find our picnic."

Sinclair prepared the coffee and Janey unpacked the chapatti-wrapped sikh kebabs which she had asked for instead of western-style sandwiches. They ate in companionable silence for a time, then Janey lay back with her eyes closed.

Through her lids the light beat and glowed; from a long way off she could hear the faint bleating of sheep. Otherwise silence. They had seen no other human being since they had left the soldier at the check post several hours earlier. On her skin she felt the blanket of the sun like mohair, warm and faintly tickling, rucked up in one corner across her legs where the shadow of a rock lay. She felt Sinclair's hand on her outflung wrist. She did not open her eyes, enjoying the moment of expectation before he kissed her.

They lay side by side, in the sun. Janey said, "Is this why you were so determined to come?"

Sinclair did not reply directly. "It's all right, isn't it?" he asked.

Janey said, "Mmmm," through closed lips, lying still and relaxed.

The breakfast picnic left Sinclair in a state of hilarity. "Perhaps it's the altitude," said Janey as he began to sing "Pa-ale hands I loved," taking one of hers from the steering wheel and laughing as she snatched it back to pull the jeep round a tight bend.

The snow-nourished grass of the mountain crest disappeared and the landscape became rocky and shaley. No greenery anywhere; small brownish scrubby bushes dotted the hillside on which goats grazed. Not until they reached Kargil in the early afternoon did they see trees again, like a green froth along the river banks.

Kargil is a small grubby town on the borderland of Moslem and Buddhist areas, Janey told Sinclair, sitting between India and central Asia and the people in its streets and bazaar showed the mix of races and religions.

Janey put the car off the road and went to a small lodging house kept by a Ladakhi. Prolonged greetings were exchanged before they were shown to a room, very narrow and dark with a bed that occupied most of the floor space. Leaving their bags there, Janey installed Sinclair in a comfortable rickety chair on a terrace at the back of the house. This niche was filled with light and warmth. A hairy Tibetan terrier lay bathing itself in the sun. The wife of the house sat pounding something in a brass mortar. Her face was like finely creased brown leather and she was wearing the long black crossover pinafore dress traditional to Tibetan women. She nodded and smiled at Sinclair, who smiled back, opened his book and dozed.

That evening a friend of Janey's came to eat with them. She was an Indian doctor who ran a clinic funded by one of the western charities and who had diagnosed and treated Janey's hepatitis two years earlier. Krishna ate fast and talked incessantly, while her husband masticated with Gladstonian slowness and said nothing. Krishna was evidently of a romantic disposition for she eyed Sinclair and Janey slyly and giggled frequently as she obliquely questioned each about the other. They bore it as well as they could and were thankful when the meal ended early as the generator which produced the town's electricity only ran for a couple of hours each evening. Silence and darkness lay over the town before ten o'clock.

Janey and Sinclair climbed the creaking stairs to their room and undressed in turn on the patch of floor not covered by bed or bags. The light of a single candle glossed Janey's hair as she sat cross-legged on the bed. Sinclair hung his shirt on a nail on the door.

"Your back, my god, your back."

He looked over his shoulder at her rather than at his torn skin. Janey was staring in horror at the long horizontal weals that barred the flesh, at the brown and purple of dying bruises that mottled it.

"You made so little of it. I didn't realise…"

"I'll make much of it now if I'm given extra sympathy and kindness."

"Fool."

"Just treat me with care."

At one point during the wakeful night Sinclair said, "I've something to tell you that'll damage your vanity."

"Mmmm?"

"You were wrong about Hugo."

"I'm never wrong. What about Hugo?"

"That Hugo was queer."

"How do you know? Sneaking about reading his love letters?"

"I would have done if there had been any to read; there weren't," said Sinclair calmly. "Do you know Ruth Quinton? She's the wife of a commercial officer. The day I came out of hospital I met her outside the house. She asked me how I was and seemed quite talkative so I invited her in for a drink and she told me about her and Hugo."

"Hugo and Ruth Quinton? I don't know who she is. What does she look like?"

"Early thirties, brown hair, plumpish. When I first met her she looked dreadful. She cried the whole time, not surprisingly I now understand. The second time her hair was loose and she looked quite pretty, cosy somehow."

"And how did Hugo get into bed with her?"

"Apparently she's quite a good photographer. Hugo was writing an article for some glossy arty or antiques magazine and he wanted photographs taken of some of his pieces to illustrate what he was doing. Ruth volunteered to do them and when they were developed Hugo was so impressed that he asked her to take pictures of his whole collection so he could catalogue and index everything properly. She used to go several times a week and he would set out various bits and pieces to be photographed. Never very many at a time: he seemed to be spinning it out. And they used to talk a lot,

Hugo explaining how each thing was made and how it was used in a Tibetan home or temple. They did the bronzes, the tangkas, the silver, the carpets, then came the clothes. I didn't notice them; perhaps you remember them. She told me that Hugo has a cupboard of costumes from all over the Tibetan area, plain woollen ones, silk and damask; men's, women's, monks'; scarves, shirts, head-dresses and jewellery as well. When they were doing the clothes, hanging them against a white sheet in the bedroom in the right combinations, Hugo suddenly wanted her to put on one of the costumes. She explained that she could not photograph herself in it as she had none of the time delay devices to do it. But Hugo wasn't interested in photographing her in it, he just wanted her to wear it. He insisted and so she put on a silk blouse and a brocade over-dress and apron and Hugo put a silver reliquary at her throat and amber and turquoise around her neck as if he were dressing a doll. She walked up and down for a bit for him to admire her. Then she demanded that he put one of the costumes on. The atmosphere must have been quite looney by then. She said it was as if the air was full of electricity and unspoken knowledge that something was going to happen. So they behaved more and more oddly, dressing up together like children until the moment that Hugo started kissing her and tearing off all the Tibetan clothes he had put on them both so carefully."

It was only much later that Janey said, "How did you make her tell you all that?"

"Make her? No. She volunteered it all. I asked her nothing about Hugo. She just sat down, with me and it all came tumbling out. She was longing to tell someone about it, every detail and I was the safest person."

"I think you're able to make people tell you anything, everything they know. You mesmerise them."

"Not everything. Everybody keeps back something. Certainly I'm told some surprising things. She told me one thing that explains why you never had a spark of sexual interest from Hugo. He was impotent."

"But you just said…"

"Sorry, had been impotent."

"And Ruth Quinton in a Tibetan chhuba turned him on again?"

"Yes. Afterwards he cried in her arms. Ow, careful, mind my ribs."

"Oh, poor Hugo. Poor, poor Hugo."

"No. Lucky Hugo. Lucky me."

Chapter 16

THE SECOND DAY'S TRAVEL took them into Ladakh proper and architecture, animals, faces, dress all indicated they had entered a Tibetan land. A huge rock carving of Maitreya loomed above them; a monastery was perched on an outcrop of rock guarding the road. To reach their goal of the Indus river they had to cross two passes both higher than the Zoji La, but neither as dramatic. The jeep sawed back and forth along the road, cutting through the hills. As they were already at such a high altitude a climb of a thousand feet to 13,500 seemed comparatively little. The arid landscape provided interest only in the colour of the ground, which was in places banded green, gold, pink and mauve.

After they had dropped to the Indus valley, villages became more frequent and they saw Tibetan houses washed white, their windows and roof lines strongly picked out in black, dotted on the level plain. In the fields irrigated from the river the villagers were working, ploughing with burly black yak or dzo. Sometimes, in the lull of a gear change before the engine revved to pull the jeep up the next incline, faint high voices singing at their work reached them across the fields. No western or even Indian dress was seen. Everyone wore what looked to Sinclair like dark red dressing gowns, kilted up with a belt to allow free movement, which he recognized as the workman's version of what Ruth Quinton had been seduced in.

Sinclair was sleepy and dozed at times; Janey was filled with excitement.

"The air," she said, "the air up here. How do we breathe on the Plains, so heavy and stuffy? It makes me choke to think of it."

"That's the wrong way round, Janey. There's less oxygen up here, not more, and oxygen is what we need."

"We use it more efficiently up here. I always feel marvelous at high altitudes." Then a trifle anxiously, "Do you feel all right?"

"No palpitations yet to add to my afflictions."

The last lap of their drive taking them to Leh, the chief town of Ladakh, was across a sandy plateau in the last light of the afternoon. The sun was so low, balancing itself on the rim of the Zanskar range to the south-west that the shadow of the jeep, enormously elongated, lifted high on stilt-like wheels, raced beside them. On the plain nearer the town they passed the Army base with its airstrip, hangars, trucks and planes in rows like a child's toys. They turned away from the river towards the north-eastern range where in the foothills at a height of ten thousand feet Leh stands.

Sinclair had already observed Janey's tendency to make

routines and traditions in her life. She had established certain patterns in her visits to India, of staying at particular places, visiting particular people, always going back searching for the same faces, remembering the people and their lives from the last time. He wondered whether these habits were imposed on her by her absorption in oriental ways, or whether India appealed so much to her because of her search for a pattern in her life.

The rooms she always stayed in at Leh were an interesting case. Sinclair, having examined them on their arrival, was not convinced that a house with running water might not be found in the town. However, Janey was familiar with her Ladakhi landlord and his wife and would not leave people she already knew for the sake of mere plumbing. Their landlady in winged hat and Tibetan dress had puffed up the stairs ahead of them to show them the glassed-in verandah, the bedroom and the bathroom. Janey had sat on the verandah talking to her while Sinclair surveyed the bucket and dry hole in the floor which symbolised the bathroom, the large bed, single chair and row of hooks which comprised the bedroom. Dolma Palsang went down to prepare the evening meal and Janey put her hand through Sinclair's arm.

"I'm glad you're here," she said.

❀❀❀

"Are you starting work today?" Sinclair asked as they breakfasted late the next morning. They were sitting beside the open windows of the verandah eating brown rolls and apricot jam and looking out over the garden below with its rows of newly planted vegetables. Beyond the garden wall was an orchard where apple trees were in blossom and through the pale fuzz of the petals ran the silver line of the horizon.

"I don't think I can work all that seriously while you're here," Janey took another mouthful and spoke through it. "What would it amuse you to do?"

"I wouldn't mind coming with you to visit your monasteries, so don't let me stop you if you want to work." Janey was leaning out of the window to drop a morsel of bread to the chained mastiff lying on the edge of the terrace below them and did not reply immediately. Sinclair waited for her to sit back in her chair and pick up her tea cup again before he said, "Didn't you tell me in Delhi you were going to a monastery called Uptak to see a lama? Why don't we go there?"

"How clever of you to remember. Yes, I am going there. In fact I hope I shall be able to spend some time there working. If you're really interested we could go while you're here. I'm hoping to see a very learned Tibetan called Lobsang Dhondup. He is the reincarnation of a Tibetan saint called Rongtsen and came to Ladakh in 1959 when the Chinese took over Tibet. I'll take my letter from Hugo to present to Rongtsen Tulku and I can make a preliminary reconnaissance of what's there. I..." She broke off, noticing Sinclair's expression. "What's the matter?"

Sinclair's voice was quiet and cold. "You have a letter from Hugo?"

"Of course, to the Incarnate Lama at Uptak. If you remember my mentioning the monastery you must remember that I've told you about that."

"No Janey. You said you had an introduction from Hugo."

"But it's the same thing." Speaking slowly and impatiently as if to a rather stupid child, "It is a letter of introduction *for* me, *from* Hugo, *to* Rongtsen Tulku." She emphasised the prepositions with insulting clarity.

"It is not the same thing at all. When did you get this letter from Hugo?"

"It was waiting for me when I arrived in Delhi. Why?"

"Because it was written by Hugo of course and just before he died. What does it say? Is it open?"

"No it is not. I have no idea what it says. It can't have any significance for you, Sinclair, so don't make such a fuss. It is simply a letter of introduction."

"How do you know it is 'simply' that if you haven't read it? It could contain any kind of information. I wish you'd told me about this before, Janey."

"It wouldn't have made the slightest difference. You're not going to open it."

"Can I see it at any rate?"

Janey looked as if she were going to refuse and then changed her mind. "You can't read it," she repeated. Nevertheless she went into the bedroom to rummage in her rucksack. She came back with a long sealed envelope which she handed to Sinclair who gazed at it in silence and then placed it with great exactness on the corner, neatly aligning the edges with the sides of the table. Janey gave a shout of laughter.

"Admit you're beaten, Sinclair," she said. "Admit it."

The superscription displayed on the upturned letter was in flowing Tibetan script.

"That'll teach you to read other people's letters," she crowed. The ending of the skirmish had left her in an excellent mood; Sinclair's face set gloomily.

"You may believe that life is so manifold and various that it cannot be chopped up into packages and so all murder investigations are futile from the start, but you must see that letter was written just before Hugo died and may contain important information."

"Sinclair, this cannot be of any use to you at all. Hugo wrote to me before I came saying he was going to give me an introduction to a man whom he knew and corresponded with in Ladakh. I'm just thankful he wrote the letter before he died."

"You have no idea what may or may not be useful."

Janey's good humour at thwarting Sinclair was disappearing fast. "Even if it were useful, it is a letter not addressed to you so you should not open it, even if you could read it."

"For God's sake, Janey, spare me that high-minded rubbish. I'm a security investigator, not a boy scout."

"Anyway, why are you so convinced that this letter is of importance to you?"

"Never mind. We'll see when your Tulku guy opens it."

"You brought up the subject of Uptak and suggested going there, then you wanted to read Hugo's letter to Rongtsen Tulku. What is all this?"

Sinclair poured himself some more tea. The gush of liquid filled the silence. As a placatory gesture he moved the pot towards Janey's cup; she snatched it away leaving a dirty dribble on the table.

"Sinclair, what is this about Uptak? I insist on knowing."

Sinclair's face was cold. "It's much better that you don't know. There are things I can't tell you and those I can I would prefer not to."

"I must know. Don't tell me what you are not allowed to, just tell me something. I won't be a—stooge anymore."

"You're not a stooge. Please don't be so melodramatic."

"If you won't explain I will not take you to Uptak and

you can't go by yourself unless you've a permit for the military zone which I very much doubt."

Sinclair sighed. From the inner pocket of his jacket hanging on his chair he extracted a piece of folding card. Janey took it from him.

"It came for Hugo while I was in hospital," he explained.

Janey looked at the address and stamp and opened it. It was written in a neat educated hand.

> Dear Hugo,
>
> We have no news of you since mid April. I hope all is well with you and that the arrangements we were making together are progressing as planned. The first transfer was received and we are very happy with the money. Will you let me know what are your plans for thc rest? If you would also notify my brother Lobsang Dhondup at Uptak of all that you have been doing he would be pleased. He is writing that he had no letter from you for six wccks.
>
> I hope you are in good health.
>
> Your friend,
> Sonam Dorje

Janey's eyes ran rapidly over the sheet of paper, then she folded it and handed it back.

"Why didn't you tell me about this when you said you wanted to come to Ladakh with me?" she said bitterly. "You had plenty of opportunity. Why didn't you explain? My God, I look so stupid. But so do you. Did you think you could only persuade me to take you if you made love to me? Why did you have to use me like this? It's so—so undignified."

Sinclair stood up, put his hands in his pockets and leaned his forehead against the glass of the verandah.

"Janey, I have not used you, at least not in the sense you mean. I did not make love to you in order to come with you and you know it. OK, I didn't tell you about this postcard and there's a lot more I'm not going to tell you. Can't you see it is my job to find these things out and it is also my job not to tell my wife or girlfriend or anyone about them." He paused, but did not look at her. She was sitting in her basket chair, knees drawn up, her feet on the edge of the seat. "They're separate, Janey, work and sex. I don't mix them. I don't go to bed with anyone for the sake of my job. I don't tell you confidential things about my work. Is that clear?"

Sinclair's experience of marital arguments led him to expect that Janey's response would be to weep or shout or accuse him, possibly to do all three in quick succession.

In fact, she said composedly, "Yes."

He looked round in surprise, forgetting his rhetorical question. She returned his gaze. "I understand your position. I agree with it. I just don't know how far I believe you."

"What can I say to make you believe me?"

"Nothing now—once you've told a lie and been found out it's too late."

"I have not told you any lies."

"You allowed me to believe what wasn't true." She watched him as he came back to the table and sat down. He took her hand.

"Janey, I didn't tell you I wanted to come to Ladakh because of Hugo. I allowed you to think it was entirely because I had fallen in love with you. I'm sorry. But you must understand what I did tell you is not any less true because of what I concealed."

"It just seems so," she said sadly.

Above them as they walked through the trees on the steep climb to Uptak Janey and Sinclair could see the backs of a large family party, women in their finest head-dresses with lappets studded with turquoises hanging down their backs. There were children too, scampering ahead of the adults and a baby in a shawl slung like a ruck-sack over its mother's shoulders. Behind them were more Ladakhis, their voices reaching up to where Janey and Sinclair stood for a moment to gasp in enough oxygen to renew their climb. There was no jeepable road to Uptak and the car had been left in the valley below. Instead they took the lung-searing way through the woods to the turn in the path where they could see the monastery stacked against the rocks of the mountain ahead.

It shone a dull white, and from its roof rose the golden symbol of the Wheel of the Law.

Janey had not realised that it was the time of the Summer Festival at Uptak. Most monasteries in Ladakh celebrate their most important and showy festivals during the winter months when there is little agricultural work to be done and people have plenty of leisure; only Hemis and Uptak hold summer ceremonies. Janey had discovered this when she had gone a day or so earlier to see if she could include Sinclair on her permit for the military zone.

"It is the end of the Spring Festival," she had been told. "Everyone will be going to the celebrations. Restrictions are relaxed for this day."

Thus they found themselves ascending the rough

path to the monastery in the early morning with parties of Ladakhis assembling for the afternoon performance.

As they came nearer to the entrance arch they saw a wall running down the slope to meet them, dividing the path into two carriageways. The wall was composed of large flat stones and as they came abreast of it, taking the left hand path, Janey stopped: "This is a mani wall," she said. "Each stone has a prayer carved on it. Look." Sinclair saw that the surface of the stone had been painstakingly scraped away to leave raised letters. "Om mane padme hum. The jewel in the lotus," Janey read. "The whole wall is a pile of prayers. It is an act of great merit to build such a wall. You must always circumambulate a holy monument like this clockwise, placing your right shoulder towards it. The same with chortens." She pointed ahead to a vast bell-shaped stone structure placed at the end of the wall. There was a line of smaller replicas leading up to an entrance arch which was a hollow chorten under which the track passed. At this point the path turned into a cobbled staircase, shallow and broad, leading up and up. Alleys branched off it to lesser buildings on either side, while the great staircase led on, inexorably sweeping up and round the hillside until it burst open into a large rectangular courtyard dominated by two imposingly carved and painted doorways. Already the space was filling with people and excitement.

"This'll be where the dances are held this afternoon," Janey remarked.

They ascended a narrow staircase out of the courtyard and found themselves on an open verandah. Here a dozen small boys, shaven headed, in neat robes, miniature monks, were seated cross-legged, with long narrow books open on their knees, their fingers following the lines, mouths moving silently. An elder boy sat on the edge of the balcony, looking out over the roof idly swinging his leg. To him Janey spoke in her slow correct Ladakhi, showing her letter to Rongtsen Tulku. His surprise was evident at being addressed in his own language by a European woman. After a pause for thought he signed to them to follow him. They were led rapidly along several winding passages and into a large hall in which perhaps fifty men were seated cross-legged facing one another with a central aisle between them. The young monk seated himself on the back form and indicated to Janey and Sinclair to do likewise.

The dim silent room was lit only by a row of butter lamps beneath three more than life size statues draped in gauzy scarves, which faced the main doors. In front of each bench was a narrow stand, as if for prayer books, and on it was placed before each man a shallow dish without handles. A small boy with a jug of brass and silver, almost as large as himself, was walking round filling the tea cups. Janey watched him going up and down the rows and quickly took out two china bowls from her duffle bag, placing one in front of Sinclair. She nodded at the boy as he came to them and he filled up their cups with a dark oily liquid.

There was a startling clash of cymbals and a low muttering growl filled the shadowy hall. Under the cover of the chant Janey whispered, "We're in the dukang, the main assembly hall. The service will finish quite soon and then we shall be able to meet Rongtsen Tulku."

Sinclair gestured to the cup, questioningly.

"Butter tea." He tasted it and made a slight grimace of distaste. Janey smiled and shook her head, sipping the salty tea and looking round noting the vast statue of Sakyamuni, the rows of tangkas hanging from the pillars, the frescoes on the rear wall. In front of the statue of the Buddha in the central position facing down the aisle was a large low throne and a lesser one beside it, both empty. The chief monk present was seated on cushions in a chair, his importance signified not only by his position and clothes but by his size as well; he was a very fat man.

At the end furthest from the chief monk were a number of boys with instruments, the most interesting being long trumpets resting on the floor and propped up for them to blow them at appropriate moments in the service. Janey ceased to look around and allowed the soft rise and fall of chanting, broken by the cymbals and trumpets, to lull and soothe her.

The end of the service took her by surprise; the monks were closing their books, standing, adjusting their robes. Their young guide led them out by a side door and told them to wait, pointing to a low-walled pen where a number of shaven heads could be seen. Sinclair raised his brows in query.

"It's the loo I think," Janey explained. "They've dashed in for a pee after all that butter tea."

The man they wanted was not there after all. Suddenly their guide turned and was speaking to a small round-headed monk. Janey watched him, realising this was the Tibetan they had come to see.

"You have a letter for me," he said in Tibetan and she handed over Hugo's envelope. He took it, reading the superscription, not opening it. "I have been waiting for this," he said. "Come with me."

He led them off down the hillside through a maze of buildings.

"What do you think of our monastery, our dukang?" he asked Janey as they walked.

"You have many fine things," she replied politely.

"Fine things, yes," he said impatiently as if she had missed the point. "More important are the religious observances. They are well done here. That is good. You saw the two thrones for the Gyalwa Rimpoche, that is the Dalai Lama, and the Head Lama. The Gyalwa Rimpoche has been once to Ladakh and he came here to occupy his throne. That was a great day for us. I had not seen him since he was a boy when I was studying in Lhasa. I used to see him at the Monlam Festival and on the days of summer when he went to his summer residence at Norbu Lingka. We have a boy Head Lama here at the moment; he is in Dharamsala with the Dalai Lama and the Treasurer is acting as head of the monastery. But he is a good man and organises things well. There are many young novices and that is the sign for the future." He turned into a low doorway and led them into his room.

The monk's cell was small, crowded with homely objects. A low bed in one corner, a bench, a low table, a small black stove with a metal chimney combined sleeping, eating and cooking equipment in one room. Books, religious objects, fine tea cups and covers, battered dekshis were arranged together on low shelves and from his position crouched near the stove the monk could reach any implement for any function. Janey and Sinclair were seated on the bed.

"Let me make you tea before I read my letter. I think you would prefer Indian tea to Tibetan." They again produced their cups and sipped their tea while the monk broke the envelope and read Hugo's spidery Tibetan script in silence. Then he put down the paper.

"You have something more to tell me, not in the letter." He made it a statement rather than a question.

Janey replied, "You probably won't know that Hugo Frencham who gave me the letter is dead. He died over three weeks ago."

She watched the round face. It was almost impossible to judge age or emotion from the features or the expression. He was not a young man, though the firm flesh was not creased and wrinkled in the way that made the villagers appear of immense age from thirty onwards. The full cheeks and slanting eyes seemed, like so many Tibetan faces, able to express only happiness and pleasure, but an air of indefinable sadness worn always in his eyes and mouth contradicted his natural cheerfulness.

"How did he die?" he asked.

"I am afraid he was murdered," Janey answered. "Stabbed. He was found in the garden of his house in Delhi early one morning."

"Do they know who did this thing?" Janey glanced at Sinclair and translated the question. He shook his head.

"This explains much," the monk said. "I have a brother, Sonam Dorje, who is now in Dharamsala. He has been expecting to hear from Hu-go." He pronounced the name as if it were two single syllable words. "I have been waiting for you as well. I knew you would be coming, but not under circumstances like these." Lobsang Dhondup paused and scanned their faces.

"Hugo had something of ours, of the Tibetans, I mean. I could almost say of mine if it were not that I have only things for my personal use, nothing more. It was something of great value. Do you know of this?"

Janey hesitated for a moment and looked at Sinclair, who could not understand the question. She looked back at the monk. "Yes," she said simply in Tibetan. She translated for Sinclair what had been said.

"What was your answer?" he asked. She smiled.

"I've already told him that we do know about it. It must be the gold he is referring to. I'm going to tell him about it, all right?"

"I depend on you, so I have to trust you. You must ask him to tell us about where it came from and how Hugo had it."

The monk watched them talk in English and said, "My brother speaks very good English and Hindi too, but I only speak Tibetan and Ladakhi. You must bear with me."

"And you with me. My Tibetan is not very good, I fear."

"No, no, very good."

"You are very kind. What you talk of we have found and it is quite safe. It was not lost or harmed by Hugo's death. Can you tell us how he came to have it? It is something we have been much puzzled about."

"It is safe. I could not believe that it could come to harm. Or at least I feared that harm might come of it and that would be my punishment for moving it from where it had been. But I sought guidance and the omens were good: how should harm come?" He stirred restlessly in his seat. "You want to know the story of the gold. It is the gold we are talking of, is it not?"

"Thirty-five bars of gold."

"Thirty-five? There were originally forty-five. That would be right. That gold is mine, though I have nothing. I am the guardian of the gold. I have guarded it for over forty years and then I agreed to give it up."

Chapter 17

MY BROTHER, Sonam Dorje, and I, Lobsang Dhondup, were born in Lhasa in the same year, within three months of one another. Sonam was the elder, just as his mother was the elder sister of mine. Our mothers were born on the country estate of a great noble family and brought to Lhasa to serve as maids to their ladies. It was in Lhasa that my mother met Jigme Ladakhi during the festival of the Lesser Prayer just after the Tibetan New Year. Our father was a trader and his home was in Leh where he lived with his brothers and their wives. After he met my mother he set up house in Lhasa. He married my mother's sister, Sonam's mother, as well, and by paying a small annual tax he was able to make them free.

I do not remember my father well as I saw him so little, for he spent long periods travelling. Another reason was that when I was four years old I was recognised as the reincarnation of the monk Rongtsen of the monastery of Gyangtang in the far west of Tibet. Gyangtang is not one of the very large or important monasteries of Tibet like Drepung or Kumbum, though it is wealthy out of proportion to its size or land holdings. Rongtsen is not one of the great reincarnations either. He was a very holy monk, a man of learning and purity who lived three hundred years ago.

When the last Incarnation died the omens told of the new one being born far to the east in Lhasa under the eye of Chenresig. The father of the new Incarnation was seen to be always moving, swinging like a pendulum between west and east. At first the monks from Gyangtang believed this must signify a nomad child, though they could not understand how the child remained in the east while the father moved to and fro. It was the Regent who told them to look among the community of traders in Lhasa and it was there that I was found.

Sonam's mother had two daughters, but my mother had no other children after I was born so she was deeply saddened as well as proud when I was recognised as Rongtsen Tulku. Because I was not strong I was allowed to remain three years in Lhasa under the charge of the monks and near my mother before I went to Gyangtang. Thus I continued to see Sonam whom I loved and admired so much, but I no longer went to school with him. I was taught by my own tutor, a monk, who introduced me to the intellectual life of Buddhism. My father travelled not only to Leh and sometimes to Yarkand but to Kashmir and to British India. He was a great admirer of you British and he wished to bring modern ideas to Tibet. You can see it was this attitude which made him decide to remove Sonam from the school in Lhasa and place him in a boarding school in Kashmir.

Poor Sonam, he was very unhappy in Srinagar at

first. He told me how he felt there. He thought he would suffocate surrounded by so much water and so much greenery. The terrible humidity of the late summer, the rain, the snow, the damp cold after the dry clear air of Tibet. And it was not just the physical differences in climate and scenery which affected him; he did not like the Indian boys with whom he studied. In Tibet we have status according to function but we do not have caste. In this school I understand Indian caste feeling was added to English ideas of class. Of these I do not know; all I know is that Sonam disliked the atmosphere and made no friends, that is until, in his thirteenth year, a new teacher came to the school. Do you know who this was? Hugo Frencham. He was a friend to Sonam, spoke kindly to him and best of all, as all good teachers, he sought to learn as well as teach. He asked Sonam about his country and religion. Sonam, I think, had never come to despise his own people but he had suppressed his thoughts of them living among strangers. It was Hugo with his interest in Tibet who taught Sonam to value his community. Hugo left Kashmir after two years and for a long time Sonam did not see him again.

What of Lobsang during these years? I also moved westward and earlier than Sonam. When I was seven years old I was taken to my monastery. Many times Incarnations are asked what they remember of their former lives and deeds. When I returned to Gyangtang for the first time in my new body I recognised the place. At once I knew I was coming to my home, as familiar and as loved as the wooden house in Lhasa where my mothers lived with Sonam and my sisters. I could see the monastery before it was truly visible across the plain with the mountains built like a high wall behind. The small speck of the monastery between wall and valley floor I could pick out in all the barrenness and space. I also knew before I was shown it Rongtsen's cave, three days' journey into the mountains to the north-west. I do not mean I could have walked there, knowing the way, but when I was taken there when I was ten and had taken my first vows I knew the paths; I had seen before the narrow overhanging cliffs, the split in the rock, though I did not know where I had seen it unless in a dream. I did not go there again until the year of the Khampa rebellion, 1959, the Earth-Pig year.

I lived in my monastery under the care of my tutor until I was fourteen and then I returned to Lhasa for my studies. It was seen that I was interested in philosophy and I was given permission to return to Lhasa to continue my work on the scriptures. It was thus I was in Lhasa in '49 when the Chinese first invaded Tibet. I remained at my studies all through that terrible time until I was eighteen and had gained the degree of Geshe; then I moved back to Gyangtang. I have never seen Lhasa since.

Sonam remained at school in Kashmir during this time until he was sixteen. My father wished him to go to university in India. My father did not like the Chinese. He always thought Tibet should look south not north and east for its contacts with the outside world. Sonam would not go. For three years after he left Kashmir he travelled with my father, as the sons of merchants have done for generations, learning to recognise goods of quality in the bazaars, to bargain, to endure the long weeks of travel. Finally he agreed to what my father wanted and went to Delhi University. He chose to study engineering and also became involved in politics and so was gradually taken far from Tibetan ways. I know little of the complexities of these matters, only what Sonam has told me. In India it was a time of friendship between India and China, 'Hindi-Chini, bhai-bhai'. So while in Tibet the Chinese tightened their control of the country and chiselled away at the religion which is our life, in India Sonam was filled with love for the progressive people that were to do so much for his own country. These ideas fused with the attitudes of my father that Tibet must change, must not stand still, so Sonam was in haste to return to Lhasa and help in building bridges, roads, hospitals, schools, to transform Tibetan society.

Building roads and bridges. Tibetans for centuries have built the strongest and most delicate bridges made of branches and twigs over chasms hundreds of feet deep. We have paths over the highest and most difficult mountains in the world and yet outsiders, foreigners, whether of east or west, think to come and teach us how to make roads and bridges. I saw Sonam only once when he came back from India and I found him much changed. He had become an Indian, no longer a Tibetan. He admired all new things; he talked a lot and laughed little; he paid little attention to religion. We were divided.

In 1959 came the revolt of the Khampas, the nomads of the east of Tibet. At that time I was at Gyangtang and Sonam and my parents and sisters were in Lhasa. The Gyalwa Rimpoche left Lhasa for India in March 1959 and when the news reached me in Gyangtang I left with some other monks who wished to follow the Gyalwa Rimpoche. For us it was quite easy. We had sister monasteries in Ladakh, so we had places to go to and be welcomed. All I had to do was make one last journey to the hermit's cave.

In following the Gyalwa Rimpoche I was the first of my family to leave Tibet, though I had never left it before, while the wandering members, my father and Sonam remained in

Lhasa. So Sonam witnessed the sufferings of the Tibetans while I was safe here at Uptak only two weeks' journey from my old monastery where my brothers were taken to concentration camps and worked as forced labourers building roads and bridges.

Sonam left Tibet in 1965. His journey out was far more dangerous than mine for by then the frontiers were well guarded on both sides after the war in '62. He never told me how our parents died. I know the large house in the traders' quarter was taken from them, that indignities and hardships were heaped upon them as capitalists and oppressors, and even their son's work with the Chinese before the Revolt could not help or protect them.

Sonam was appalled by what happened in Tibet, not just to our parents but to all the people. It was the deliberate attempt to wipe out a way of life which horrified him most. He remembered the teaching that Hugo had given him at school in Kashmir to honour and value the ways of his community and in Tibet this means the ways of Buddhism, for if the practices of religion are removed from Tibetans there is nothing left of their tradition and way of life. The Chinese abolished all religious houses and ceremonies and put the monks and nuns to forced labour and destroyed our country.

Sonam came out of Tibet sick. For many months he lay ill in Leh and when he had recovered he had made the decision to become a monk. It is not necessary to go to a monastery as a child as I did; you can turn to religion at any time in your life. Sonam went to Dharamsala where the Gyalwa Rimpoche lives now in his exile, and took his vows.

He is not a student of the ideas and mysteries of his religion. He still wants action rather than meditation as his means to gain merit. He has worked for years to help the Tibetans in India to provide schools, medical assistance, lamas to guide them, but he is very hostile to outside help. He has rejected his experiences as a young man, our father's philosophy that Tibet must look outside herself for help and learning. To Sonam this has brought nothing but misery and suffering to our people. It is a diversion from our old ways of self-reliance to which we must return if we are ever to regain anything. Among Tibetans in India has come much dependence on charity, money collected abroad. Very often it is arranged how this money much needed by our people should be spent. So Tibetans proud and independent, are like beggars in the world community with others spending money for us as if we were children. Sonam cannot like this. He works all the time to make us able to manage our own affairs, making co-operatives that produce things that we can sell. Money is always needed to set up these projects and to look after our people and it was need for money that brought about these events.

I must return for a moment to myself and my monastery in Tibet. I told you that Gyangtang was wealthy out of proportion to its size and numbers and now I must explain why. In Tibet we have many beliefs which appear strange to people of other religions and one which I do not think many others share is that we should not dig deep into the earth, as this releases the demons and evil spirits that inhabit the nether regions. To plough the earth is of course natural; to mine it is forbidden, so minerals and metals have not been taken from the land. In west Tibet is a small gold field which is part of the possessions of my monastery and, fortunately for us, the gold is on the surface and could be collected by merely digging shallow trenches. This has made us over many generations a wealthy foundation.

When I decided to leave Gyangtang I did not know what to do with the store of gold that we kept in the monastery. I did not want to leave it there for the Chinese, but at the same time to remove it from Tibet, part of Tibetan earth and substance, I did not want to do that either. So I hid as much gold as I could take.

The monk Rongtsen of whom I am the reincarnation spent years in meditation in a cave sacred to Padmasamabhava containing a pure spring, high up in the mountains. The cave has been used for meditation by the following Incarnations and I have already told you it was one of the signs of my former lives that I recognised it when I went there as a boy often.

It was in this cave that I hid the Gyangtang gold and there it stayed from 1959 until this winter. The idea of moving it and using it was not, of course, mine. I think perhaps it was originally Hugo's, made in his conversations with Sonam (for Hugo and Sonam had met again) and it was Sonam who put the idea to me. I meditated deeply on this matter and sought for guidance from brothers and teachers in Dharamsala and it was eventually agreed that if the gold could be recovered it would be a legitimate use of it to sell it and employ the funds to benefit our people in India.

So who should retrieve the gold? I placed it in the hermit's cave, should I go? Sonam would not allow this and insisted as the initiator of the idea and as an experienced traveller of the high passes from his days as a merchant, that he should make the journey and take the risks, if I would tell him the way to the cave.

Sonam made his journey in the snowy season. This is

not the right time for crossing the mountains; it was chosen because the movements of the troops on either side of the border are much reduced. They limit themselves to picket duty and do not roam the mountainsides as freely as they do when the summer comes.

He left here just before the Winter Festival and was gone for two months. When he returned it was with a story of great difficulties. It is certain that the demons that live in the mountains had been angered. A terrible storm with howlings and wailings in the air had appeared when he was at the cave and forced him to stay there for several days. To pass through the Indian lines he had to travel at night and it was necessary to wait again for some time till the moon was right. In spite of all his care and his knowledge of the mountains he fell, breaking his leg. How he managed to bind his leg and then to haul himself on to his mule I cannot imagine. I only know I could not recognise my brother in the man who arrived with the gold. His hair had grown, he had a beard. He was as thin as a winter tree as he had had to eke out his tsampa day by day; his face was that of an old man with the lines of his suffering. We have a doctor of Tibetan medicine in Uptak who set the leg, though he could not prevent it from shortening. Sonam now walks with a limp.

Sonam was eager to return to Delhi with the gold and he wrote to Hugo to tell him of his return. Hugo wrote of his anxiety for Sonam. He wanted him to go back to India as soon as possible and not to wait three further months until the road opened. He said he had a friend with contacts in the Indian Army who could arrange for Sonam to fly on an Army plane out of Leh. So when Sonam was stronger this was arranged.

The gold we wrapped in kidskin and placed in two tin

boxes from the bazaar in Leh. Sonam took it on the plane with him to Delhi.

I have not seen my brother since he left with the gold. I know that, according to the arrangements, Hugo was to sell the gold and that some was sold. Then I heard a few days ago from Sonam that he had heard nothing from Hugo for several weeks and did not know what was happening.

I wonder whether the movement of the gold was not an error. The demons on the mountains were angered and the gold has brought a release of evil, a wave of greed that washes through the world. Sonam's leg is permanently shortened. Hugo is dead. I can only wait for what will come to me for my part in this.

There was a long pause when Lobsang Dhondup had finished speaking. Then Janey said, "Do you know the name of the man who arranged Sonam's flight out of Ladakh?"

Lobsang roused himself from his thoughts. "Yes," he replied. "It was an Indian called Ranjit Singh, a friend of Hugo who had been in the Army. Do you know this man?"

Chapter 18

THE HUGE QUADRANGLE had filled up since they first arrived. Ladakhis in their finest clothes occupied every horizontal surface and, it seemed, some of the vertical ones too. The cloister opposite the two imposing entrances to the temples was packed with people who were being forced back from the ceremonial area by lamas carrying a low trellis-work fence which they were using as a crowd barrier. All the roofs, steps and balconies which overlooked the courtyard were densely crowded with humanity. Above the empty pavement of the courtyard soared two tall poles with brilliantly coloured prayer flags floating from them.

Sinclair and Janey were conducted along a series of passages and stairs, through the courtyard and eventually out onto a small ledge which allowed them to look down the length of the acting space with an excellent view of the steps leading from the dukang. Immediately below them the musicians were gathered and, by peering down, they could see the cymbals and drums, horns and trumpets, and their players. They were joined on their ledge by a group of Ladakhis, evidently of some importance, and it was clear that throughout the courtyard the last comers were fitting themselves into their places.

The music had already begun. Its beginning was unrecognisable. Individual instruments were tuning up and practising notes and phrases which at some stage developed into a full community of sound. Trumpets and cymbals brayed and clashed as down the steps of the dukang came a procession of monks in fine silk robes with elaborate headdresses, swinging censers so that the air was scented with the peppery smell of incense. They fanned out as they reached the pavement and with the music still sounding, a slow pattern of colour and sound was woven together.

This formed an overture; into the space emptied by the monks rushed grotesque masked figures, leaping, turning, jostling in no order. The huge masks worn by many of the dancers dwarfed their bodies and made them more bizarre than their horrific faces alone could do. Frenzied curls carved out of wood, bulging eyes; bared fangs made the heads monstrous. The demons carried hand-drums and rattles which filled out the noise of the orchestra to represent the malice of evil in the world.

With astonishing simultaneity the apparently wild and random cries and movements ceased and in the silence came the tingling of the smallest of cymbals. As the shivering sound died away the demons, shrieking, fled and the procession of lamas returned. The area thus cleared of evil was reoccupied by comic creatures, buffoons who tripped one another up, hit each other on the back, made gestures of simple obscenity and screamed with laughter at their own antics.

They were succeeded by pitiful creatures, almost naked, who ran to and fro, lost and terrified, their hands held out as if blind and searching for their way. They whistled with high haunting notes as they fled around the courtyard. The demons reappeared on the stage and tormented the lost souls, terrifying them further, chasing and cornering them. Then again the silence; the tremor of the cymbals; the return of the holy men; the flight of the demons.

Janey was wedged into her place by the soft, immovable shape of a stout Ladakhi lady on one side and the tall form of Sinclair on the other. For a while she ceased to watch the whirling, distressed souls and the lumbering scowling forces of evil and scanned the audience. The expressions of absorbed interest, fear, and pity on the broad faces around her showed the Ladakhis' intense concentration on the hours of dance and mime.

Two demons were now in conflict, a rivalry of competitive dance. Each was trying to seize a corpse-like doll which lay in the centre of the quadrangle. One, snatching at the head-dress, ribbons, staff of the other, defeated him and danced in triumph. The crowd groaned at his victory. Framed between the two flag poles was the entrance to the dukang. Down the steps was now coming a palanquin roofed in yellow silk. Above the doorway was the balcony of the upper apartments where, seated in state, were the special visitors to the ceremony. A party of Indians was there, some of them in uniform, and a magnificently dressed Ladakhi with a long turquoise in one ear.

The victorious demon was slashing at the limp doll

with a sword. Out of the palanquin, escorted by an umbrella-bearing monk came a figure with the serene moon face of a buddha. A burst of sound from the musicians was followed by silence as everybody waited for the inevitable conflict.

Janey watched her Ladakhi neighbour, whose eyes were wrinkled up to narrow her vision on to the confrontation before her. Opposite her she could see small children clinging to a balustrade in terror of the allegory which they could not understand. Even the Indians in the balcony over the dukang were leaning forward in their seats, straining to see.

Even the Indians. Her gaze passed along the faces in the second row revealed by the leaning forward of the men in front; passed over, recognised, knew, before her brain, distinct seconds behind, could formulate questions or explanations. Ranjit Singh.

"Sinclair," she exclaimed loudly, grasping his arm in both hands. At that moment a long call came from the trumpets, blanketing her voice in its overwhelming sound. Sinclair responded to the pressure of her fingers, not her voice, looking down in amusement thinking she was seized with the tension of the dance. Her mouth moved soundlessly against the competing cymbals; he shook his head in puzzlement. She put her lips to his ear and said into it, "Ranjit Singh. Over there in the balcony above the steps."

At her first word he was frowning, searching the balcony on the other side with his glance.

"I can't see him. Are you sure?"

"Yes, yes. Wait a minute. When they lean forward, between the third and fourth from the left. Look now."

As if suddenly focused Ranjit Singh's head sprang into

view, looking straight at them. As the rhythmic chants of the monks of the golden palanquin battled in the air with the wild music of the demons they stared at one another. Janey waved and the next minute Ranjit Singh was hidden by the body in front of him.

"Don't do that." Sinclair's voice was angry.

"Why not?"

"We must leave. Come on, Janey." Sinclair grabbed her wrist and turned hastily from the ledge of the balcony; immediately other bodies took over their positions. To move any further was another matter; the press of people around them made it almost impossible to pass.

"We can't get out, Sinclair. Even if we leave the balcony the staircase goes down into the courtyard and the way out is at the other end. We'll have to wait till it's over."

They eventually struggled to the steep stairs which led from the balcony and sat down on the narrow wooden rungs. Janey crouched one step lower than Sinclair.

"Now, what is this, Sinclair? You must tell me what's going on."

Sinclair smoothed his hair in a characteristic gesture of frustration. "Yes, I think I must. I don't like seeing Ranjit Singh here. And even more I don't like his seeing us."

"Ranjit? What have you got against him?"

"It's a very long story. He was deeply involved with Hugo in Delhi. The two of them ran an antiques exporting business on the shady side of the law. I imagine Ranjit Singh organised the Indian side and Hugo the London one. I found out a good deal about Ranjit in Delhi but I could see no connection between him and the gold. Today Lobsang Dhondup reveals the connection and the man turns up in the very place the gold came from. I don't like it."

"But does this mean you think Ranjit had something to do with Hugo's death?"

Sinclair paused before answering. "I always felt that Hugo's death was bound up with the gold; until today I didn't see how there could be any link with Ranjit Singh. It now looks as if Ranjit learned about the gold when he helped to transport it and Sonam Dorje to Delhi. I already knew that he had been to Hamid in Bombay to find out what Hugo was doing with it, just as I did. He was at the Turnells' party and was one of the last people to be seen talking to Hugo, though he himself did not admit to this. He could have walked next door, killed him and returned to the party without anybody noticing. In fact, I am almost certain that is what he did."

"Ranjit—I can't believe it. It's crazy. He and Hugo were great friends. They'd been in the Army together before Independence. Do you realise what you're saying?"

"I know exactly what I'm saying. Don't think that Ranjit couldn't kill. He's a dangerous and ruthless man. I know from experience."

"Experience? You mean he…?"

"Yes, he had me beaten up."

Janey turned to Sinclair in astonishment and saw him regarding her detachedly, assessing the quality of her surprise. She ran both hands distractedly and angrily through her hair.

"You infuriate me, Sinclair. You make use of me; you don't tell me anything; you lie to me…"

"I never lie, Janey."

"You told me you didn't know why you were beaten up. If that's not a lie, I don't know what is."

"I told you no one in Delhi was interested in finding out, not that I couldn't guess myself."

"You're so..." She gestured impatiently. "So bloody calm. You're telling me that Hugo was involved in a smuggling racket with Ranjit who, you say, beat you up. It's preposterous. I can't believe it. And what's worse," she finished, "you're eyeing me as if you think I could be in it with them." She beat her fist angrily on the step while Sinclair watched her, making no effort to reply to her tirade. She regained control of her temper and said more calmly, "Now, answer me, Sinclair. Why was Hugo involved in all this?"

"To accumulate money."

"Money? What for? He had more than he needed."

"Until today I thought it was for himself. Now, from what Lobsang Dhondup has told us, it seems as if the gold at least was not for his own benefit but for the Tibetans."

"And Ranjit Singh? Why do you think he had you beaten up?"

"The day before I was kidnapped I met Ranjit Singh at the airport and he was certainly annoyed at the attention he was receiving from me. While I was at the airport a small thing happened. We were attacked—no that's too strong a word—approached by a rabid dog. I started to run away from it. Ranjit killed it with his stick. I saw the contempt in his face. He wrote me down as someone who would run if threatened. The next day I went back again to the airport and I think he must have heard of my continued enquiries for it was just after that I was beaten up."

"All right," conceded janey. "I can imagine Ranjit losing his temper and striking someone. I can even imagine him arranging to have someone beaten as savagely as you were. But how could he kill Hugo, an old friend? Why should he do it?"

"Look at it like this. Hugo and Ranjit for several years had been doing profitable business exporting stuff from

India and sharing out the proceeds—on what percentage we don't know, but they were certainly both profiting. Then Hugo lays hands on a huge haul of Tibetan gold, and, moreover, he invokes Ranjit's influence to move it by military plane out of Ladakh. I can't help admiring Hugo's cheek; he was naïve though. He must have thought he could manipulate Ranjit with impunity: he was mistaken. Possibly a sharp-eyed clerk, like the one that spotted me at the Cargo Area in the airport on my second visit, noticed the very heavy tins that Sonam Dorje brought with him from Ladakh. Possibly Ranjit had asked someone to find out what Hugo was up to, asking for one of his Tibetan monks to be flown urgently out of Ladakh in mid-winter. However it was, I think we can be sure that Ranjit Singh discovered that something of importance had come from Ladakh to Hugo and he wanted a share in it. He may not have realised at first what it was. When he tackled Hugo he was obviously told to keep his hands off. We know Hugo was not making money out of this particular consignment; he was doing it on behalf of his Tibetans and he was not going to allow Ranjit in on it. I think they must have fallen out over that: Ranjit wanting a share of the gold, Hugo trying to keep him out of it."

Janey had found some chocolate in the pocket of her jacket. It had been melted by the heat of her body and reset; embedded with its own silver paper and rimmed with pocket fluff, its consumption comfortingly filled the mouth and the time as they waited for the ceremonies to finish.

"What's he doing here now," Janey demanded as she licked up the last crumbs of chocolate. "Why has he come to Ladakh?"

"Still looking for the gold I imagine," said Sinclair. "He

knows it came from Ladakh in the first place. He has probably traced it back to Uptak and come to find out more."

The music still rose from the courtyard, with less strength now, as though it could not do anything so definite as stop, but would simply fade away, still playing, into realms where human ears could no longer hear it.

The atmosphere of evening and ending affected the audience. Children started to call and cry and a gentle ebbing towards the great staircase and the entrance chorten began. Janey and Sinclair joined the crowds on the way out. The movement down the shallow steps was slow and languorous, the voices low and muted. The two Europeans kept to the centre of the path, hoping that their distinguishing features and dress would be hidden among the wide turquoise-studded head-dresses of the women, the rakishly tilted, high-crowned hats of the men. They did not hurry or push, allowing the slow surge of the crowd to carry them along. The procession almost halted as the path narrowed at the entrance gate.

As they shuffled forward Sinclair, marginally taller, glimpsed through the tall hats that surrounded them the figure of the Indian raised on some steps to scrutinise the faces of the departing audience. He stopped, grabbed Janey and struggled against the pressure of the crowd to the wall.

"He's waiting at the gate. Can we find another way out?"

"There's bound to be a back exit. There's usually a very steep track that cuts off all the corners of the zigzag path. We'd need to ask Lobsang Dhondup or one of the monks."

"Come on then. Let's go back and do that. We don't want to be caught by him here."

Panic filled Janey as she began to move back up the

cobbled stairs. It was as if she were running on the spot for, though her limbs were attempting to propel her forward, the downward press of the crowd made even the slowest progress difficult. Fighting the current of bodies, buffeted by shoulders and baskets as if by the waves and boulders of a stream, she reached the entrance to the courtyard again and turned to look for Sinclair. She could see no sign of his pale head among the bobbing head-dresses below. She hesitated for a second then moved in the direction of Lobsang Dhondup's room.

The courtyard had by now almost emptied. A few Ladakhis still stood in groups about the edge; the musicians were moving their instruments up the steps into the dukang. There was no Sinclair. She looked back down the stairs and saw, not more than three steps below, the glossy black head of Ranjit Singh. She swung round and ran across the courtyard and up the stairs at the side.

Looking back she could not decide why she acted in this way. She had no doubt that by obeying her impulse of flight she determined what followed. Sometimes she wondered if she had held her ground, feigned pleasure and surprise at seeing a friend from Delhi in so remote a place, whether things might not have turned out very differently. While Sinclair always pooh-poohed this, Janey remembered his tale of the mange-ridden dog at Delhi airport. Flight in a victim stirs an inevitable response in the predator.

As she clambered up the steep stairs, raising her knees high to clear each step, she heard Ranjit Singh below her. She reached the verandah at the top and raced along it. The one idea in her panicking mind was to hide, to find somewhere quiet and safe until she could emerge later.

At the end of the verandah she squeezed through a

narrow archway on to a flat roof on which brass posts shone gold in the evening light. Set back on the roof was a building with its door ajar, its long Tibetan padlock lying on the stone flags. She slipped through the door, pulling it to gently after her. She could hear footsteps on the roof stones and hurriedly moved away from the door.

She stood still for a few moments allowing her gasping breath and thudding heart to return to a more normal rhythm. She was in a dusty darkness only illuminated by the flickering light of several butter lamps which burned in a row in front of a large image in the centre of the room. The edges of the hall merged back into smudgy dimness.

As her eyes became accustomed to the light, she could see crowding in upon her the clutter of objects and images which crammed the shrine. Most clearly lit by the butter lamps was a carving, reaching up to the ceiling, of a grotesque, black creature whose snarling mouth and bulging eyes revealed it as one of the fierce manifestations of a Buddhist deity. Beneath its spread feet, whose sharp toes expressed its cruel energy and power, lay the prostrate form of a dead man. This was not the peaceful meditative face of Buddhism but the representation of the savage tantric rites which characterise Tibetan worship. Gleams of light fell on the frescoes around the walls, picking out necklaces of skulls, flayed bodies, brandished knives, frantic many-limbed copulation.

Janey moved forward, then started back in shock at a soft leathery touch on her cheek that seemed to have come from above. Looking up she could see a dead bird, a stork or heron, its legs dangling, its wings spread, hanging from the ceiling, still stirring faintly with the life given by her movement. She shuddered. Hanging with it in the upper darkness were mysterious shapes which gradually resolved themselves into bows, old guns with long slim barrels, antique helmets made of polished leather, one of them cleft by an ancient axe blow.

She knew enough to recognise where she was. This was the gonkang, the temple of the guardian divinities, the fierce deities in whose protection the monastery and monks lay. The gonkang was very holy; women were not allowed to enter. Never before had she penetrated inside. She remembered once before trying to persuade a friendly monk to let her into one. He would have been glad to receive a tip but he would not let her enter.

She moved quietly to the back of the gonkang and squatted behind the huge carving, hidden from the door. The monstrous images in the darkness didn't frighten her in themselves; yet she felt the religious horror of the sacred place and a sense of sacrilege in finding herself in a forbidden shrine. And, in addition, was the real fear, greater, more immediate than anything else, of the footsteps outside the door.

She listened to them pass the gonkang. They were going much more slowly now, as if Ranjit Singh realised that she had gone to ground somewhere nearby. She tried to visualise the flat roof outside. Was there a way out at the far side? If there was he would go on, thinking she was still ahead of him; if not he would retrace his steps looking for the point at which she had hidden herself. Perhaps she should slip out now and run back the way she had come, making for Lobsang's room and Sinclair. She rose from her squatting position and started cautiously round the wooden statue.

In her first step she froze. Through the fretted wood which made up the base of the statue in front of her she saw a thin slice of daylight appear and disappear between the double doors. She remained quite still, forcing her breath to slide silently and evenly through her nose. There was a long pause.

Through the thick, dust-laden air she heard her name, "Janey", in a hoarse whisper.

More clearly, "Janey, I know you're here. Where are you?"

Finally, peremptorily, "Janey."

She did not stir; her ears strained for sounds. The Mahakala in front of her was now more a hindrance than a hiding place for it obscured her view of the empty centre of the room. Ranjit must either decide to search further or leave again for lack of reply. That was too much to hope for; she must work out which way within the gonkang he was advancing and retreat ahead of him to the door.

There was no noise at all; the lamps burning before the image consumed their oil without a sound, throwing up a faint glimmer onto the objects of death hanging from the ceiling. Janey realised in that age of quietness that Ranjit Singh was doing what she was doing, standing waiting for her, by sound or movement, to reveal herself to him. It was turning into a game of chicken. She must remain still and exploit her advantage: she knew he was there while he only guessed that she was.

For an achingly long time the rhythms of her body seemed to try to betray her. Her heart was thundering inside her chest; her breath was hard to catch and she needed to gulp air; there was a choking knot in her throat.

Ranjit Singh moved. She heard a shuffling footstep, rolling dust and grit beneath its sole. He was circling the room anti-clockwise, very slowly, a pace at a time. This way he could hope to frighten her into flight and still reach the door before her. She must wait until he had reached the row of images and had passed behind the Mahakala; then for her the dash to the door would be no further than for him. She was younger, lighter; she must be able to reach it before him. Fighting down the panicking desire to rush blindly towards the great doors she waited. No man could have trod more cautiously than Ranjit Singh. For a moment his dark bulk was revealed in the light of the butter lamps. She watched the far end of the row of images like a runner watching the starter's flag.

She was right in all her calculations; only the door defeated her. As she saw Ranjit Singh edging past the base of the Mahakala she leapt towards the exit. Ranjit Singh was in any case facing the wrong direction and so that gave her an additional advantage, but when she reached the doors she could not find the latch or handle in the dim light. For a desperate few seconds her hands fumbled up and down the central division before seizing on the heavy iron bar. She was unsure of the manipulations of this and as her trembling hands tugged and pulled fruitlessly she was grabbed from behind. Ranjit Singh's arm came round her throat and took her shoulder, pulling her round to face him. He wasted no time on preliminaries.

"Now I've got you Janey Somers. Gave you and that detective friend of yours a shock to see me here, what?" he said. "Well, I know a lot more about this business than you might think, Janey Somers, and I know exactly what you and your boyfriend are up to, so don't think you can shake me off."

A wave of nausea almost to faintness swept over Janey and how she managed to speak coherently she was never afterwards sure.

"...No idea what you're talking about, Ranjit," was what she said, hardly an intelligent or even truthful statement under the circumstances, though it did at least make sense.

"You've no idea... You're right, my gel. You go off in my car to meet my jeweller and question him about gold. You go to Bombay and talk to that fat Moslem Hamid and listen to gossip about me. You're right you've no idea if you think you can do that without me knowing."

Janey was feeling fear for the first time in her life. Ranjit Singh was no taller than she was and his talking face was within inches of hers. She could see the separate springy hairs of his military moustache above the raging and distorted mouth. Drops of spittle fell on her cheek. She felt distanced from the scene so that though she saw dimly the angry face in front of her, felt the powerful grip of his fingers in her flesh, the words he spoke made no sense and her mind seemed unable to take them in. It was as if she were watching a difficult play in an unfamiliar language.

Ranjit's voice dropped to venomous sibilance.

"I warned Sinclair in a way I thought he'd take some notice of. I was wrong. Now, just you listen to me. That gold is mine. Hugo and I were business partners and the gold should be mine as the surviving partner. If you know where that gold is you'd better tell me because it belongs to me and I'm going to have it. If you don't know where it is, you'd better stop looking for it. This is India you know; it's not like England. I can do a great deal and get away with it here, so if you don't want to end up like our poor friend Hugo, keep out of things that don't concern you." Janey swallowed painfully and tried to turn her head away from the pressure of Ranjit's hand on her throat. "I was at Alan Turnell's party that night. You know that,

Janey, don't you? I had the police officer in charge of the case moved because he was too matey with that demmed Sinclair, and he was making too many enquiries about me. Because I did for Hugo, Janey, and I'll do for you too, if you don't tell me where the gold is." He shook her hard and her neck recoiled agonisingly. "I think the rest of the gold is up here and I think that Sinclair of yours has come up here to find it. I know it came from here; it was all part of a deal between Hugo and me. It has nothing to do with you and Sinclair and I want you out of it. Do you understand me, Janey?"

She jerked her shoulder as hard as she could.

"Ranjit, I am up here for my work. I come here every summer, as you know very well. Sinclair is here because of me. Hc is going back to London soon and he's here to spend some time with me. We're lovers. It has nothing to do with any gold. Now, will you let me go."

She pulled away from him with all her strength and as she did so Ranjit's other hand shot out and clasped her neck.

Chapter 19

FRAMED IN THE DOORWAY stood Lobsang Dhondup, his bare arms outstretched to grasp the leaves of the door on either side of him. Ranjit Singh angrily dropped his hands from Janey's neck and turned to face the intruder. Janey's body worked faster than her mind, for as soon as she was released she doubled up and pushed under the arm of the monk and out of the gonkang. As she ran she could hear irate complaints of disrespect and sacrilege. She did not wait to see how Ranjit Singh coped with the accusations.

She reached the great courtyard in a few seconds and found it almost empty. While she had been in the gonkang the spectators had all departed, leaving only groups of monks clearing away some of the debris of the ceremonies. The staircase too was freed of its sluggishly flowing crowd and this time Janey was able to run down the long slope, zigzagging to avoid the few last parties of

Ladakhis. She had seen no sign of Sinclair in the courtyard and prayed he had not gone back to Lobsang's room for she had decided to make for the jeep. She continued to run through the chorten arch and past the mani wall. Reaching the hillside track she slowed to a walk, pressing a hand to her side against the tearing stitch there. Going down a steep slope is more difficult than climbing she found and for most of the way she was forced to maintain a cautious pace. Where the track ran almost level she broke into a trot again; once or twice she saw a short steep path cutting off the corner of a turn and took it, in places scrambling down on her bottom. Even on the roughest parts she walked faster than the steadily plodding Ladakhis whom she overtook with a wave or word of greeting. As she ran, "Sinclair, Sinclair, please be there," circled in her head like the words inside a prayer wheel.

The sound of the river filled the air as she reached the wood. The path was wider now and much smoother. She had started to run again and was jogging quite fast when, rounding a corner, she saw blocking the way an old blue Land Rover. There was no driver with it, so she stopped and inspected it briefly, feeling at once that this must be Ranjit Singh's vehicle. It was an elderly short wheelbase Land Rover with a canvas top. Peering over the tailgate she could see a bedding roll and other luggage, including a tin trunk labelled Brig. R Singh.

The last quarter of a mile was the worst. The stitch in her left side had returned, the prayer wheel revolved with its infuriating jingle inside her head and under it lurked the question of what she should do if Sinclair was not there. She emerged from the wood and below her, like a toy, the jeep was parked on the edge of the metalled road where the track to Uptak branched off. Its doors were shut and there was no sign of Sinclair.

The car keys formed a small hard knot in her jeans pocket. Her breath was coming in long retching sobs as she continued to run, faster now, towards the car. That morning she had turned it and left it facing back towards Leh so the driver's door was nearest to her now. She ran straight at it to yank it open and throw herself in. She had already grabbed the handle when she heard her name spoken and Sinclair strolled round the bonnet.

❀❀❀

Janey abandoned the safety of the door handle and ran at Sinclair. He patted her back for a few moments as if burping a baby before she detached herself and sat down on the bumper to regain her breath. With all her pride in her independence Janey was surprised and rather embarrassed by her own behaviour. Sinclair's unruffled appearance and air of vague civil service calm had seemed infinitely reassuring at a moment when she had despaired of his being there and was visualising the alternatives of a return to the monastery or a meeting with Ranjit out on the desolate road.

Sinclair did not allow Janey long to recover. Without waiting to hear of any adventures she might have had he took the keys from her and, in spite of her protests about her licence, her insurance and his health, started the car. They drove fast down the plain towards Leh. The sun had already set below the hills on their left beyond the groove in which the Indus flowed and the immensely clear blue of the Tibetan sky was darkening rapidly, intensifying its colour until the blueness had gone and the darkness remained. The golden beams of their headlights bobbed ahead of them as Janey gave Sinclair an account of her experiences in the gonkang.

"He killed Hugo, you were quite right. He 'did for him' he said. I don't know if he meant he killed him himself or if he meant the murder was carried out by some bully boys, the ones he used on you. He admitted that he had you beaten up—'warned you off' he called it—and I'm sure he would have murdered me if Lobsang Dhondup hadn't come in."

"I doubt it," Sinclair said calmly.

"You doubt it. You weren't there. You didn't have his hands round your throat."

"I'm sure he might murder you if it served his purpose. I don't see that it would have done anything for him to kill you then. Frighten you into telling him what you know, yes; murder, no."

"He thinks we are still looking for the gold and that's why we are here. He wants us out and he wants you to stop interfering. He's angry and dangerous."

It wasn't until several hours later when they were back in Leh and were eating some delicious broth in Dolma Palsang's warm kitchen that Janey said, "So what are we going to do?"

Sinclair broke off a piece of brown, floury bap and dipped it into the soup.

"We'll have to go back. Tomorrow."

Janey put down her spoon. "Sinclair, I can't. I've work to do." A mulish expression appeared on her face. "You can go; I'm staying here." Sinclair seemed untroubled and did not cease to gulp down his food.

"I'll hire a jeep in the town in the morning." Janey looked at him doubtfully, uneasy at his acquiescence. "We'll have to hope that Ranjit decides to follow me rather than to hang around in Ladakh and prize out the secret of the gold from you. Do you know where it is, by the way?"

"No, I suppose… Damn you, Sinclair."

"We'll start at six and go as far as we can. Do you think we could reach Kashmir in one day?"

"I've never done it in a day before," she replied. "If we started really early I should think we could. Earlier than six though. We'll probably have to sleep in Sonamarg."

"OK, let's make a five o'clock start."

"What am I to say to Dolma Palsang?" Janey wailed.

"Don't make difficulties. I thought you were the imaginative one. Say anything you like"

It was still dark next morning as they loaded blankets and bedding rolls into the back of the jeep. Janey was leaving her books and some clothes at Apple Blossom Cottage. She had told Jigme Namgyal and his wife that she was returning in a few days and had asked them to keep the room for her. Dolma Palsang, unperturbed, had provided rolls, flasks of soup and coffee and a bag of dried apricots as comforts for the journey.

"With any luck we'll be in Sonamarg tonight," said Janey as she took the wheel.

❀❀❀

Luck was not with them and that evening they had not even reached Kargil where they had spent their first night together on the journey up only a few days earlier.

The first puncture was at Basgo, a scruffy village dominated by a great ruined fort, once the home of the kings of Ladakh. Janey was crouching forward over the steering wheel, trying to point out the castle and drive at the same time when the heavy lurching and bumping of the jeep indicated the nature of their disaster. Janey took this first mishap calmly and efficiently. The tool kit was pulled out from under the luggage, the jack fitted. Janey did most of the work, giving terse instructions to an amused Sinclair who was relegated to the role of nurse assisting a highly competent surgeon. Janey jacked up the jeep, flicking the wheel to see if she had managed to lift it clear of the ground.

Sinclair saw that offers of help would only annoy her so he sat on a stone by the roadside and stared back at the crowd of children who had gathered to watch what was going on. Their flat faces were caked with dirt and crusted snot channels ridged their upper lips. They regarded Sinclair with utmost solemnity, ignoring Janey struggling with the jeep. Sinclair recalled the lines of women working in the fields and realised that the wheel had come full circle: his self-restraint in not taking charge of their breakdown would be seen by these children as the sign of his male superiority as he sat by while his woman worked.

"Janey, is there anything..." he began.

"Oh, shit, this blasted spanner won't fit. Look."

One of Janey's explosive frustration rages had started.

"Why, oh why, can't they ever provide the right tools. When I'm back in Srinagar I shall tell that Mohammed who hired this jeep to me." She threw the wheel spanner on to the ground and left unsaid the words she would use to the unfortunate Mohammed. The children's round brown eyes swivelled from her to Sinclair and back again.

"Here, let me look." Sinclair picked up the discarded

tool. He had too much respect for Janey's efficiency to have much hope of succeeding where she had failed and indeed neither end of the spanner would fit the nuts of the punctured wheel. One end was too small, the other end just too large, so that when pressure was placed on the spanner to loosen the screw it jerked round, slipping over the corners of the bolt.

The wheel took two hours to change, involved almost the whole population of Basgo as well as a Sikh mechanic from the Development Commission and was done so easily in the end that both Janey and Sinclair felt extremely foolish.

In the first place Janey asked the children if there was a garage in the village. Shy and dubious negatives were eventually produced and a loan from a passing vehicle seemed the only answer, when one of the children volunteered that the Development Engineer might be able to help and an enthusiastic hunt for him in and around the village was begun.

He was at length found and arrived at the head of a growing crowd of larger children and adults. He turned out to be a young Sikh with an immaculately tied turban and a bag of tools. None of his implements would fit the wheel nuts and Sinclair could see that Janey was close to tears of rage and frustration. The Sikh then looked again at the original tool and, remarking that it was almost the right size, he scooped a little dust from the road's edge into the cup of the spanner and fitted it onto the nut. It turned and the nut turned with it. There was a sigh of admiration from the spectators and a cry of thanks from Janey. The Sikh courteously undid the nuts, removed the wheel and replaced it with the spare. Janey, acknowledging a proven supremacy, made no attempt to assist.

"Where will you have this mended?" he asked as he lifted off the damaged tyre.

"Kargil, I suppose," said Janey.

"Leh's nearer."

"I know, but we can't go back. We'll have to hope for the best."

The Sikh shrugged with graceful fatalism. He knew what would happen.

❀❀❀

"What do you think Ranjit's doing now?" Janey asked. They had reached the point where the road leaves the Indus valley and starts the climb to the Fatu La. Janey dropped into second and started the long crawl out of the valley bottom.

"I hope," said Sinclair, "he's still swanning round Uptak trying to find out where the gold is. He has traced it to the monastery. It won't take him too long to find out that Rongtsen Tulku is Sonam's brother. I hope it will take him just long enough for us to reach Srinagar and get on to a plane to Delhi. Seeing us at Uptak yesterday must have made him even more sure that he was close to the gold."

Janey fed the wheel from hand to hand; the car swung right round and the engine began its steadily increasing roar towards third gear.

"And what will Lobsang say to him when Ranjit does work out who he is and that he is the source of the gold? I doubt if he'd tell him the story he told us: we did have Hugo's letter to introduce us, after all. I suppose he might answer questions about us. He might say that you had the gold in Delhi if he were asked directly."

"That's why I want to be back in Delhi as soon as possible. Once Ranjit Singh knows that we have the gold I think we are at risk."

"What are we going back for? What are you going to do about it?"

"I'm going to make a report to Verma in the Delhi Police pointing out the racket that Hugo and Ranjit were in, the fact that Ranjit was at the Turnells' party, had both opportunity and motive for killing Hugo, had me beaten up, threatened you and—there's not much left to say. I doubt if they'll take any notice of it in any case."

"And what about the gold?"

"The gold's a very tricky problem. Morally it belongs to the Tibetans in Dharamsala. Legally it belongs to the Indian Government as it was smuggled into the country and is therefore liable for confiscation. It was in Hugo's possession at the time of his death and possibly his heirs might have some claim on it, not to mention HMG which does not permit British citizens to hold stocks of gold bullion."

"It would be better to say nothing to the Indians about the gold. I really don't see why they should have it. Or your lot either. The Tibetans should have it. It belongs to them. It was Sonam Dorje who took all the risks to get it."

Sinclair laughed. "Legal concepts seem to have no validity in your mind, my pet. Legally the Tibetans have almost no claim to speak of. And it's hard to see how an accusation against Ranjit can be made convincing without mention of the gold since it has motivated him throughout. He won't want the Indian Government to have it, any more than you do, but he'd probably rather the Indians had it than the Tibetans. In the end it'll come down to what British relations with the Indians are like at the moment. It might be decided to make a clean breast of it and hand it over, or it might be thought better to dispose of it quietly and have no fuss, in which case the Tibetans might yet be the winners."

Sinclair stopped speaking and Janey concentrated on the next couple of hairpins which came in close succession. Then he said, "Whatever happens, I don't like leaving you in India, Janey. You've made a very nasty enemy in Ranjit and I have little hope of seeing him behind bars. I'm almost sure that it was his influence which had Battacharia moved from Hugo's case."

"Yes, that's right. That's what he said to me yesterday in the gonkang." Janey shuddered at the memory. "What can he do to me? Once he knows what's happened to the gold and that he had no hope of gaining it I won't be of any further interest to him, will I?"

"There's revenge. Why did he kill Hugo before he had his share of the gold from him, before he even knew where it was?"

"That's odd, isn't it? Did he do it just because Hugo refused to cut him in? Oh Lord, you involved me in all this. I've been coming peacefully to India for years until you turned up and created havoc."

Sinclair watched Janey's sharp profile outlined against the light from the driver's window. She was looking intently at the road with her usual concentration on whatever she was doing, and he knew she was frightened.

She had put up only the briefest resistance to returning to Delhi with him; she had anxiously determined to travel on to Kargil in spite of having no spare wheel in the car. Her encounter with Ranjit Singh had affected her more deeply than she had wanted to say. Just as with Hugo's death, she had distanced herself from the events in the gonkang by speaking of them lightly. She had talked of

Ranjit with a joking moral indignation: not only had he murdered Hugo, beaten up Sinclair, he had finally tried to throttle her. Sinclair was now beginning to know the signs that revealed truer feelings than the concealing candour with which she normally faced people. She always drove with impatient speed which on their way up had been tempered on the empty uplands with an enjoyment of the clarity and emptiness of sky and land. Now she no longer allowed the jeep to cruise on the straight stretches as she looked around her. She drove fast and tensely as if she felt a presence at her back.

Chapter 20

THE SECOND PUNCTURE occurred on a bare hillside a few miles beyond the highest point on the road. It was still early afternoon; the sun shone from a cloudless sky; there was no one to be seen. They were high above the valleys where the Ladakhis work and sing; the road stretched in either direction and on it nothing moved. Janey turned off the engine and the silence flooded back into their heads. Sinclair looked into the blueness above, listening for larks; he heard only the faint clicking of the cooling car. Janey beat her fists against the steering wheel in her anger.

They drank some coffee and ate some of the rolls.

"We'd better take the wheel off at any rate," said Janey. "Then we'll be ready when something passes us. There's an army camp a few miles along the road," she added. "I'll take both tyres in there and have them vulcanised."

Together, using the Sikh mechanic's trick, they removed the second punctured tyre and extracted the first from the rear.

"The first car that passes I'll ask for a lift to the camp."

"Why don't I go?"

"Because I speak Hindi," Janey returned succinctly and convincingly. Sinclair resigned himself to continuing in a subordinate role.

It was a long wait. At first, they sat in glum silence, chewing on dried apricots. Then Sinclair taught Janey to play Botticelli and he found that it cheered her up and passed the time as effectively as it had done when he was travelling with tired and disgruntled children. Sinclair was trying to answer: "Did you murder your lover by mistake?" when the distant revving of a climbing lorry could be heard.

"At last," exclaimed Janey, standing up and rolling the wheels to prop them against the front of the jeep.

"It's going the wrong way," Sinclair said, as it became obvious where the noise was coming from.

"That doesn't matter."

"Will he go back for us?"

"I don't know. We can only ask."

At length a labouring lorry appeared over the crest some half a mile away and crept towards them. Janey flagged it down and it stopped promptly, its driver listening to Janey's rapid Hindi with evident interest. It was a standard Indian truck with wooden sides vividly decorated with paintings of birds and animals and 'OK TATA' inscribed on its tailgate. Janey stepped back from the cab as the driver withdrew his head and restarted the engine.

"He's going to turn and take me," she informed Sinclair.

Janey and the two wheels were stowed in the back. Glad of action, she waved cheerfully as the lorry set off the way it had come.

❀❀❀

For Sinclair the afternoon passed slowly. He read a bit and walked up and down keeping the jacked-up jeep in view. He could imagine Janey persuading people to mend the two punctures, chatting them up, drinking tea while the job was being done. He was feeling cold and, wrapping a rug round himself, he fell into an uncomfortable doze. He woke suddenly when the lorry delivered Janey and the two mended wheels at about five. She was in a good humour and allowed Sinclair to refit one of the wheels and unjack the jeep.

"I found a dak bungalow near the camp," she said. "I've arranged a room for the night and some food. I bet you're starving. I know I am. It's the most primitive place yet. I hope you'll survive the experience. I really couldn't face the Namika La in the dark. We'll be up early tomorrow and be in Srinagar before dark."

The dak bungalow was indeed primitive. A room with a slit of a window and no light, furnished with two charpoys, was the bedroom; a tap and bucket was the bathroom. Janey saw Sinclair's face and said, "Don't look like that. Dak bungalows are only for officials. It's owing to my charm that you're here at all."

"It's not that. It's just that Ranjit Singh's friends put me off charpoys for life."

"Oh that. I'll put down the bedding roll. It'll feel just like any ordinary bed."

In spite of the simplicity of the building the chowkidar provided them with a large and filling meal of rice, dal, subzi, chapattis. He stood with them as they ate to pile up their plates with more food, complaining as he did so that it was too cold up here in the mountains to set the dahi, the yoghurt, which he felt would have rounded off what he was able to serve them.

With the bedding roll down Sinclair lay stretched on one of the charpoys watching Janey in the light of a single candle. The bed was not uncomfortable and, though it was too dark to read and too early to sleep, he was content to rest. Not so Janey, who prowled around the tiny room and along the verandah outside in the dark, nervously, restlessly.

"Don't worry, Janey," Sinclair said at last. "Ranjit's miles away from here."

"I hope he is. It's just that we planned to be miles away from here by tonight. I don't like failing in what we set out to do."

Her excuse for her anxiety did not ring true and she returned to the subject the next morning, as they drove off in the misty cold of the dawn.

"I hope it won't matter that we've lost a day. What do you think?"

"I shouldn't think it'll matter much. We must assume Ranjit has left Uptak by now. It depends what he decides to do. He could probably take an army flight and be back in Delhi before us, though I don't think he has much to gain by that. More likely he'll try to catch up with us. I should think he's at least half a day behind."

Janey swooped into a dip, changing gear at the up-slope.

"We'll stay ahead," she said confidently. "The lorry driver came over Zoji La the day before yesterday and it was quite clear."

The second day's drive seemed at first less hazardous than the first. They reached and passed Kargil without mishap and as they turned south-west, at the meeting of the Suru and Dras rivers, Janey said, "This is the last lap now."

Some time later Sinclair noticed that Janey was unusually silent and had frequently been glancing in her rear view mirror.

"What's the matter?" he asked quietly.

"I don't know. Yes I do. A mile or so back I thought—I hope I was imagining it—I thought I saw a Land Rover on the crest of a ridge behind us. I haven't seen anything since and it was a good way away."

"You concentrate on the road in front. I'll look behind."

Sinclair swivelled in his seat and looked across the luggage through the rolled up back-flap. Only half a mile of road was visible and that was empty. They were climbing and as the road lifted them he could see the string of the track curving round the hillside below. After ten minutes Janey asked, "Was I imagining it?"

"Perhaps. I haven't seen anything yet."

As he spoke he saw a shape crawl over the edge of the furthest loop of the road.

"Stop. Let's use the glasses." Janey pulled up and feverishly rummaged for the binoculars under the canvas that protected the luggage from dust. Sinclair took them from her and focused them, moving them up and down to find the bit of road he wanted.

"It's not the Land Rover," he reported. "They're green lorries. Must be the Army. My God, more of them. It's a convoy."

"Here, let me look," Janey was tugging at his arm. She took the glasses from him. "Yes, you're right. It is a convoy. But I was sure it was…" Sinclair was amused to observe how Janey had to confirm everything for herself. "Yes, there. Look at the end." The binoculars changed hands once again and Sinclair saw at the tail of the long line of Army lorries a blue Land Rover.

"I knew it," Janey wailed. "The convoy must have been in a dip when I saw the Land Rover on the crest."

"Let's go," said Sinclair. "That convoy must have started from the camp soon after us. It'll slow the Land Rover up for a bit so we must press on. The last thing we want is for Ranjit to catch up with us on an empty road." He opened the driver's door. "I'll drive. You're tired." Janey grumbled her way into the passenger seat.

The road ahead was quite straight, rising only slowly and for some way they made good speed, increasing their lead on the lumbering Army vehicles.

"Oh, what now?" Janey cried.

A lowered barrier blocked the way; a line of lorries was drawn up on the grass and a couple of army tents made a small encampment.

The jeep slithered to a stop in front of the barrier arm and Janey was out almost before the engine was switched off. She walked over to the jawan on duty and questioned him. Sinclair could see that his responses were very short in spite of her persistence. Soon she came back.

"The road's closed. He won't say why; he doesn't know for how long. Hopeless." She wandered off again to speak to some of the lorry drivers. When she returned she reported that they had set off from Kargil at first light and had been at the check point since early morning. They were sleeping or playing cards, obviously prepared for a long wait.

Sinclair climbed out to stretch his legs; when he came

back he found Janey in the driver's seat again. They played Botticelli for a while and watched a Sikh soldier who had washed his knee-length hair drying it in the sun, throwing it to and fro over his head. This sight distracted Janey for a short time, then she became restless again.

"The convoy wasn't that far behind us. Ranjit'll be here soon. What shall we do?"

"Nothing," said Sinclair tranquilly. "It may be for the best to have it out here. He can hardly murder you here in front of all these witnesses, if that's what you're worried about."

From behind them came the sound of a car travelling at speed.

"That's him," said Janey.

A Jonga, a big Indian Army jeep, braking hard, overtook their parked car and halted, nose to the barrier. From the passenger side came a shout. The jawan raised the barrier and the jeep moved off in a flurry of stones. Within seconds it had rounded the curve of the hill and was gone. The jawan stood watching it, the barrier arm still up.

Suddenly Janey turned the ignition.

"If they can go so can we," she muttered and the jeep shot under the barrier. Sinclair was almost precipitated through the windscreen; the jawan gave a wail of protest; Janey did not stop.

"I expect you think I shouldn't have done that," she remarked defiantly.

Sinclair did not respond.

"It's fatuous keeping us there all day. Look, this road is perfectly all right. Nothing wrong at all. What nonsense!"

However, as they climbed, the snow crept down on them, approaching closer and closer to the edges of the road until they were bumping along in second gear through ice ridges with snow piled high on either side of them. After about half an hour of very slow progress Janey said crossly, "If the Jonga can manage we must be able to."

A little further on the narrow track bounded by its walls of ice opened out into a snowfield. The Army jeep was parked there with several others beside a small wooden hut. A jawan waved them in and signalled to them to park. They climbed out stiffly shivering in their thin sweaters. Janey dug into the bags and dragged out an anorak and a Husky. As they were struggling into them, they were greeted by a plump Indian in uniform.

"Jolly cold up here, isn't it? Come inside and warm up. There's a paraffin stove in there." He offered his hand to Sinclair. "Major Bhatia, officer in charge, Srinagar-Leh military road."

Sinclair shook it firmly. "Sinclair of the British High Commission, New Delhi. And this is Miss Janey Somers of London University, a student of Tibetan language and culture." The Major bowed, shook hands again and ushered them into the hut.

"I am afraid you must be waiting here a jiffy. A bad avalanche yesterday on my road and I have two snow shovellers out clearing the way. It's a good day today, freezing hard, and so I'm not expecting any more falls. Another couple of hours or so and we'll be open again for business. I hope you won't mind waiting here."

Sinclair assured him of their gratitude for a warm place to rest, and the Major disappeared leaving them in a small dark room, containing a narrow bed, a chair and a paraffin fire.

"You don't deserve to meet anyone as good as the

Major," Sinclair observed, ruffling Janey's hair as she huddled over the heater. "You defy his orders, risk being caught in an avalanche and blocking his road and he invites you in and keeps you warm. You're luckier than you deserve." Janey was unrepentant.

"I'm not sorry I went through the barrier. I couldn't wait there for Ranjit to catch us up. It's much better to be up here, for the moment the snow ploughs have finished, we can drive on."

There was a knock on the door which, when opened, revealed a jawan carrying a tray with three plates, followed by the Major.

"You're jolly hungry. Hot food will be doing you good." He distributed the plates and dismissed the batman. Janey was given the chair, Sinclair the bed; the Major stood, forking in his food.

"Good sausages, eh? I am bringing these up for myself to add some variety to food." The meal was an odd mixture, consisting of rice, dal and sausages; nevertheless hot and filling.

Janey and Sinclair spent two hours in the stuffy warmth of the hut, while the Major was out supervising the clearing of what he called proprietorially 'his' road. Eventually he came back to say, "The machines are almost through to other side. If you go carefully you should be able to manage."

They hastily reassumed the warm clothes they had discarded in the hut. As they were about to go out, the Major politely holding open the door for Janey, the field telephone rang, a hoarse purring sound. The Major spoke into it sharply, "Yes, yes. Well, if he must… Yes, clear in the next hour… No lorries. No one else at all today."

The Major, as he accompanied them across the hard

frozen patch in front of the huts said, "Another car anxious to leave Ladakh tonight. I've allowed that one up, but no more. I can't be having stranded lorries and people dying on my road."

Janey glanced nervously at Sinclair. "Another car, Major? Ours is a jeep so we won't block your road, I promise you."

"No, no, I shall see you're all right. And the other one will be all right too. It's a Land Rover." He climbed into his jeep not noticing Janey's horrified expression. "You come behind me. We'll have to wait a bit on the top, and the moment it's clear you'll be away."

Janey sat in the driver's seat shivering as she watched the Major's Jonga leading off. "We'll be through to Sonamarg before him, do you think?" she asked uselessly.

"This is a bloody awful place for him to catch up with us. I doubt we'll be over the pass before he's up here. An hour to finish clearing, the Major said; that gives Ranjit plenty of time to drive up from the road block, if that's where he is. At least if we're right up where the avalanche hit the road there'll be no delay in driving off as soon as the snow ploughs have come to the end."

They followed the Major slowly, bumping and occasionally skidding up the snowpacked road. The jeep ahead of them came to a halt beside a huge machine with an extravagantly tall chimney. Ahead of them a narrow defile had been cut through a smooth slope of snow. The Major wanted to show off his toys.

"Come this way," he shouted. He led them up from the road so that they could see how the avalanche had tumbled thousands of tons of snow across the road as it ran horizontally across the slope. The even fall was now gashed by the path cut out by the snow shovellers and at the furthest edge of the slope could be seen a spray of snow bursting into the air from a growling machine hidden in its own ravine.

"I have two machines for snow-clearing. Only that one," pointing to the snow spray in the distance, "is any good when the snow's this deep. It blows the snow eighty feet into the air. It's almost at its limit now."

Janey had her ears cocked for the sound of a car behind them while she narrowed her eyes at the distant snowblasting.

"How much longer will it take?" she asked bluntly.

"Not much longer," the Major said vaguely.

After about ten minutes the cold had penetrated through Janey's sweater and she could feel her flesh shrinking and turning icy inside her clothes. Dancing and stamping she made her way back to the car. She sat at the wheel rigid with cold and worry, gazing at the sweep of the second hand of her watch until its creeping finger lulled her into a trance. Shouts and waves from above recalled her to the present. She saw the Major and Sinclair formally shaking one another by the hand. Elaborate farewell rituals were under way. She started the jeep's engine and began to edge forward. Sinclair climbed in.

"Go carefully," he instructed her. Janey gripped the wheel and glared ahead.

As they entered the snow tunnel the brilliant light of snow and sky was cut suddenly to a strange underwater glow. Sixty or seventy feet above their heads a pencil of blue traced the rim of the snow cliffs. The road was solid snow impacted by the caterpillar tracks of the snow-shoveller. They crept along, Janey's knuckles glowing white with tension. Almost half way through, the surface became softer and they saw in front of them a river flowing fast and shallow across the road from underneath the ice wall.

"How can it do that?" Janey exclaimed. "Why isn't it frozen?"

"It just isn't," Sinclair snapped. "Drive across it."

The jeep bucketed nose-down into the water and then up again swerving and slithering so that, as Janey accelerated out of the dip, the tail swung round.

She pulled the wheel carefully and the jeep obediently straightened itself.

"I wonder how the Major knows when this lot is due to fall again," Janey speculated gloomily.

"That's the least of our worries," said Sinclair. He had turned to look back as the jeep moved out of its skid and at the entrance to the snow tunnel he had seen a blue Land Rover. He said nothing to the girl and she, concentrating intently on the road ahead, was not looking much in her mirror. The snow walls ahead of them curved; they turned the corner shutting out the unwelcome rear view.

Parked on the edge of the road leaving just enough room for them to pass as they emerged from the snow tunnel was the snow-blasting monster. They hooted and waved to its driver. The road surface was now hard and gravelly, steeply sloping, running with water. Janey pumped the brakes furiously and the jeep jerked bumpily down to the first bend. Their speed quickened and they shot down to the next hairpin, stones spinning from under their wheels.

"Easy, Janey."

"We have that madman on our heels."

"I know, I know, but it'll do us no good to escape him by taking a short cut two thousand feet to the bottom."

As they rounded the hundred and eighty degree turn

Sinclair glimpsed the sky hanging below him; there was no sign of the valley. Janey slowed down, using brakes and gears and they took the next two turns at a safer pace. The snow was lying thinner here and trees could be seen beneath them. As they approached the umpteenth hairpin a shower of stones spinning down from the road ledge above hit the track in front of them. They drove through it with pebbles spattering against the sides of the jeep like the ricochets from a bullet.

"There's somebody behind us. Have a look, Sinclair."

As she spoke Janey accelerated again. There was no one on the stretch immediately behind, as Sinclair, on the mountainside on that sweep, craned up. He could see only the dark edge of the road scoring the hill until it went out of view.

"It's impossible to see a car on the road above until it comes round the bend and is on the same stretch as us."

"And then it's too late."

On one long slope, just before they made the next turn, they saw the blue Land Rover whip round the corner behind them. Janey groaned.

"He's gaining on us. We haven't a chance. What does he want?"

"Keep calm. Keep going." Sinclair slewed round in his seat watching through the back-flap. They negotiated the next bend without seeing the Land Rover come on to the straight behind them. Ranjit Singh must have taken the zigzag very fast for they were still some yards from the next hairpin when he appeared swooping down on them. Through the narrow windscreen Sinclair could see his hands placed high on the steering wheel. Only a few yards behind them now, Ranjit was hooting his horn, a threatening, honking sound.

Janey held grimly on to the steering wheel, brought the jeep down into second and turned smartly through a hundred and eighty degrees. She was back into third and accelerating before she glanced into her mirror and said, "Where's he gone? Where is he?"

Ranjit, concentrating on catching up with Janey, had started to turn too late and had ridden the Land Rover up on to the high curved bank at the outer edge of the arc. The furious revving of his engine echoed against the bare rocks of the mountainside.

"He's stopped, run against the road edge, stalled, I think. We've gained a little time."

The jeep was already into its decelerating mode, a popping gurgle on a descending scale, as they approached the next corkscrew and passed out of view of Ranjit's Land Rover.

Sinclair, uncomfortably craning his neck to keep watch through the back-flap, could not but wish he were driving. He could not, in honesty, say that he would have driven faster or more skilfully, for Janey was experienced both with the Indian jeep and the Himalayan roads and handled them well. It was simply that the activity of turning the wheel, manipulating the gears, concentrating on the road was something to do, an easier part than just watching and waiting.

Janey was pushing the jeep as hard as she could, accelerating out of the bends and putting on as much speed as possible on the straight, delaying her braking and gearing down to the last safe moment before the road made another of its terrifying swings to reverse the direction of its descent.

The blue Land Rover had not put its nose round the upper bend before they had twirled round the lower one, spinning stones behind them as Janey cut into the centre of the turn.

"There's one good thing," she remarked. "We know there can't be anything coming up thanks to the avalanche. Think of the hell of meeting a lorry on one of these corners, where's Ranjit?" she finished without a pause.

"No sign. Keep going. He's dropped right back."

But this was not to be so for long. As they both knew, but neither put into words, the Land Rover was a faster car than the jeep and its cornering was neater. Ranjit might be behind them by the length of a zigzag but he would not remain so.

He caught them up more quickly than they expected. The next straight was very long and steep and, before they had reached the lower turn, Ranjit had appeared round the upper corner. Janey saw this and her moment's anxious glance in the mirror, held by the sight of the blue nose behind them, cost them accuracy in taking the next bend. It was a right hander and instead of taking advantage of the empty road and cutting into it early, using the right side of the road, she pulled on the steering wheel too late. The two nearside wheels caught on the loose gravel in the run off ditch on the outer edge of the turn. The jeep skidded and had slid broadside on to the road several yards down hill before Janey corrected course, changed gear and set off again.

Sinclair had managed not to exclaim as the binoculars lying loose in the back smacked into his knuckles and he saw road and rock disappear from the frame of the backflap and the pure blue emptiness of the late afternoon sky come into view.

"Oh God, sorry, sorry."

Janey had frightened herself. The whirling car, the way

that earth on her right and sky on her left had violently changed places, suddenly reduced the blue snub-nosed threat of the Land Rover behind.

Ranjit swung round the corner a few seconds later, gaining with every yard. This time he did not sound his horn; he took the inner, right-hand lane and began to overtake.

"He can't do this. There isn't room for two cars here. He'll force us over the edge."

Sinclair, on the precipice side, could see nothing beyond the grey crumbly shale of the berm. They were hanging in the air it seemed. Only whitewashed stones marked the fall hundreds of feet to the river below.

"What does he want?" cried Janey. "Shall I stop? Shall I stop?" Her hcsitation cost them further yards' lead.

"No, keep going. Keep calm," Sinclair urged her. "Don't bother about him. Just drive and stay on the road." As he looked to the rear it seemed the silver grille of the Land Rover was about to drive through the jeep's back-flap as if into a snugly fitting garage. Sinclair could see Ranjit's moustache, the sunglasses covering his eyes through the gleam on the tilted windscreen. He waved to him, signalling him to come in behind. Ranjit made no sign that he had seen his gestures; he did not obey them.

The bonnet of the Land Rover was nosing between them and the cliff wall. It was now level with the back wheels of the jeep. The next corner, a left hander, was only a few yards ahead.

"I can't take it," Janey shouted frantically. "I'll have to stop."

Instead of slowing, however, she accelerated into the turn, feverishly pulling at the wheel. As the front of the jeep came round she jammed on the brakes and stopped abruptly. Her plan had been to keep the safe inner track which was now hers with the left hand swing of the road and, by stopping, to allow the Land Rover to shoot past.

It did not work out like that. Ranjit had not managed to overtake on the right-hand slope because of Janey's last minute acceleration. Already on the wrong side of the road he took the corner wide, failing to pull round sharply enough.

Janey was never to forget those few moments in which the Land Rover, by every rule, should have appeared to view, first in the driver's window, then in the windscreen, dust briefly clouding its outlines as it came to a halt in front of them. Its absence was a strange counterpoint to her anticipation. The impact of that time was irrevocably printed on her mind, yet it passed so quickly. She had barely turned her head or shaped her lips in question before she heard the crashing, bellowing plunge as the Land Rover made its sideways leap wide of the curve, and made its first contact with the rocks of the hillside.

Janey was out of the car, and across the road, before Sinclair. She heard him shouting behind her.

"Don't go too near the edge, Janey. It may be weakened."

She could see the Land Rover's tracks in the gravel. The two offside wheels had run on to the extreme unprotected rim of the road, their marks, just below the edge, ended abruptly, showing where the centrifugal force of the Land Rover's turn had tipped its weight beyond its point of balance and toppled it roof-first down the hillside.

Sinclair ran up to join her where she stood looking

down. Below them was not a cliff but a precipitous shaley slope, unclimbable because of the loose rocks that covered it. Some distance further down trees were growing quite thickly and there was another sign of the accident. One of the tall conifers was scarred by the Land Rover's passing. A gash on its lichened trunk showed where the bark had been sheered off exposing the naked wood beneath.

Almost as soon as Sinclair was there, Janey tore back to the jeep. She pressed the back of her hand to her mouth to choke back a wave of nausea. She restarted the engine and drove off, changing gear with a hand that trembled and fumbled for the stick. They rounded the next hairpin. At the far end of the straight, lying in the road was a wheel, sheared off in the fall.

Janey moaned, "How much further can it have gone?"

As they turned the bend Sinclair, looking up from the passenger seat, shouted, "Stop, Janey."

The slope above them was gentler and they could see the Land Rover wedged on its side between two trees. It had clearly rolled over a number of times in its descent and had come to rest with its three remaining wheels facing downhill.

Janey jerked on the hand brake and flung herself out of the car leaving her door open behind her. She cleared the deep drainage ditch that ran on the inside of the road and started to scramble up the bank using both hands and feet.

"Janey," called Sinclair despairingly. "There could be petrol about. It might explode. Janey come back."

She did not obey him, so he followed her up the shingly slope, grabbing tough little plants for leverage in hauling himself up. Janey was standing by the exposed underside of the Land Rover when Sinclair, panting heavily, reached her. He sniffed the air. The reek of petrol, penetrating and spiritous as alcohol, surrounded them like a miasma. The petrol cap had gone and a dark shining smear on the Land Rover's side showed that it had lost some fuel on its way down. That hole was now staunched by the car's position on its side, but a more sinister seepage could be seen ebbing from the holed jerry cans anchored above the front bumper.

"You can see him through the window. He's been flung over to the passenger side. If you give me a leg up I'll try to open the driver's door."

"Janey, this isn't safe. There's petrol everywhere."

She ignored him, clambering on to the upturned car and tugging at the handle in its shell-shaped recess. Either the effort of lifting the door upwards was too great for her or the door itself was jammed and distorted by the fall.

"Come down, Janey," Sinclair ordered. "I'm going in through the back."

Janey was there before him. The metal struts that had shaped and supported the roof were crushed and buckled. The back entrance to the Land Rover was a tangle of canvas through which Janey crawled, climbing over the tumbled luggage that had been stowed between the side benches.

In the front seat she saw that Ranjit's legs were still trapped under the steering wheel and his body was hanging upside down from his snared thighs. His torso was twisted at the waist and again at the neck; his head was wedged forward by the passenger door.

Janey gazed at the contorted body and was reminded of Hugo's terrible grimace when she had turned his body over that first morning in Delhi. Ranjit's eyes were open and staring, his mouth was set in a fierce grin, exposing white wolfish teeth under his cavalry moustache. She could see within, dark pink, his tongue.

"I think he's dead." Lying on her stomach across an upturned trunk, she put a shrinking, tentative hand on to his chest, unable to feel any beat through the thick, shoulder-padded sweater.

The eyelids trembled. The movement was not as much as a blink, yet unmistakable. Ranjit's eyes, Janey saw were not the deep, light-absorbing black of most Indians', but hazel flecked with gold. She had not noticed their strange colour before, even in the gonkang. There was no recognition in them, no consciousness, but there was life.

"Sinclair, he's alive." She spoke in no more than a whisper, as if she were afraid of frightening away the flicker of existence.

"Come out, Janey." She crawled backwards.

"He's not dead, Sinclair. What are we to do?"

"Let me go in."

The hole made by Janey was too small to admit Sinclair and they lost time in pulling out one or two small bags blocked the way. He was inside for longer than Janey who, as she waited for him stood by the rear of the Land Rover, constantly clasping and unclasping her hands, the movement somehow consuming a small but necessary amount of the adrenalin of terror and shock.

At last Sinclair's feet, legs, torso, head, emerged from the Land Rover.

"What can we do? Shall we try to get him out?"

Sinclair straightened himself up. "I think we'll have to find help. You're right, he is just alive. I could feel a faint pulse. But God knows what he's broken or what his internal injuries are. How far are we from the bottom of the road?"

"We're miles. At least three quarters of an hour's drive. And there'll only be a few jawans and a sergeant, no doctor."

"That's more use than just the two of us."

"Can't we do anything? It's... it's so horrible to think of him hanging like that."

"We could try to get him clear of the Land Rover. If we cut through the canvas by the cab..."

"Let's try that at least. There's a knife in the jeep."

The events of the next few minutes happened too fast to separate into order in the memory. Janey turned her back on the Land Rover and began to slither down towards the road. She made a diagonal course to her right where some more trees offered handholds and support. Suddenly she heard a shout from behind and a roar of rocks as they chased one another in a solid cascade down the slope. She teetered as she tried to see what was happening, slipped, grabbed the trunk of a sapling and clung to it.

The Land Rover passed her, not falling nor rolling, riding the rock-fall like a boat on fast water. She cried out. She could hear Sinclair's voice above her.

The Land Rover hit the bank of the drainage ditch and turned over for the last time on to the road. The orange flame appeared almost at once from under the bonnet, flowing like liquid to engulf the whole car.

Janey was screaming. She could hear her own voice, though not what it cried, nor why.

Sinclair passed her, crouched, allowing the falling rocks to carry him, scrambling, sliding until he made a leap which carried him over the ditch to the edge of the road. Janey watched in terror and bewilderment as she saw his form against the fire. Then he disappeared behind the jeep.

There was an explosion from the Land Rover. Burning fragments arced like tracers over the lip of the road; the flames grew and branched like trees. Suddenly the jeep jumped backwards, reversing at high speed round the bend above the exploding car.

Janey crouched on the slope watching the horrible parody of a Hindu funeral pyre, with petrol for ghee, the black rubber of the tyres for the logs of sandalwood and herself and Sinclair, untouchables, as the Mahabrahmans to conduct the funeral rites.

At some point Sinclair, whom she had heard shouting to her from above, came and dragged her up the hillside. Clutching one another they pulled themselves up to the road and again Janey huddled looking through the trees to the fire below. Sinclair put a rug round her shoulders and only then did she realise that she was shivering in uncontrollable spasms.

❀❀❀

They remained there while night fell and the dense black smoke was consumed within the darkness. They could not go on because the burning Land Rover left no space on the narrow road for them to pass. They did not speak for a very long time, not voicing their questions, fears, regrets, relief, contenting themselves with the comfort of a close silence. It was Janey who said at last, "What a terrible end."

Sinclair said nothing. He did not try to minimise the horror of Ranjit's death nor to reassure her that it must have been quick, or without suffering. They both knew too well it would not be true.

"Why?" Janey whispered. "Why was he chasing us like that? Nothing is worth the risk he took and lost."

"The gold. It always comes back to that. He must have learned, or worked out, that we had the gold. In Uptak he was still looking for it; he must have realised it was not in Ladakh after all, but in Delhi with me."

"And what about Hugo? Will you be able to get any further with that? Will you ever know now if Ranjit really murdered him?"

"I don't suppose so now. Isn't that what you're always saying? I'm a greater believer in certainties than you are but I know when things are never going to become clearer. We have to live with a level of uncertainty."

Chapter 21

ALAN TURNELL took off his half-moon glasses. He only ever wore them for reading and removed them as soon as he could: spectacles were ageing and he looked quite distinguished enough without them. He tapped them thoughtfully on the papers which lay on his blotter and looked at Sinclair who was sitting on one of the black imitation-leather armchairs. For this interview Alan had felt the need to remain behind his desk.

"I must say you're looking extraordinarily well, very—er—relaxed. Just as if you'd had a tranquil few days on a houseboat on Lake Nageen. Instead of…" He let his voice trail off. It was usually better to leave unspoken the details of the kinds of activities that Sinclair had been up to.

Sinclair was indeed lounging in a very abandoned way in the Minister's armchair. His long legs were spread; his hands dangled loose; the bruises on his face had gone and so had the rigidity with which he had held his body when Alan had last seen him before he left for Kashmir.

"Oh, yes," said Sinclair. "I'm fit enough by now."

Alan paid no attention. His comment on Sinclair's health had been routine; his mind was already on the question of the report which lay in front of him.

"Hugo's death has turned up quite a lot of surprises, most of them unpleasant ones for us. It doesn't look too good that you have been able to root out blackmail by the Russians, private dealings which may or may not be eligible for the term smuggling and probably a lot more too. Makes us look a bit slack as far as London is concerned. And there is the question of our relations with the Indians. So we may have to make a little in the way of—er—a presentational alteration before we can let your report go forward to all the interested departments in Whitehall." He paused. "Are you with me, Sinclair?"

Sinclair seemed to wake up. "Oh, I'm with you, Alan. What is it, particularly, that you think requires some—er—presentational adjustment?" Sinclair still slouched; he looked as if he hardly cared. Alan did not like the slouching, which showed some fundamental lack of respect towards him or his job or the Foreign Office. On the other hand it might indicate a lack of interest which would allow him to arrange things as he pleased. He did not answer Sinclair's question directly.

"First is the matter of Dolgov. Now, you'll be given lots of stars from your own side for spotting him and even more from SIS for offering him up on a plate. I don't think I'm being indiscreet in saying that things have been moving fast on that front while you've been away. Charlie Croom is like a dog with two tails. We, that is, I know H.E. is very keen to write adding our commendations to theirs. We missed all this going on under our noses and you ferreted it out in a few days." Sinclair felt that the animal metaphors which permeated Alan's speech conveyed his distaste with the whole sordid business.

"That's very handsome of you, Alan. In fact it was only Hugo's death which made that relationship interesting and forced Dolgov to break cover. Not much credit there for me."

Alan warmed a little at this. It seemed as if Sinclair, who under the meek, civil service exterior, was an oddity, was going to play this one properly.

"No, no. The letter's drafted and it'll go. No doubt of it, you did very well on that one.

"Then we come to the business of Hugo's murder. Now, this is much trickier." He fixed his spectacles back on his nose and flicked through the typescript. "You'll agree with me that your brief was the security aspect rather than the—er—actual death, yes? Yes now, you've presented a case here which suggests that Ranjit Singh was the murderer of Hugo Frencham. You show that you uncovered evidence of Hugo's and Ranjit's collaboration over several years in exporting Indian art objects and antiques, some of which may have been in contravention of Indian law. You suggest they fell out over a large consignment of gold which Hugo had—er—acquired and that Ranjit Singh followed Hugo home from my party on Monday 30th April and murdered him in his garden during an argument about the gold. You further suggest that Ranjit was responsible for removing a sympathetic police officer from Hugo's case; for breaking into Bungalow 2 to search for the gold; for the assault on you on May 13th and for pursuing you and Jane Somers from Ladakh with violent intent, if I understand right." Alan stopped.

"I think you can be said to have understood my report," Sinclair commented when it became clear that Alan was waiting for him to say something.

"Now we come to the matter of the gold..." Alan went on.

"In fact," Sinclair interrupted, "the gold comes in much earlier. None of the rest is explicable without mention of the gold. That's why Hugo let himself be blackmailed. Dolgov said that in June last year Hugo needed time and was prepared to pay for it. The time he needed was to smuggle the gold out of Tibet which he was planning with Sonam Dorje. And Ranjit's part is only understandable in terms of the gold. He arranged Sonam Dorje's flight out of Ladakh by military plane. He heard that Hugo was selling gold and guessed how he came by it. He was furious that Hugo had made use of him and had not cut him in on the profits. This was, of course, because Hugo was making no profit at all. The proceeds of the sale of the gold went straight into the Bombay bank account of a Tibetan relief organisation. Ranjit clearly did not know this, or, if he did, couldn't believe it. He thought he had a right to a share in the gold and, after Hugo's death, to it all."

Alan listened to what he said and then remarked coldly, "I'm sure your analysis of the motives of the various characters involved is highly plausible. However, we cannot accept the judgments you make in your report. What I am concerned with is the consequence of your recommendations. You advocate the submission of that part of your text dealing with Hugo's death to 'the appropriate Indian authorities'." Quotation marks were indicated by the tone of Alan's voice, suggesting disgust at Sinclair's prose style. "I am afraid, Sinclair, that we feel that we cannot agree to this." He waited as if for protest from Sinclair, who said nothing. "In order to make any sense of your accusations against Ranjit, a highly respected and influential man as you must be aware, we would have to make known, at the very least, Hugo's export business with him and, at worst, Hugo's part in the gold smuggling. Hugo is dead. Ranjit is dead. I can see no good in raking over their relationship; justice cannot be served and positive harm could be done. The Indians would be extremely displeased if they knew what Hugo had been doing—and the matter of the gold would be very serious indeed. I feel that your interpretation of events is highly speculative and that the most likely explanation of Hugo's death is that he disturbed a burglar. The missing objects confirm this hypothesis, and so does the break-in which occurred while you were living at Bungalow 2. This is supported by Inspector Verma. So in consideration of the embarrassment that would accrue to HMG we have decided not to follow your recommendations on Hugo's murder. Instead, Inspector Verma's Interim Report will be forwarded to Security Department in Whitehall."

Sinclair looked neither surprised not upset. He merely said, "So what happens to the gold?"

Again, Alan avoided the direct answer. "We've heard from England about Hugo's will. A slightly odd one, not totally unexpected. The V&A will be gnashing its teeth, I imagine," he added cryptically. "Hugo's money goes into a fund for the benefit of the Tibetan community in India—some kind of educational trust I think. His collection is to be kept together and is to form part of a Museum of the Tibetan Heritage which is projected. Now, the new Head of Chancery has been appointed and, of course, Bungalow 2 will have to be emptied and redecorated.

Maggie's willing to supervise the packing. So I think the thing for you to do is to see that everything—absolutely everything—that was in the house at Hugo's death is back there so it can all be packed up and sent to the Tibetans in Dharamsala. Perhaps you would notify your contact there, Sonam Dorje, isn't it, who made that extraordinary journey? I'm sure Hugo's solicitors will be arranging matters at their end."

"Ah, I see. Or rather, I don't see. A little diplomatic winking goes on. The gold is put back into the house, is packed up and sent off to the Tibetans, who thus in a roundabout way regain what is theirs."

"Yes," said Alan reflectively, "though I think it is really unnecessary to spell things out so clearly. It's best that we know nothing about it. The Tibetans are going to have the problem of unloading the gold on to the Indian market. We'll just have to hope they're not caught and that the Indians never have a whiff of what Hugo was up to. Even if they do we'll deny it and with Hugo dead there's not much they can do." He leaned over and offered the papers to Sinclair. "So there's one more thing I must ask you to do, Sinclair. We need something for our files and this clearly won't do. Could you rewrite this before you go, whenever that is? No gold, mind. I'm wiping it from my memory. And if you're wise you'll do the same."

Sinclair took the papers and started to separate some sheets from the front. "I'll give you this section on Dolgov for your files, that should do."

"But what about Hugo's murder?"

"You said yourself my brief was security. Well, that covers it. I don't want to put my name to any fairy story, so I'll keep the rest. Better to have a blank on the file."

Alan, looking as though anything was better than a blank on the file, took back the proffered sheets. "You'll be off soon, I expect," he said. "Come for a drink before you go. Maggie'll give you a ring." Thus dismissed, Sinclair left.

"How did it go?" asked Janey from her usual position on the verandah as Sinclair dumped two heavy parcels in the sitting room before stepping out on to the terrace. He put his hand on her head, feeling the thick curls between his fingers.

"Fine. Everything just as I wanted."

"Clever you. How did you do it?"

"Wasn't difficult. I wrote a report recommending complete frankness. That's bound to be popular with a diplomat, for a start. I suggested sharing the dirt with the Indians and it had Alan standing on tip-toe to keep out of the muck. It leaves the High Commission looking bloody silly both with the Indians and with London, so they've decided to buy me off with lots of praise for...with lots of praise and cover everything else up. The interrupted burglary theory is back in fashion and Verma's going to support it. Alan did suggest I should write a report which 'explained' everything. Very clever that—a fall guy ready with a signed confession if anything came out. I wasn't having any so he'll have to pad out the files in some other way." He sank down onto the sofa next to her. "Why do you sit out here in this filthy heat?"

"You know I love it. So between you, you've solved it all, wrapped it all up. There's nothing to choose between them: your theory about Ranjit, Alan's theory of the interrupted burglary. The best one was Lobsang Dhondup's—the release of evil with the removal of the gold from Tibet. The demons were angered."

Sinclair wiped his brow with his forearm. "Janey, don't pick a quarrel with me. You were the one who said the truth of that evening would never be known. I agree with you. Now Ranjit's dead we won't know, so we're just going to let it lie."

"It's still too neat," Janey complained. "You rationalize everything, order it, divide it up: the gold, the Tibetans, Ranjit, Hugo. You write a list and tick them off. They're summed up and dealt with. It shouldn't be like that. It's much more complicated."

"Janey, you're supposed to be an academic not a mystic. How else in heaven's name can the case be treated?"

There was an obstinate pause, then Sinclair said, "Come and see what I've brought back from the High Commission."

He led her inside and undid the parcels, flicking back the lid of the tin box and removing the kidskin just as he had that evening in Hugo's bedroom. Janey picked up one piece of gold and let it roll heavily into the curl of her fingers.

"What is to happen to it?"

"Hugo's left his estate to a Tibetan educational trust apparently. Everything is to go into a museum in Dharamsala."

"Do you remember Kalsang Lhawang and the monk? They said the Tibetan things were to go to a special Tibetan place. Hugo must have told them what he never mentioned to us, me. So the Tibetans will get their gold back at last."

"Yes, I've made Alan see that there's nothing else to

do but to let it go to Dharamsala without any fuss. You may call it writing a list and ticking it off. I'd say that I'd managed more or less to see that it has all come out fairly, even if not according to the exact letter of the law. And as for tidying things away neatly, it's anything but neat in my view. I said to you before, I've had to learn your lesson and accept a degree of uncertainty."

"All for this. Hugo, Sonam Dorje, Ranjit."

They were silent. Janey's mind went back to the glowing pyre and its heavy shroud of black smoke above which they had sat for so long until they had been rescued by an Army lorry sent up from the post at the bottom of the road. Every night she dreamed of that burst of orange flame, the white and gold which had burned within it. She would wake sweating and panting with an image of terror imprinted on the darkness of her eyelids, and lie awake, a hand on the living back beside her, listening to the harsh purr of the air conditioning until her pulse subsided and she had reasoned herself out of her dream and into wakefulness. She would try to understand the source of her nightmare and why Ranjit's twisted neck and open eyes troubled her so much more than the memory of Hugo's curled body on the lawn.

She had decided that a clue lay in Sonam Dorje's words which she had repeated to Sinclair. It was in Ranjit's rage distorted face in the gonkang, in the tangled body inside the Land Rover, she had recognised the evil released that he had spoken of and she had feared it. The usual optimism with which she met the world, her belief in human decency and kindness had been profoundly undermined by her glimpse at a wilfulness and greed which risked everything.

❁❁❁

In the foyer of the Chandragupt Hotel where they had just had lunch, Janey and Sinclair shook hands with Battacharia. Sinclair had been determined to see and thank the energetic little police officer before he left Delhi and, with Janey's help, had tracked him down without much difficulty. The girl on the switchboard at the Police Headquarters was no longer on the lookout to divert anyone from Inspector Battacharia, so when Janey rang and asked in Hindi to speak to him she was put through at once and arrangements to meet for lunch had been made.

With oriental delicacy no reference had been made by any of them to Hugo's death nor to the manner in which the files had been closed. Their conversation was only on neutral topics.

Sinclair had looked out of the darkened glass of the restaurant windows on to the unnaturally blue lozenge of the swimming pool. He could not tell Janey about Dolgov, yet to lunch there with her within sight of Hugo's and Dolgov's meeting place gave him a secret amusement, a satisfying sense of completion, one job at least well done and finished. It was the only strand of what had happened in India that had been neatly finished off. His attempts at tidying up other ends had not been a success. When he called on Ruth Quinton, for instance, he had failed to find her in. And there was, above all, Janey.

After their goodbyes had been said, addresses exchanged, hospitality offered for future years, Battacharia departed leaving Janey and Sinclair with two clear hours before Sinclair had to be at the airport for his flight to London.

Janey dealt briskly with the problem.

"You've seen nothing while you've been here. You might as well have been in Canada or Australia." She hailed a scooter rickshaw and gave her directions.

Sinclair had been waiting for an opportunity to talk to Janey, putting off doing so every time occasion arose for fear of what the definition of words would produce. He found himself seduced by oriental inexplicitness; within the undefined, hope was possible.

The rattle of the rickshaw defied speech. The unresolved remained. Janey pointed to three little domes on a mosque, pink and white striped olives pierced by cocktail sticks. She did not attempt to speak above the noise of their passage.

When they had arrived and paid off the rickshaw she led him through arches and along a tree-lined walk into a vast walled enclosure. The brilliant heat of the afternoon clamped on their heads like a helmet; complete silence and stillness had fallen. In the shade, students sat cross-legged in front of books open on the grass. A large Indian family picnicking under the trees lay as if asleep.

In the centre of the walled garden rose on a high arched platform a great domed building of austere dark red stone. Without disturbing the silence they climbed on to the platform and entered the tomb.

Inside it was dark and cool; the sun threaded the jhallees with long needles of light. Janey sat down in one of the window recesses and the fretwork embroidered her dress with its intricate shadow.

"You're going back tomorrow?" Sinclair did not need to ask; he had heard her on the phone the previous day.

Janey was peering through the tracery at the trees of the garden. On one she could see a couple of monkeys grooming each other with neat contented movements.

"Yes. I should be in Srinagar by nine at the latest. But I don't think I'll leave for Leh till the next day. The road should be quite avalanche-free by this time."

"I'm sorry I disrupted your work so badly. You weren't warned what you were letting yourself in for. It wasn't meant to turn out as it did."

"Nonsense, Sinclair," Janey said crossly. "You didn't plan Ranjit's bursting in upon us. Don't apologise."

Sinclair looked at the achingly bright world outside the tomb. There was not much time left.

"Anyway I shall miss you, on the drive and in Ladakh."

"Janey." Sinclair started to speak. The carefully rehearsed points that he wanted to make jumbled themselves together and came out in any order. Teresa was Roman Catholic, he told her. She would certainly not divorce him. If he tried to divorce her she might oppose it. He did not know enough about the divorce laws; it could take ages. There were the children, money, the house…

Janey was laughing. "Sinclair, Sinclair, stop."

He had done everything the wrong way round. He should have started with her, her wishes, her feelings, her future; he had been too nervous even to approach them.

"Don't worry. Really, don't worry. I shall be home in October. You can tell me then about your plans. I don't mind. I just flow along, as you know."

"You flow. I plan."

"Then plan, go ahead. But don't worry."

Sinclair leaned against the wall. Through the thin cotton of the shirt Janey had bought for him in Khan Market all those weeks ago he felt the chill of the stone that never saw the sun.

"I can't plan without you."

"Plan on my coming back—in October—to England. That'll be a start."

Chapter 22

JANEY RETURNED TO THE BUNGALOW from the airport to spend her last night in Delhi. She had managed to book a flight to Kashmir early next morning to pick up the jeep and return to Ladakh. Jogiram had promised to wake her at five, and to call a taxi for her. Though she had insisted she could wake herself, he was adamant that he would be there to see her off a second time.

No one was in the house. Hugo's things were being packed and Jogiram had spent the day supervising the Chinese removers, who had sat on the floor coating objects with infinite patience in tissue paper, newspaper, straw. They had all gone home for the day leaving half-filled tea chests in almost every room. The drawing-room in particular was a scene of desolation. The books had gone from the shelves and the smaller objects were already safely in the packing cases; pictures were stacked in size order, propped against walls or chairs. Piles of wrapping paper and rolls of corrugated cardboard lay on the floor with the lids of the unsealed tea chests against them. Janey stood in the sitting room looking at the ordered untidiness as Hugo's personality was systematically stripped from the house. A new Head of Chancery was expected in a few weeks. The house would be redecorated, wiped clean of his predecessor before he arrived. As she debated what to do and where to go—a Hindi movie perhaps, a debased taste which she occasionally indulged in Delhi—she heard a knock on the door. For a moment she did not move, thinking to play possum, but at a second tap she walked through the hall and opened the door.

In front of her stood a woman in a pink sun dress, plump and brown, her hair loose, hanging to her shoulders. There was a pause as neither spoke, then Janey said, "You must be Ruth Quinton. Come in." The visitor looked embarrassed, flustered; hesitatingly she stepped across the threshold.

"Yes, I'm Ruth Quinton and I know you're Janey Somers, aren't you? I—I didn't know you were still here. I came—I was—I thought I might find Jogiram."

"No, I told him to go when the packers left. I'm on my own."

Janey led the way into the sitting room and cleared a space on the sofa.

"It's my last night. I'm leaving tomorrow."

"You're going back to London with Mr Sinclair?"

"No, I'm going back to Ladakh tomorrow morning. Sinclair has gone already; this afternoon in fact."

"Mr Sinclair's gone? I thought he might be here. I came..."

Mrs Quinton had sat down on the sofa, on the edge of the cushion, as if uneasy, about to take flight. She seemed to be trying to think of something, or decide what to do next. Janey sat on the arm of a chair and looked with curiosity at the figure in front of her. The plump face was soft, its expression wary and indecisive; the mouth was clearly marked, full-lipped, looking like that of another person, a different character, one more definite and powerful than the anxious-eyed woman who sat nervously creasing her handkerchief

Janey broke the silence. "What did you want to ask Jogiram? Is it anything I can help with? Or can I give him a message? I'm going to see him in the morning before I go."

Her guest remained distrait. "No, it doesn't matter really..." Her voice faded away. She was looking round the room, noticing where the faint dust marks outlined the absent pictures; her eyes moved to the empty table tops, the bare shelves.

Janey felt a sudden rush of pity for her visitor. Her own depression at saying goodbye to Sinclair rose in her again. For her it was only a question of time. She would see him again in a few months. For poor Ruth Quinton Hugo had gone for ever. She could not even openly grieve. She had perhaps needed to come to the house to see it again before Hugo's things were packed up and sent away for good.

"It's miserable, isn't it?" Janey gestured to the muddle of boxes and packing materials. "Did you want to have a last look round while Hugo's stuff is still here or see anything in particular?" She stopped at the embarrassed surprise in Ruth's face and with some embarrassment herself said, "I'm sorry. It must look like a betrayed confidence to you and in a way it is, I suppose. Sinclair told me—about you and Hugo I mean. It was in such a way... I mean he and I..." Janey, normally so articulate, broke off. She could not explain to Ruth or anyone else how the telling of a confidence of someone else's love affair had become part of her own. "Naturally, I wouldn't talk of it to anyone else. I shouldn't have spoken of it to you, I know. I knew Hugo too and you must feel..."

What Ruth must feel also defeated Janey's powers of fluent expression. Her listener was no longer looking absently round the room, her eyes were fixed on janey's face.

"Mr Sinclair told you about Hugo and me? He went to stay in Kashmir with you after he was hurt, didn't he?" Janey was relieved to feel that it was accepted that the tale had been told as lovers' confidences not as gossip. "He's an odd man, isn't he? He understood more about Hugo, even though he'd never met him, than anyone else who'd known him for years. I suppose that's why I told him. I needed—wanted to know what he was doing about Hugo's death. I came to the house to see him. He didn't tell me anything, of course, but he talked about Hugo's things, the Tibetan stuff. That's why I told him about Hugo and me." She paused and said as if to herself, "I wonder how much more he knew." Then to Janey, "It really was Mr Sinclair I came to see."

"I'm sorry you missed him," Janey said conventionally. To compensate for Sinclair's absence she added impulsively, "Look why don't you take a keepsake of Hugo before everything is packed. All the Tibetan bits are going to a museum, you know, and I think the rest'll be sold." She jumped up, delighted with her own idea. "They've almost finished down here, but they have not done upstairs yet. What would you like? Let's go up and have a look."

Ruth followed her up the stairs, saying uneasily, "It's like stealing. I don't know that I should take anything..."

"Nonsense," said Janey, "Hugo would have wanted it. Anyway quite a lot of stuff was broken in the burglary so one more piece missing'll make no difference."

They walked into the big bedroom where once Ruth and Hugo had dressed up in Tibetan clothes, where Janey and Sinclair had found the box of gold. It was still tidy, untouched. She opened the wardrobe.

"What about the clothes? Would you want them? Sinclair told me..."

"No, no. They'd be—well, they'd be hard to explain."

"Yes, I suppose so. Then some jewellery, an amulet or earrings? Let's look at those. Where did Hugo keep them?"

They found a brass bound wooden chest at the bottom of the wardrobe and opened it up, Janey rifling through the compartments like a child going through its mother's jewel box for dressing up. Ruth Quinton sat on the edge of the bed with none of Janey's enthusiasm and concentration. She reluctantly identified a reliquary as one she had worn, after half-heartedly examining and rejecting various other trinkets.

"It's so pretty," Janey said thrusting the little silver and turquoise box at her. "Look it has the Wheel of Truth on it, three double wheels one inside the other. It's one of the symbols of the eight Blessings of the Buddha. Let it be that. No one'll ever know, and you should have something." She shut the wooden case and started to drag it back to the wardrobe.

Ruth had her bag open. It was a large canvas affair with bamboo handles. She put the reliquary inside and then said, "If I'm taking this I must give back something of Hugo's that I've had all this time. That's really why I came. I wanted to give this to Mr Sinclair."

She drew something out of the bottom of the bag and placed it on the bed. Janey, turning from the wardrobe saw a small silver statue of the Buddha, serene faced, one finger gently touching the earth below his folded legs, poised tranquilly on the smooth cream cover. She stretched out her hand and picked it up, balancing the figure in her palm.

"Isn't this the Buddha they were looking for and never found?" she said almost without thinking. "It must be the one Hugo... How do you come to have it?"

Recalling the scene afterwards Janey was amazed that she had felt neither fear nor even surprise. For though she knew what the answer must be her tone was as matter of fact as if she were asking the whereabouts of something quite trivial. Ruth's response was equally undramatic.

"I've had it all the time," she replied. "From the night Hugo died. I mean I took it home with me, without realising it I suppose. And then I couldn't throw it away, somehow I felt I had to hold on to it. I knew it was stupid. I have been waiting for Mr Sinclair to come and find it."

Janey thought of Sinclair's account of the tears at his first meeting with the Quintons, of the unsolicited outpourings about Ruth's affair with Hugo.

"Why did you bring it back this evening? Were you really going to give it to Sinclair if he had been here?"

"I had to tell someone. There have been such terrible stories about Hugo in the compound, about him being a sort of racketeer and even worse stories about...about odd sex. Based on nothing. How people can say these things when they've all known Hugo all this time. I couldn't bear it any longer. I must straighten it all out. You'd think the crime was in being murdered. Nothing said about the person who did it—just smears and innuendos about poor Hugo."

"Sinclair's gone back to London, as I told you. I've just come back from seeing him off. He thinks that the matter is finished as far as he's concerned and in fact he never was here to investigate the…the death as such. If you want to talk, do you want to tell me? I know I'm not official but it might help to sort things out in your mind."

Ruth stood up from the edge of the bed and walked over to the window looking down on the sprawling branches of bougainvillea that sprang over the roof of the verandah. She remained there for several minutes until Janey said gently, "What happened that night?"

Ruth turned back and sat down on the easy chair with her back to the light. Her round face looked deflated and drawn. She put her hands to her head.

"It was an accident you know—though I'd be bound to say that, wouldn't I?" She pushed back her hair and let her hands fall to her lap. "I can't explain about what happened that night without talking about Hugo and me. I don't know what Mr Sinclair described to you. It was a dream—Hugo and me—a fantasy. I still can't understand it when I look back on it, but I can see it couldn't have lasted. When you're dreaming you feel as if the dream'll go on for ever, it's for real. Then you wake up and all the things that seemed so sensible and right in the dream are shown to be all wrong. Hugo and me for a start. I mean I'm not a…a…" She was floundering for words, her hands fluttering. "I'm not a sexy person. I'm not like that, never have been. With Hugo—well, that was one of the things that seemed right in the dream that when you look at afterwards turn out to be all wrong. I suppose we'd have woken out of it one way or another. What actually did it was—I got pregnant."

She stopped for so long at this point that Janey said tentatively, "You mean you weren't sure whether the baby was Hugo's or your husband's?"

Ruth looked at her as if only just remembering her presence.

"Oh, no, I knew it was Hugo's. My husband can't have children. We've been married seven years, you know. People always assume it's me—funny, isn't it, the way not having children, like having them, is always blamed on the woman. It isn't me, it's Frank. We had all the tests done years ago and that's when we found out. I'd've liked to adopt but he wouldn't hear of it. Well, that's neither here nor there now." She paused again, smoothing her cotton dress across her knees. "So you can see I knew whose it was and I knew what it would mean to Frank. I told Hugo that I wanted to leave Frank and move in with him. It just seemed the most sensible thing. I loved him. It was his baby. He wasn't married. There weren't any other children. I mean it could've been much worse. God knows, you see some messy break-ups. This one looked so easy. But Hugo wouldn't."

"He wouldn't?"

"He wouldn't let me or listen to me or anything. He said—oh, the arguments we had—he said he was too old for me. I'd be shackling myself to an—an old age pensioner. He was fifty-six and I was thirty-two: the age difference was too great. He would be retired in four years: it wouldn't be fair on me."

Ruth had spoken with complete calm up till this point; as she retailed Hugo's persuasions tears started to slip down her face.

Janey leaned towards her. "Look, I could do with a drink, couldn't you? I think there's a bit of whisky in the house and maybe some gin and sherry. What'll you have? I'll bring some whisky for us both. You stay here. This is the most comfortable place there is."

She was back a few minutes later with a tray, a bottle, glasses and some water, and poured out the peaty liquid for them. Ruth took the glass quite collectedly and sipped while the tears continued to fall silently.

"I wouldn't have taken any notice of him," she went on eventually. "Things like that are only said to be contradicted—or they are normally—but Hugo meant them. He meant he didn't want to marry me. I could see it at once even though we argued about it for weeks. Not long, but it seemed ages—and you haven't long when there's a baby on the way. I don't know why I went on when right from the start I knew he didn't want me. Underneath all his excuses that it would be bad for me, he was afraid, for himself, terrified. You can't force a man to marry you. What would be the point? As I couldn't go to Hugo I had to stay with Frank and that meant an abortion. Hugo suggested it at the beginning when I told him; at first I wouldn't listen. It was all very well for him. He thought we could go back to things as they were and continue just as if nothing had happened."

She took another sip of her whisky and the tears fell from her cheeks on to her dress in bright beads. "No, that's not fair to him. He didn't really think like that. But it didn't mean to him what it meant to me."

"Didn't you," Janey said hesitantly, "didn't you think of going it alone. Without Hugo or Frank?"

"Well, I did, but oh, it was too difficult. How was I to live? I was a secretary before I married but I'm so rusty now no one would give me a job. And where would I go? We haven't a house in England and I couldn't see my mother taking me in. What could I do? I felt so helpless. It had to be one or the other of them and if it wasn't Hugo it had to be Frank. So I had the abortion. Hugo arranged it. I wouldn't have known what to do but he knew everything about India. It wasn't a bad place, not the terrible back street slum you always think of. It was a clinic in Nizamuddin, just a respectable looking house, clean enough for India. Frank was away for ten days on a tour of the Punjab so I went off there one morning and it was all over by lunch-time. I came home in the evening and no one knew I'd been away; no one cared. That was the Friday. I stayed in all that weekend. Oh, it was awful, the worst time, much worse than later. I cried all the time, I couldn't stop myself. I thought about—what you said—going it alone. I knew that's what I should've done. I mean, I'm not a career woman. I should have a family to look after and Hugo took that chance away from me. I thought I should've told Frank and kept the baby as his, though I knew it was impossible: he'd never, never forgive me if he found out."

She was still crying but the tears hardly affected her voice at all. She made no effort to check or blot them and they dripped off her jaw onto her shoulder, making little pools above her collar bones.

"Hugo came to see me that weekend. He was very kind and gentle, but I could see it was all over. I think he was relieved. Frank was due back on the Wednesday so Hugo said he would come again on the Monday night, straight from the office, to see how I was. But he didn't come. I keep wondering if he had come, would it all have been different; perhaps he would be alive now. I knew he was going out and I supposed he'd been held up at work and then had had to go straight on to the dinner. I wanted to see him again so much, just once before Frank came home because then that would be it, over, finished. We wouldn't meet again except, you know, casually. So I thought I'd slip into the house and wait until he got back from the party. I knew where the servants always keep the back door key so I let myself in and went onto the verandah to wait for him. He came very quickly, in fact it all happened so quickly that later I couldn't believe so much so terrible could be crammed into so short a time." Her voice changed from its quiet even tones and became breathy and short.

"I was in the garden. I thought he'd be hours. Then the next thing I knew he was calling me. He knew I was there. He came out on to the verandah and he was carrying that with him",—she gestured to the statue which still lay, calmly and elegantly mounted on the bed—"and a little silver knife."

She raised her hands to her tear-swollen face; her eyes were dry now. "He just wanted me to go home, be quiet, rest. He had no idea why I'd come or what it meant, what anything meant. He sat down at the verandah table and I could see him looking at the figure and the knife. That's what had brought him home early. He wanted me to go so that he could concentrate on them. I started crying again; I couldn't stop. I picked up the things and threw them into the garden, shouted at him to look at me, think about me, pay attention to me. He was so angry. He got up to look for the pieces of silver. The knife was nearest, it hadn't gone far at all. I reached it first and grabbed it and he came to take it away from me. I had the handle in my hands and he was pulling it from me. I don't know how it happened but it did. I don't even know where the knife went into him. He fell with hardly a sound. I was so terrified I think I was out of my mind. I ran. I got back to the flat. I saw no one—which was lucky, I wasn't trying to hide. I was running and weeping. If anyone had seen me... When I was home I washed myself—there was not much blood. And then I thought, supposing Hugo isn't dead but lying there bleeding and bleeding. So I went back."

"Back here? When was this?"

"Oh, I don't know. It must have been quite a bit later. The cars had gone from the Turnells' drive. I went into the garden and Hugo was lying there, a bit curled up as if he were asleep. He seemed dead. I mean I'd never seen anyone dead before. I thought he must be dead—there was no breath or heart beat so I couldn't do any good by calling for help and so I thought I'd better... Well, I mean, it couldn't hurt Hugo, could it, so I found a cloth and wiped the table and the door handles. I hadn't touched much because I'd gone straight out into the garden. Then I thought I'd make it look like a burglary. The knife was on the ground so I took that and the statue and a big fancy trumpet from the sitting room and I threw them into the mali's compost heap and covered them all over. I knew they wouldn't find them there for ages. But not the statue—for some reason I couldn't. So I took it home with me."

She sat in her chair eyes closed, no longer speaking, relaxed and spent. Janey was sitting on the floor cross-legged studying the texture of the carpet. They remained in silence for a long time.

Eventually Ruth said, "What shall I do?"

"What do you think you should do?"

"I don't know. That's why I came to see Mr Sinclair."

There was another long pause before Janey said, "Sinclair isn't here and isn't coming back. You either have to decide to tell what you've just told me to someone else—I don't know who to suggest—your husband—"

"Oh no."

"—or someone in authority like—er—Bryan Lenton or Alan Turnell. Or do nothing."

Ruth did not ask Janey to speak for her, nor did she beg her not to tell. There was no need, for there was an unspoken assumption between the two of them that in some way what Ruth said to Janey was a confidence, like speaking to herself. It was partly because of the absent Sinclair to whom Ruth had spoken before, who had told Janey and bound them together in a secret which he himself would not have acknowledged.

Ruth prepared to leave. Frank was at a reception, she explained and was due home about nine. Janey saw her off from the front door and watched her, a moving shadow in the dark, until she was round the curve of the road on her way back to the flats. Then she climbed the stairs and returned to Hugo's bedroom. Holding the silver statue, she stood where Ruth had stood, looking over the pink waterfall of bougainvillea to the spot where she had found Hugo that morning almost a month ago.

She thought over the story she had heard that evening. Was it any nearer the truth than the conjectures that she and Sinclair had built for themselves, than the story Ranjit had hissed at her in the gonkang at Uptak? She wondered whether Ruth would tell someone else, or whether the cathartic effect of recounting the story—a story—to her would be enough to seal it off for ever.

Janey carried the statue downstairs. The garden was dark, the same thick tropical darkness as the night of Hugo's death. She went out by the back door into the vegetable patch behind the jhallee. She could see the neat rows of lettuces and the deep irrigation trenches between them. A narrow path led to the incinerator and compost heap. A faintly pungent smell of decay filled her nostrils and drew her on.

Why had Hugo died? Each person who had become involved she thought, had found for himself an interpretation for Hugo's death.

Alan Turnell had made an interrupted burglar the official explanation. For him the Head of Chancery had been struck down in one of those random collisions of fate for which no cause beyond coincidence can be found.

Lobsang Dhondup depersonalised the events and saw the gold as unleashing evil, greed, power into the world, like a boulder thrown into a pond which raises a wave that washes to and fro swamping those who cannot withstand it. Presumably he would regard the violent deaths of Hugo and Ranjit as signs of their attachment to the causes of rebirth, desire, ignorance, anger.

And to her alone had been offered Ruth Quinton's story. Was she to say Hugo died, not for the gold, nor his greed, nor his breaking of the rules, but for his failure to Ruth?

She contemplated the dim heap in front of her. In Sinclair's world of deduction and proof, the turning over of the compost heap would produce the knife, or not, and so tell her whether she had heard the truth from the sick woman grieving for a baby and a lover, any more than from Ranjit Singh determined to frighten her with lie or truth. Could truth be found under a pile of decomposing vegetation?

She had no intention of digging through the compost

pile. She did not want to turn back to the beginning and read again the story of Hugo's death, this time with certainty. She had brought no implement out with her, only the Buddha in her hand. Scuffing her foot at the rotting edge of the heap she breathed in the putrefaction.

She did not want, or need, the certainty that finding the ritual knife would give, for in Ruth's story she had recognised a truth about Hugo.

Inside the house again she looked for the last time at the figure of the Buddha. He touched the earth which replied to his hand, "I am his witness."

She slowly wrapped it in layers of paper and laid it gently on the top of the packing case in which, that morning, she and Sinclair had placed the gold.

GLOSSARY

Ayah	child's nurse
Badmash	rogue, villain
Banja	shopkeeper, merchant
Bhai	brother
Bidi	cigarette
Burra sahib	'great lord'; Anglo-Indian slang for a high British official, head of a district or household
Chapatti	unleavened bread
Chappals	sandals
Charpoy	four-legged string bed
Chhota-hazri	early morning tea, 'little breakfast'
Chhuba	Tibetan gown, usually dark red, worn by both men and women
Chorten	Tibetan shrine
Chowkidar	watchman
Chuprassy	messenger
Churidars	tight trousers
Dacoit	bandit

Dacoity	theft, banditry
Dahi	yoghurt
Dak bungalow	rest house for travelling officials
Dal	lentil purée
Dekshi	saucepan without handles
Dhoti	cotton loin-cloth which hangs to the knees
Dhow	Arab sailing vessel
Dukang	Tibetan temple
Dzo	cross between a yak and an ox
Gonkang	Tibetan temple of guardian divinities
Goonda	hooligan
Insh'allah	God willing
Jawan	private soldier
Jhallee	screen of pierced bricks, often arranged in highly decorative patterns
Jheels	lakes
Ji	sir
Khansamah	cook
Kurta	long loose overshirt
Lakh	one hundred thousand
Lathi	staff, truncheon
Luddoos	round sweets made of milk and sugar
Mahabrahman	an Untouchable with special functions at funerals
Mahakala	the great black God, a guardian divinity of Tibet
Mali	gardener
Mani wall	wall built of carved stones
Nimbu	lime
Nullah	ditch
Paan	digestif of betel-nut, lime and spices chewed after eating

Pugree	cotton scarf worn wrapped around face and neck
Puja	prayer
Punkah	fan
Shikara	canopied boat propelled by a boatman with one heart-shaped oar
Subzi	vegetables
Tangka	Tibetan devotional wall hanging painted on cloth bordered with silk
Tola	unit of weight
Tonga	two-wheeled horse-drawn vehicle
Tsampa	barley flour
Yiddag	one of the six forms of existence in Tibetan Buddhist belief, a creature of insatiable greed with a swollen belly and tiny mouth

"ELIZABETH IRONSIDE" is in fact a pseudonym for Lady Catherine Manning. A graduate of Oxford University, Lady Manning holds a doctorate in Economic History, and is married to Sir David Manning, until recently the British ambassador to the United States. For nearly 15 years she kept her "double life" a secret, attending writers' events as "Elizabeth Ironside," and informing only close friends and family members (and the British Foreign Office) about her career as a novelist. She finally blew her cover in 1999, at a publication-party in Tel Aviv, where her husband was serving as ambassador.

As a "diplomatic spouse," Lady Manning has lived in India, Russia, Poland, and France, as well as Israel, and most recently in Washington, DC, and her travels have greatly informed her work as a writer. The Mannings currently live in London.

As "Elizabeth Ironside" Lady Manning is the author of five stand-alone mystery novels. *A Very Private Enterprise,* published here for the first time in the U.S., originally came out in England in 1985, when it was named Best First Mystery of the Year by the British Crime Writers Association. Her second novel, *Death in the Garden*, was shortlisted for the CWA's Gold Dagger award for Best Mystery of 1995. It was first published in the United States in 2005, by Felony & Mayhem, and was named one of the 12 best books of the year by National Public Radio. *The Accomplice,* the third of Ms. "Ironside's" books, was published in the U.S. in 2006 by Felony & Mayhem, which expects to bring out the first American editions of *A Good Death* and *The Art of Deception* in 2008 and 2009, respectively.